THE
SURGEON

BOOKS BY LESLIE WOLFE

LESLIE WOLFE

THE
SURGEON

GRAND
CENTRAL

NEW YORK   BOSTON

Grand Central Publishing
Hachette Book Group
1290 Avenue of the Americas, New York, NY 10104
grandcentralpublishing.com
twitter.com/grandcentralpub

Originally published in 2023 by Bookouture, an imprint of StoryFire Ltd.

First Grand Central Publishing Edition: June 2023

Grand Central Publishing is a division of Hachette Book Group, Inc. The Grand Central Publishing name and logo is a trademark of Hachette Book Group, Inc.

The publisher is not responsible for websites (or their content) that are not owned by the publisher.

The Hachette Speakers Bureau provides a wide range of authors for speaking events. To find out more, go to hachettespeakersbureau.com or email HachetteSpeakers@hbgusa.com.

Grand Central Publishing books may be purchased in bulk for business, educational, or promotional use. For information, please contact your local bookseller or the Hachette Book Group Special Markets Department at special.markets@hbgusa.com.

Library of Congress Cataloging-in-Publication Data has been applied for.

ISBN 9781538767375 (trade paperback)

Printed in the United States of America

LSC-C

Printing 1, 2023

A special thank you to my New York City legal eagle and friend, Mark Freyberg, who expertly guided me through the intricacies of the judicial system.

An enthusiastic thank you to Dr. Deborah (Debbi) Joule for her friendship and thoughtful advice. She made my research into the intricacies of cardiovascular surgery a far less daunting task. Her expertise and passion for precision and detail made writing this novel a fantastic experience.

ONE
THE PATIENT

What have I done?

The thought races through my mind, searing and weakening my body. The rush of adrenaline fills my muscles with the urge to run, to escape, but there's nowhere to go. Shaky and weak, I let myself slide to the floor; the cold, tiled wall against my back the only support I have. For a moment, I stare at my hands, barely recognizing them, as if I'd never before seen them sheathed in surgical gloves covered with blood. They feel foreign to me: a stranger's hands attached to my body by some inexplicable mistake.

A faint, steady beep is sounding incessantly over the constant whoosh of air conditioning. I wish I could summon the strength to ask them to turn it off. The operating room is at a standstill, all eyes riveted on me, widened and tense above face masks.

Only one pair of eyes is glaring, drilling into mine whenever there's a chance, the steel-blue irises deathly cold behind thick lenses and a face shield. Dr. Robert Bolger, still seated by the anesthesia machine, doesn't need to say anything. We've said to each other everything that needed to be said. Too much, even.

"Turn that thing off," Madison whispers. Lee Chen presses a button, and the ghastly sound is muted. Then she approaches me and crouches by my side. Her hand reaches for my shoulder but stops short of touching me. "Dr. Wiley?" she whispers, her hand still hovering. "Anne? Come on, let's go."

I shake my head slowly, staring at the floor. I remember with perfect accuracy the properties of the polymer coating they apply on all the operating room floors. Useless information taking space in my brain for no reason, since I'm the surgeon, the end user of these blue mosaic floors, not someone who decides what coating should be used.

"Anne?" Madison says my name again, her voice reassuring, filled with warmth.

"No," I whisper back. "I can't."

A bloody lap sponge has fallen from the table, staining the pristine floor inches away from the tip of my right foot. I fold my leg underneath me, staring at the sponge as if the bloodstain on it could come after me.

Madison withdraws under the fuming glare of Dr. Bolger.

He sighs and turns off his equipment, deepening the silence of the tense room. "Well, I guess we're done here." He stands with a frustrated groan and throws the echocardiologist Dr. Dean a loaded look. "Let's grab a cup of coffee to rinse off the memory of this disaster."

Dr. Dean throws me a quick glance as if asking for my approval. He probably feels guilty for being singled out by Bolger. I barely notice.

I don't react. I can't.

My mind is elsewhere, reliving moment by moment what has happened since this morning.

The day started well for me, without a sign of what was to come. A capricious, windy spring morning that made my daily jog more of an exercise in willpower than in physical endurance. Chicago has a way of showing its residents some tough love, with chilly wind gusts that cut to the bone, so to speak—there's no surgery involved; just weather and people's perceptions of it.

Like the past couple of weeks, I ran the usual three-mile loop through Lincoln Park looking at elms and buckthorns with renewed hope that I'd find a budding leaf, no matter how small. I was ready for spring and flowering gardens and warmer sunshine. Nothing else was on my mind; at six thirty in the morning, it seemed to be just an ordinary Thursday. Deceptively so.

At about seven thirty, I drove into the hospital employee parking level, taking my reserved numbered spot. I had reviewed the details about the day's surgery a final time the night before from the comfort of my home office, another set routine I have.

The procedure on schedule was an ascending aortic aneurysm. The patient, a fifty-nine-year-old male by the name of Caleb Donaghy. We were scheduled to start at ten sharp.

I'd met Caleb Donaghy twice before. The first time was during a consult. His cardiologist had found a large aneurysm and referred him to us for surgical repair. I remembered that consult clearly. The patient was understandably scared by the findings, and became more so with every word I said. He kept his arms crossed firmly at his chest as if protecting his heart from my scalpel. His unkempt beard had streaks of yellowish gray, and the same gray adorned his temples, as much as I could see from under the ball cap he had refused to take off. I let him keep it.

He was morose and argumentative for a while, disputing everything I said. What had he done to deserve the aneurysm? His parents had only recently died, and not of any heart-related issues. Only after spending a good fifteen minutes managing his anxiety was I able to evaluate him.

That was the first time we met.

Then I saw him again last night, after completing the surgical planning session with my team. Caleb Donaghy had been admitted two days before and had all his blood tests redrawn. He was sitting upright in his bed, stained Cubs ball cap on his head, arms folded, leaning against the pillows doing absolutely nothing when I came in. The TV was off, there were no magazines on his bed, his phone was placed face-down on his night table. The room smelled faintly of stale tobacco and boozy sweat. He was brooding, miserable, and alone. And he was pissed. He'd just learned they were going to shave his beard and chest in pre-op. To add insult to injury, someone in hospital administration had swung by and asked him if he was a registered organ donor. For seven long minutes, he told me in various ways he wasn't going to let himself be sold for parts. He knew what we, doctors, did to people like him, who had no family left to sue us and no money to matter. We took their organs and transplanted them into the highest bidders. Why else would entire buildings in our hospital be named after Chicago's wealthiest?

I promised him that wasn't the case. He wouldn't listen. Then I told him that all he had to do was say no and organ transplant stopped being a possibility in case of a negative surgery outcome. Which is surgeon lingo for death on the table. That silenced him in an instant.

But that was yesterday.

This morning, Madison had my coffee ready for me when I got to the office. She's the best surgical nurse I've worked with, and my personal assistant when she's not scrubbed in.

Madison; Lee Chen, the talented second surgical nurse on

my team; Tim Crosley, the cardiovascular perfusionist who operates the heart and lung machine we call the pump; and Dr. Francis Dean, the echocardiologist, are part of my permanent surgical team. Then it's the luck of the draw with anesthesiologists, and I drew the short and very annoying straw with Dr. Bolger. There's something off-putting about him. Could be his undisguised misogyny. Rumors have it he's been written up twice by the hospital administration for sexist diatribes insisting women don't belong in a clinical setting anywhere above the nursing profession. Contempt for women seeps through his pores, although recently he's grown more careful about letting it show. He's also an arrogant son of a bitch, albeit an excellent anesthesiologist. His professional achievements fuel his hubris and dilute the resolve of the hospital administration when dealing with his behavioral issues. That's who Dr. Bolger is.

When we're in surgery together, I always try to make it work as well as possible, for the good of the patient and the surgical team.

It never works. It takes two to dance in harmony.

I remember swearing under my breath when I saw his name on the schedule, then pushed the issue out of my mind.

Dr. Bolger was already in the operating room when I came in. "Good morning," I said, not expecting an answer. None came, just a quick nod and a side glance from behind the surgical drape that separates his world from mine, before he turned his attention back to the equipment cart at his right. The anesthesia machine helps him deliver precise doses. He controls the patient's airway from behind that protective drape. During surgery, I rarely, if ever, get to see my patients' faces.

My focus is on their hearts.

I'm forty-one and I've been doing this for twelve years, since I finished my general surgery residency. I moved to cardiothoracic right after that, and I never looked back. It's what I've always wanted to do. And I've never lost a patient on the table.

Not until today.

The thought of that hits me in the stomach like a fist.

For an instant, pulled back into the grim present moment, I look around me and try to register what I'm seeing. The surgical lights are off. Madison is still there, looking at me with concern. Lee Chen is sitting on his stool, ready to spring to his feet when needed. Tim Crosley is seated by the pump, his back hunched, his head hung low. If he could, he'd probably rest his forehead against his hands, but he's still working, still keeping sterile. As long as that pump's whirring, he's on duty.

My thoughts race back to the surgery. The operating room was filled with excited chatter, like normal. Virginia Gonzales, the semi-scrubbed nurse who runs back and forth, keeping us all organized and bringing us what we need, was sharing her experience with online dating. She's just been through a terrible divorce. She'd recently decided she could still go out there and meet people. I admired that resilience in her, and secretly hoped it wasn't desperation at the thought of living an entirely lonely life. But her first Tinder match had proven to be a man who'd misrepresented himself dramatically, and everyone on the team was laughing as she shared the details. He'd said he was a transportation executive, when he was in fact a truck driver. Nothing wrong with that, Ginny was quick to say, but the man had never heard of flossing, and during the twenty-five-minute encounter he'd let it slip he used hookers while he was on the road. Cheap ones, he immediately reassured a stunned Ginny.

Hearing her speak, I couldn't help thinking how grateful I was for my husband and my marriage. I'd die a hermit if I had to date again.

A quick bout of laughter erupted in the operating room when Ginny added, "I just ran out of there."

Dr. Bolger glared at her. "Let's try to have some professionalism in here, if at all possible," he said, speaking slowly, pacing his words for impact. "If I'm not asking for too much."

I refrained from arguing with him. Everyone was working, doing their jobs. Surgical teams perform best when they have a way to let off some steam. If there's silence in an operating room, if no one's sharing a story, if the music isn't playing, then something's going terribly wrong.

I'd rather have them laughing all day long. That's how you keep death at bay. It's worked for me anyway. So far.

"What will you have?" Madison asked me, standing by the stereo.

"Um, let me think." The early morning jog had me thinking of The Beatles. "Do you have 'Here Comes the Sun'?"

Madison grinned from behind her mask; I could see it in her eyes. She loved them. "I've got the entire greatest hits collection right here."

"Punch it," I said, moving between equipment and the operating table until I reached my station, by the patient's chest. Music filled the room.

Humming along, I held out my hand and the scalpel landed firmly in it. No need for me to ask; Madison knows how I work. I'm sure she can read my mind, although that possibility isn't scientifically proven.

From the first incision—a vertical line at the center of his breastbone—every step of the procedure was routine.

The sternotomy to expose the heart.

Opening the pericardium, the thin wrapping around the heart, and exposing the aneurysm.

It was big, one of the biggest I'd seen. But I knew that already from prior imaging studies. We were prepared for it.

"On pump," I said, instructing Tim to start circulating the patient's blood through the heart and lung machine.

"Cross clamp in position," I announced. "Cold flush," I asked. A cold solution of potassium was administered into the

chambers of the heart. I flushed the exterior of the heart generously with the solution, knowing the cold fluid preserved the
heart tissue while we worked. Within seconds, the heart
stopped, its death-like stillness announced by the droning sound
we were waiting for. The sound of flatline, or the absence of a
heartbeat.

With the heart perfectly still, I started working to replace
the aortic aneurysm with a graft. It took me almost an entire
Beatles album to finish sewing it in.

It feels strange how I remember the cold above all else. It's
always cold in the operating room. The air conditioning system
blows air at sixty-two degrees. The cold flush that lowers the
heart temperature and renders it still is delivered at forty
degrees, barely above freezing. My fingers become numb after a
while, but I move as fast as I can. Yet today it seemed colder
than usual, the only premonition I can say I had.

I don't believe in them. I have my reasons.

When I was done with the sewing of the graft, I examined
my work closely, checking if the stitching was tight enough. The
final test would be when the blood started rushing through that
graft. Then I'd see if there were any leaks and fix them. Usually
there weren't. For now, I was satisfied.

"Warm saline," I asked. Those two words marked the end of
the cardioplegia stage of the surgery, when the heart is perfectly
still. I flushed the organ generously with warm saline solution,
relishing the feeling of warmth on my frozen fingers, then used
suction to get rid of the excess solution. "Releasing clamp."

The clamp clattered when it landed on the pile of used
instruments. I held my breath, knowing this was the moment of
truth.

The heart remained perfectly still.

Not fibrillating, not barely beating. Nothing. Just perfectly
still.

And that almost never happens.

"Starting resuscitation," I announced. Madison gestured toward the stereo and Ginny turned it off, then started a second timer with large, red digital numbers. Silence filled the room, an ominous, unwanted silence underlined by the flatline droning of the heart monitor. "Epinephrine, stat."

"Epi in," Dr. Bolger confirmed.

The shot of epi should've done something. It didn't. I massaged the heart quickly, feeling it completely unresponsive under the pressure.

"Paddles," I asked, my voice tense, impatient. Madison put the paddles in my hands. Placing them carefully on opposing sides of the heart, I called, "Clear," and pushed the button. A brief interruption in the steady droning, then the sound of bad news was back.

I tried that a few more times, then returned to massaging the heart with my hands. "I need another shot of epi. Time?"

"Seventeen minutes," Madison announced, grimly.

"Damn it to hell," I mumbled under my breath. "Come on, Caleb, stay with me."

For a couple of minutes, I kept on with the massage, but nothing happened. The pump still kept his blood oxygenated and delivered to his organs, but the heart was another issue. Its tissue was no longer preserved by the cold potassium solution. With every passing minute, it was deteriorating, its chances of ever beating again waning fast.

"Come on, already! Live!" I snapped. "Come back."

I felt the urge to look at the patient's face as if it could hold some answers. I took a small step past the surgical drape—and froze, mouth agape under the mask, hand stuck in midair. I believe I gasped, but I don't think anyone noticed under the hum of air conditioning, the whirring of the pump, and the blaring of the monitor.

I recognized that man.

My blood turned to ice.

The face I'd seen yesterday and hadn't recognized was now clean-shaven. The ball cap was gone, his bald forehead marked by a port-wine stain on the right side. The birthmark was an irregular shape of red splashed across his forehead as if someone had spilled some wine there.

It took all my willpower to step back behind the drape. Breathing deeply, thankful for the cool air that kept my mind from going crazy, I abandoned the paddles on the table and stared at the heart that refused to beat.

"Time?" I asked again, this time my voice choked.

"Twenty-one minutes," Madison replied.

I slipped my hands into the chest and massaged the heart, knowing very well the heart compressions I was delivering wouldn't work.

I forced one more breath of air out of my chest, then said, "I'm calling it."

"What?" Dr. Bolger sprang to his feet. "Are you insane? Keep going."

I was expecting that. "I could do that, but he won't come back, Robert. We tried everything. The heart's not even giving me the tiniest flutter."

His steely eyes threw poisonous darts at me. "Giving up already? Why? Are your pretty little hands tired, sweetheart?"

I let that one go. It wouldn't help anyone if we argued over the open chest of Caleb Donaghy. "My case, my call." I held his seething gaze steadily for a moment. "Time of death, one forty-seven p.m."

Heavy silence took over the room. Then people started shifting around, collecting instruments, peeling off gloves, turning off equipment. Only Tim stayed in place, the pump still working, still preserving Caleb's organs and tissues.

"It's unbelievable what happened here today," Dr. Bolger said. "You're unbelievable. Pathetic even. You didn't just lose your cherry... you threw it away."

The sexualized reference to the fact that I'd never lost a patient before left me wondering how much of his disdain was in fact envy. But that thought went away quickly.

Then reality hit me like a freight train.

What have I done? Have I just killed a man?

TWO

DINNER

Paula Fuselier almost ran from the cab's door to the Langham Hotel entrance, her heels clacking loudly against the smooth, slippery sidewalk. She slowed briefly on entering the lobby to avoid knocking over an elderly woman pulling a Louis Vuitton wheelie, then resumed her sprint after giving the time displayed on her phone a concerned look.

She was two minutes late already. Her boss had said four, sharp. He'd actually used the word *sharp* twice. That was how important it was for her to make it on time.

The sound of clacking heels caught the attention of a receptionist when she was still a few yards away from the front desk. He smiled patiently as if to say there was no need to rush. She stopped in place, ready to bolt.

"Travelle?" she asked, shouting the restaurant's name over the busy lobby.

The receptionist's grin widened. "Second floor." He pointed to the bank of elevators. The clacking of her rushed heels against the shiny marble floor resumed, echoing indecently in the vast lobby. Once she reached the elevators, she pressed the call button a few times, impatiently, the heel of her right shoe stomping in the rhythm of her rushing, anxious heartbeat.

"Sorry I'm late." She heard a man's voice she recognized. Just as the elevator doors opened, she turned and saw her boss, Mitch Hobbs, smiling sternly by her side. The smile didn't touch his eyes. "Thankfully, it almost never happens when I'm due in court."

Her cheeks caught fire under her makeup. The innuendo was unequivocal. Her boss always noticed lateness, even if only by a few minutes. Or any other misconduct, no matter how inconsequential. The Cook County state's attorney wasn't someone who tolerated underperformance.

Yet she breathed with relief. It was better this way than the nightmarish alternative: her boss waiting for her at the most exquisite dining choice within the five-star hotel, rapping his fingers against the starched tablecloth, waiting on his subordinate to show some bloody respect and turn up on time.

She managed an awkward smile and a whispered apology as she stepped into the elevator. Then she hesitated for a moment before pressing the elevator button, finding herself struggling to steady her hand.

As the elevator set in motion, she gave her reflection a quick look. Despite the unexpected invitation and the short notice, her long, brown hair looked perfect, as if she'd just stepped out of a salon, gathered loosely in the back with a gold pearl clip that left a few strands free to frame her face. Her makeup was pristine after touching it up in the cab on the way over. The business pantsuit was just right, a perfect shade of navy blue that matched her satin blouse. The collar of that blouse, skillfully designed into a bow with long ends, was out of shape a little, hanging crookedly to the side. Nervous, she rearranged it quickly, with furtive movements, behind her boss's back, while hoping the rebel, slippery ends of the bow wouldn't find their way into a bowl of soup.

She had no idea what the unexpected invitation was about.

Her boss was all business in a very intense way. She'd worked for him for eight years, and before Mitchell Dwight Hobbs was elected to lead the State's Attorney Office for the second most populous county in the United States, she'd worked for his predecessor. Her entire career had been about bringing justice to the streets of Chicago. Since the day she'd passed her bar exam and turned down several private law firm offers in favor of the State Prosecutor's Office, she had dedicated her life to something that mattered: justice for everyone, for the underprivileged, for people who rarely found a strong voice to speak on their behalf.

She wanted to be that voice more than anything else. That passion fueled her record of convictions, second only to the state attorney's. She'd earned herself a nickname in the crime world of Chicago. They called her the Pit Viper—deadly if one crossed her path. She secretly loved that nickname. It told her she was succeeding.

The posh restaurant had a standing reservation in her boss's name. He was well known there. Seemingly at home in the large dining room, Hobbs led her to a table by the window, gestured a silent invitation, then sat across from her. It didn't have a starched, white tablecloth as she'd imagined. The perfectly spotless lacquered finish revealed the wood grain and harmonized to perfection with the rest of the decor.

A waiter appeared instantly, delivering a tray with chilled Pellegrino water and two tall glasses. Another one delivered the long menus, placing them across their plates with a smooth gesture.

For a moment, Paula was grateful to hide her quizzical look from her boss's scrutiny. The choices were all mouthwatering, but she didn't feel she could eat anything, the knot in her stomach tense and painful as if she'd swallowed a stone.

Hobbs didn't need more than a few seconds to make up his

mind. He placed the menu back on the table and the waiter promptly appeared with a notepad in his hand.

"I'll have the steak, Willie," Hobbs said, then turned to her. "How about you?"

Paula swallowed with difficulty. "A salad should be fine. I'm not really that hungry."

Hobbs placed his hand on the table's shiny surface with a muted thud, a gesture she knew well from prosecution strategy meetings and endless case reviews. "Nonsense." He swiftly raised his glance toward the waiter. "She'll have the hanger steak too. That's what hunters eat."

"Yes, sir," the waiter replied. "How would you like it cooked?"

"Medium, with a touch of blood," he said, a smile stretching his lips. That grin and the glint in his eyes when he talked of hunters and meat and blood removed the banality from his appearance, the sense of benevolence induced by his silver metallic glasses and almost permanent smile, showing his true colors for a mere second. When his eyes locked on to hers, they still glinted. "Because that's what hunters do. They draw blood."

Paula felt a shiver down her spine. Uneasiness unfurled in her gut. She placed her hands in her lap, folded neatly, and replied without blinking, "How very true."

Willie vanished just as quietly as he'd arrived, leaving a moment of uncomfortable silence between them. Paula refrained from taking a sip of water, knowing Hobbs was watching her every move. Appearing as relaxed and casual as she could possibly fake it, she waited as if she had no cares in the world.

"Well, I'll dive right into it," Hobbs eventually said, with a sigh. "Since we started late."

Paula managed a timid smile instead of a groan and an eye-roll. Four minutes. That was all. But he was right, nevertheless.

"I've been watching you, Ms. Fuselier," Hobbs said, taking the glass of water and rotating it with careful movements as if to get rid of the bubbles. "You don't know how to lose." He grinned at her for a brief moment, then turned serious. "I love that in an ASA. I *need* that in *all* my ASAs, but I only get it in some."

Paula allowed herself to breathe, slowly emptying her lungs of the trapped air inside, then filling them up again.

"But there's something about you I don't understand."

Her eyebrows shot up. "Maybe I can explain."

He gestured with his hand, an unspoken request to be patient. "Some cases, you take them to court and win, deliver the convictions elegantly and effortlessly. But other cases, like the Kestner theft last month, you go after them with a vengeance, with an appetite for blood."

Paula swallowed, keeping her eyes fixed on her boss's face. What was this about? He could've asked her about that in the office. She held back, allowing him to ask his question.

"What was different about the Kestner case?" Mitch Hobbs watched her intently, like a predator ready to pounce. "Is it personal?"

A beat of tense silence. "It's all about the victim, sir," she replied, casually. "If the victim is underprivileged—in this case an orphaned child who'd just matured out of the foster system without a dime—then I throw the book at the perp." She leaned toward him, placing her hands on the edge of the table. "Can you imagine how hard it was for that young boy to raise the money for a beat-up Honda? What that jalopy would've meant to him? A slightly better job, maybe even a place to sleep if he ended up in the street somehow. Times are uncertain for every-one." Her thin, manicured fingers found the seam of her napkin and toyed with it absent-mindedly. "That Honda meant way more to him than the half a million stolen from some corporate tycoon's cryptocurrency account in last month's headliner case."

"Ah, I see," Hobbs said. "Do you know what that is?"

A bit surprised, Paula shook her head.

"You're a natural. That's political capital in raw form. It's like gold ore, raw, beautiful, unprocessed. Real, as opposed to fake. Seriously hard to find."

She watched him, unsure where the conversation was going. He didn't seem upset by her silence though.

"I believe you could be the future of this office, Paula. Starting today, with your promotion to head of the Criminal Prosecutions Bureau, I will coach you to someday take my place."

Slack-jawed, Paula stared at him for a brief moment. It didn't seem real, but Mitchell Hobbs was not a man who'd make a joke about the office he held proudly. "I don't know what to say," she managed, painfully aware she was frowning: hardly the appropriate response to receiving news of a promotion.

"'Thank you' would be nice."

She smiled, nervously. "Thank you, sir. I appreciate the vote of confidence. I wasn't expecting this. I'm the—"

"Youngest head of criminal prosecutions ever?"

She nodded, eyeing the waiter approaching with two large plates balanced on his arm. Hardly the time to interrupt their conversation.

"Only by a couple of years, Paula. I looked it up." He leaned back, allowing Willie to place the steak in front of him, then unfolded his napkin and laid it on his knee. "I'm confident you'll do fine. Yes, there will be some ruffled feathers, and probably Parsons will huff and puff and then hit the private sector for a seven-figure paycheck, but you'll sit opposing counsel and hand him his own ass for lunch every time you cross paths in court." He stabbed the steak with his fork and cut a large piece. Juices flowed, staining the plate the color of blood. "Right?"

She tasted a bite of mashed potatoes. It was delicious, buttery and creamy and soft as if mixed with air. "Absolutely."

The thought of facing a frustrated, motivated, and financially incentivized Parsons in court scared her for a split second, then a smile bloomed on her lips. He was nothing but an entitled asshole, a third-generation lawyer with a Harvard education, growing overconfident with age. He didn't have her gumption. "Bring it on." Whatever the smug son of a bitch was going to get, he well deserved it. She wanted to jump off her chair and dance around the table.

Hobbs checked the time and frowned a little, then gestured at Paula's steak. "Dig in. You have precisely eight minutes to finish your meal."

Her brow ruffled again. "What's in eight minutes?"

Hobbs smiled crookedly. "Your party." He beckoned the waiter. "Have a bottle of champagne brought over at four thirty, sharp. Four glasses. If our guests arrive early, please seat them in the lounge until we're done."

Willie bowed his head and disappeared. The restaurant was starting to get busy, but he seemed assigned to their table, rarely more than a few feet away.

Paula cut a piece of steak and chewed it slowly, savoring the exquisite taste. *Eight minutes? And who is arriving?* For a moment, she felt tempted to ask, but decided to keep her cool and wait. With Hobbs, the job interview was never over. She could still screw it up.

"You start in May. Tannehill is retiring next month." Hobbs finished his steak to the last bite, chewing enthusiastically.

"I didn't know that," Paula replied without thinking. She instantly regretted it. She couldn't afford to appear clueless.

Hobbs pushed his plate to the side. Willie appeared and took it away. "Now, let's talk long term."

Paula's hand stopped in midair, her fork inches away from her lips. She slowly put it down, listening.

"You'll have three months to get the hang of it, three months on-the-job training if you will, followed by one year of probation. I'll hold you to higher standards than I hold any of your peers. I expect you to deliver better, faster, and more above the line than anyone else who's ever prosecuted a criminal case in this county."

She took a sip of water. "Understood."

"If you struggle, don't keep it a secret. Ask for help. That's how I started. The job isn't easy."

She nodded. "Thank you, I will." She paused for a moment, doubting if she should ask. "How about my team, sir?"

He nodded in lieu of an answer. "You can call me Mitch." His eyes glinted again, lightning-fast, before his gaze went back to its usual chill beam. "Not now. Starting in May."

She chuckled, then picked up the last piece of mouthwatering steak and put it in her mouth. "Thank you," she said, after she finished her meal. "For everything. Especially for believing in me."

"Make me proud, Paula." He checked the time, then gestured toward Willie. It was four thirty.

Willie disappeared, then returned carrying a silver champagne bucket filled with ice and wrapped in a white napkin, setting it on the table. A gold-wrapped bottleneck peeked from inside. Above the edge of the napkin, the side of the ice bucket was etched with the hotel name in fine, barely discernible lettering.

Moments later, a man and a woman approached their table with hesitant smiles on their faces.

Paula stood and welcomed them. The woman, Marie Eckley, had been her assistant for seven years. She was a bright and skillful attorney and a recent empty nester after raising two sons on her own. The man, Adam Costilla, was a former Chicago PD detective who'd joined the State's Attorney Office as lead investigator. About five years ago, when Adam, a bulky and cynical cop who spoke in his own version of Italian-accented shorthand slang that no one understood, had joined their office, she'd recognized the value of having a street-smart cop on her side. She saved for him the most challenging cases, the headline grabbers, and the most loaded investigations. He loved her for that, for saving him from the "slow and painful death by boredom," as he'd named it.

"Thanks for coming," Paula said, responding to Marie's enthusiastic hug. "Just wait until you hear the news. You'll love this."

Hobbs watched the interactions with keen attention, not leaving his seat, a bit of impatience seeping through his gestures.

"Mr. Hobbs," Adam Costilla said, shaking the state's attorney's hand, "thanks for having us. What are we drinking to?"

"It's a who, not a what," Hobbs replied, nodding in Paula's direction. He was inviting her to make the announcement.

"Effective May, I'm the new head of criminal prosecutions," Paula announced, her voice a bit shaky from the excitement. The words still didn't ring true; it seemed impossible somehow. "And you guys helped me get there." She had to raise her voice a little over Marie's congratulations and Adam's open-mouthed laughter and enthusiastic interjections. "So, you're coming with me to the fifth floor."

"Taking that elevator up, baby," Adam cheered, fist-pumping the air. "Yeah!" Marie touched his arm and he fell quiet, throwing Hobbs a sheepish glance but still grinning as he pulled out a chair and sat.

Willie approached and uncorked the champagne, the loud pop raising another round of cheers. This time Paula chimed in, under the state's attorney's reserved gaze. Flutes were filled three quarters and clinked in the air.

"Congratulations," Hobbs said, taking the glass to his lips but barely touching the liquid. "And don't imagine I'll be cutting any of you any slack."

Paula's phone chimed and her smile waned for a moment,

before seeing the sender's name. Then her smile returned, lopsided and loaded, as she read the message.

You're having dinner with another man and I'm crazy jealous. Can I join you? the message read. The sender's name shown was *Mr. Mayor*, as she'd stored it in her phone's memory. She knew who he was... no one else needed to. Even if he wasn't the mayor yet.

Frowning a little without realizing, she quickly typed her reply. *You know you don't wanna be here. Why even ask?*

Adam's heavy pat on her shoulder startled her, and she almost dropped the phone. "It's what you get for all those long nights and hard work. But it takes a special kind of someone to remember their team when they move up." She slid the phone safely into her pocket. When she lifted her eyes, she met Hobbs's steeled, unreadable gaze.

Her boss rose from the table, holding his hand in the air to stop Adam from following suit. He ran his hand quickly down his Armani tie as if to check if it was still in place, then buttoned his suit jacket. "I have to run, but please carry on. I'm sure you have lots to talk about."

Paula stood and shook his hand over the table. "Thank you, sir. For everything. I promise you won't be sorry."

He didn't say anything, just looked at her as if to see if she really meant what she said. Then he turned and walked out of the restaurant at a brisk pace.

"Whew, the man is intense," Adam said, raising his glass and inviting the others to join him. Glasses clinked merrily a second time. "To the woman, the legend, our one and only Pit Viper."

Marie gasped and covered her mouth with her hand. "Adam!"

Paula grinned. "It's okay. We all made that nickname happen."

"I still hate it," Marie replied. "It's a terrible thing to call someone."

Paula's phone chimed. Another message from Mr. Mayor—short, cryptic, full of promise. *HL #1098*

Her eyes wandered to the ice bucket, where the letters HOTEL LANGHAM were finely etched under tiny droplets of water. She smiled, a satisfied smile that swelled her chest with the thrill of anticipation. Somewhere in that hotel, on the tenth floor, the future mayor of Chicago was about to get naked and wait for her in bed, rock hard, counting every minute until she joined him. The perfect ending to a perfect day.

She picked up her glass and held it out for Adam to top it off.

He quickly obliged. "Aren't you the cat who ate the canary?" he quipped, looking at her with intelligent eyes sparking with curiosity.

She didn't flinch. "Really?" She set her glass down. A droplet of Krug Grande Cuvée splashed onto the gleaming wood finish. She resisted the urge to wipe it dry. "I'm in no hurry, guys. Let's order something to eat." She smiled to herself, a tiny smile at the thought of her lover waiting for her, wanting her more with each passing minute.

THREE
INTROSPECTION

The operating room seems even colder than before, now that most of the people who bring it to life every day are gone. Only Madison remains, crouched by my side, and Tim Crosley, still seated by the pump, staring at his feet.

My teeth chattering, I try to get up, but fail. Weakness has spread through my body like glue, holding me still, paralyzing me. Yet I can't take my eyes off the patient's head, a barely visible shape behind the drape. I feel drawn to him, the need to see his face again overpowering, defeating the urge to lie down on the blue, frozen floor.

The operating room looks different with the surgical lights off. Lit like any other procedure room, by ceiling-mounted lights that lend a bluish hue to everything, it seems lifeless, a foregone conclusion of failure and defeat.

Just like Caleb Donaghy.

I've never lost a patient before.

The emptiness I feel is harrowing. My thoughts race erratically, trying to make sense of what just happened. I reach for the edge of a cart, hoping to hold on to it for support as I struggle to get up. Instead, I find Madison's arm. I cling to it with my trembling hand, still clad in a bloodstained glove, thankful for her being there yet unable to look her in the eye.

Tim leaves his post by the pump and rushes to help me up. After I manage to stand, neither lets go until I whisper, "I'm fine. Really." But I'm not. I can barely support my weight, unsteady and unbalanced like a windblown castaway.

The effort to stand forces my mind to focus. I remember things I have to do, patients I have to see.

"Um, the Williamson bypass?" I ask, my voice hoarse, my throat constricted and parchment dry.

"It's been rescheduled," Madison whispers. "Dr. Seldon took it. Nothing to worry about, sweetie."

I nod. Dr. Seldon won't judge. He was my fellowship mentor. I learned most of what I know from him. My patient is in good hands. *My other patient... the one who's still alive.*

I stare at Caleb Donaghy's body, afraid to look at him, even more afraid to look inside myself.

Madison touches my arm gently. "Come on, let's get you home."

I shake my head, still staring at my patient's body, pulled toward it by an unseen force I cannot defeat.

One tiny step at a time, I draw close, my breath caught in my lungs, unable to escape. Against all reason, I expect him to wake up and point a tobacco-stained finger at me, accusing, threatening.

But he's perfectly motionless under heaps of surgical Steri-Drapes and bloodstained lap sponges, his heart perfectly still in the open chest. My hands were in there only minutes earlier, working hard to bring life to it, willing it back to normal sinus rhythm, giving him my very best.

Until I'd seen his face.

Retracing my earlier steps in a daze, I move past the surgical drape that separates the head from the rest of the body.

The splash of red on his pale forehead draws my eyes like a

magnet. A unique birthmark I'd recognized the moment I first saw it, when I was still hoping to bring Caleb Donaghy back to life. The port-wine stain that haunted my nightmares for years.

How could I have seen this patient twice before today, and not known who he was?

I squeeze my eyes shut and grab the side of the operating table with both hands. The room is spinning around me, faster and faster, while I desperately try to steady myself. Then I realize I've been holding my breath, trapping air into my lungs and refusing to let it out, in a frozen gasp that won't end.

It takes all my willpower to force air in and out of my lungs a few times, until the room steadies, and some strength returns to my weakened limbs. When I open my eyes, the first thing I see is the port-wine birthmark on my patient's forehead. It has the same effect on me again.

Paralyzing. Seeding unspeakable dread in my chest. Filling my blood with ice. Not a clinical possibility, but it feels as if those ice crystals are made of steel and have sharp edges that cut me from within.

How could I not recognize him?

He wore that damned ball cap every time we met. I didn't ask him to take it off. I had no reason to. And the beard—hiding the features of the man I'd seen once and hoped I'd see again, at least once.

Many patients wear beards, and there's nothing wrong with that.

Until there is.

I draw closer and study his birthmark in detail. *Can I be wrong about who Caleb Donaghy is?*

Without realizing, I shake my head slowly, eyes still riveted on the red-stained skin.

"Let's get you out of here," Madison whispers.

I raise my hand, pleading silently for a little more time. On the other side of the operating table, Tim is shutting down the pump, its fading whirring the last sound I can hear except for the thumping of my own heart. There will be no organ harvesting. My patient hadn't given consent.

But that seems like years ago.

I'm not wrong. I'd recognize that port-wine stain a hundred years from now. I've seen it in my mind so many times, always precisely, its shape unfaded in my memory: a large, irregular shape, somewhat resembling a handwritten, embellished R, and three smaller spots, as if wine drops were actually falling from the left edge of the letter, almost touching the eyebrow.

I close my eyes again and picture him clearly. Yesterday, he wore his ball cap low, the visor shielding his eyes as if he were out in the piercing spring sun, not in a dimly lit hospital room.

I have to ask myself, as I draw another lungful of cold air: *Did learning who he is make a difference in the OR?*

The answer, brutally honest, resonates loudly in my mind. For a moment, I throw Madison a worried look as if she can hear my thoughts and judge me on them. Be horrified by them. But she's meeting my gaze with nothing but kindness, her eyes filled with understanding.

Had I known who Caleb Donaghy was before the surgery, I would've asked a colleague to take over for me. No one frowns about that; it's standard procedure not to operate on friends, family, or anyone who could compromise the surgeon's ability to perform in the operating room. It would've been easy. And had Caleb survived, I would've—

I don't know what I would've done.

But I didn't know who he was before opening his chest and holding his heart in my hand.

Did I hesitate? Did I make a mistake?

With a nervous frown, I peel off my gloves and throw them in the biohazard bin, then turn to Madison. "Fresh gloves, please."

She doesn't budge. "Anne, let's just—"

"Please," I repeat, pushing more determination into my voice.

She brings me a fresh pair of gloves after replacing hers, following procedure to the letter, as if the patient were still alive. Then she helps me put my gloves on while I stare at the patient's chest.

Quickly, I inspect the work I did, looking for nicks, damaged tissue, anything that could explain why his heart refused to restart. I don't find anything. I remain still, my hands stuck in midair above the open chest, unable to answer a single, crucial question.

Was his heart viable after surgery, and did I deliver a final blow, after learning who my patient was?

My head hangs low under the weight of the implications.

Before looking at his face, after all the sewing was complete and warm saline had flushed the heart, I had tried to resuscitate him for more than fifteen minutes.

And that is a documented fact.

I throw the cameras above my head an intense glance. All procedures are recorded these days, from multiple angles, the feeds synchronized with critical statistics, such as time codes and patient vitals. If I have any doubts, I can always watch the recording.

But that doesn't change the fact that once I knew who my patient was, I wanted him dead.

FOUR
DRIVE

I watch helplessly as two orderlies roll away the table with Caleb Donaghy's body hidden under the fresh, blue sheet Madison just unfolded. Young, carefree Charons dressed in dark blue scrubs and making quick work of their task, they don't say anything to me, just throw me a pitiful glance and then quickly look away. One of them is wearing earbuds, probably listening to music or perhaps a game. To him, it's just a normal day at work.

I'm not the first surgeon whose work they've come to haul away to the morgue. I won't be the last. It's a small miracle if I'll be the last one today. The hospital I work in is one of the largest in the country and has an impeccable reputation, but people still die. A bitter chuckle escapes my lips as I remember I was recently recognized for being a key part of that reputation, my perfect record contributing to the hospital's prestige as a place of choice for heart surgery. The lowest cardiothoracic operative mortality rate in the state, and among the top ten lowest in the nation, after places like Stanford, Mass General, and the Mayo Clinic.

I used to be a part of that success. Now I stare at the two

orderlies wheeling my dead patient to the service elevator and from there, to the basement morgue. A rush cleanup job, no one willing to let too many eyes land on the unfortunate. No good ever comes from that.

One death, among so many success stories, reunited families, and fulfilled dreams my work made possible.

Just one death. And yet, it weighs so heavily on my mind.

"You're going home now," Madison states firmly, grabbing my elbow and leading me out of the operating room.

I follow her order without objection. With Caleb Donaghy's body gone, I have no reason to be in the cold, deserted operating room anymore. It smells of death and blood and new plastic. I start peeling off my gloves and mask, then the disposable scrubs, all in one swift move, and roll everything into a ball, which I dump in the large bin by the door. The gesture is familiar, ingrained into me with the smell of disinfectant soap and the feel of nitrile gloves on my skin. It grounds me, helps me carry on, a mindless wanderer though a sequence of well-rehearsed moves.

"Let me get you an Uber," Madison offers, as soon as we reach my office.

The peacefulness of the familiar room with its bookshelves full of medical journals and surgery treatises, with the large desk by the window and the leather chair that has welcomed me countless times after lengthy surgeries, and the large sofa I sometimes doze off on when pulling a seventy-two-hour shift, is exactly what I need. I falter toward the sofa, my eyes half-closed, weary to the bone. I yearn for the soft blanket that hangs on its back, neatly folded, just ready to be used. It's got Golden Retriever puppies on it, yellow and cuddly. I'd like to wrap it around myself and sink my face into it, to forget everything for a few merciful minutes.

Madison intercepts me with a firm grip. "Nope. You're going home. You'll thank me tomorrow."

This time I resist, or at least I try to. I pull back, frowning weakly. That simple gesture demands too much energy. "Just for a little bit, Maddie, please. If I could just lie down for a little while—" Somehow, she's like a parent and I'm the stubborn child, and I'm comfortable with the role for today, when I need someone else to be in charge; when I know I could strengthen my voice and glare for a split second and she'd rush out of there and give me peace, if I really trusted myself to make that decision.

Just for once, it's okay to let someone else decide.

She shakes her head. "You know the drill, Anne. It exists for your own benefit. You're going home, and you're not coming in tomorrow. It's the rule."

The thought of dealing with the hospital administrator, the fiercely rigorous and driven Dr. Jody Meriwether, or M, as almost everyone calls her, brings a pang of migraine pain right at the center of my forehead. I don't recall who gave her that nickname: it was during my residency, and her reputation preceded her. The nickname M had stuck, inspired by the James Bond movies in which it took an M to hold the unstoppable 007 in check.

Even recent grads knew her name and feared her more than their respective rotation specialists.

I'm no exception, not even after fourteen years working in the hospital she runs like à white-bearded admiral would a tight battleship. I'm still afraid to face her. One look at me and she'd instantly know something is wrong. Well, something other than a patient dying under my knife.

Thanks to Madison, I don't have to face her today. Suddenly afraid that M might walk into my office and question me until I tell her what I've done, I snatch my purse and jacket and walk past my assistant. She watches me with a slightly gaping mouth and round eyes, probably unsure why she won the round so fast. I'm not exactly famous for being easy to manage.

Seemingly not trusting me, she escorts me to the elevators. "Are you okay to drive?" she asks, sizing me up as if I've been drinking.

I'm not okay. I haven't been okay since I've seen my patient's face, the unmistakable port-wine stain on his forehead. But the thought of sharing car space with a stranger for the next twenty-five minutes seems unbearable. Just as stripping off surgical scrubs has become something I can execute in my sleep, I hope that the drive home will be the same. Routine. Easy. I've been taking the same road home for more years than I care to remember, ever since I finished med school. So I nod, mustering all my willpower to give Madison a reassuring look she seems to believe. She hugs me just as the elevator doors whir open.

Then I'm on my own. At last.

The parking garage is deserted and almost completely dark, the few and far apart light fixtures too weak to fight the early dusk of the March evening. Not many shifts end at five thirty in the afternoon; thankfully, I don't have to make small talk with anyone on the way to my car.

But I don't fully breathe until I close the car door behind me, sealing my bubble shut from the rest of the world. I start the engine and immediately turn the heating knob as high as it can go, reaching with trembling, frozen fingers for the dashboard vents.

Finally alone, I can let the mask drop. Tears spring from my eyes and my mouth gapes open crookedly in a silent scream. At first, I rub my hands together in front of the heated jets of air to warm them up, but then the gesture turns into obsessive clasping and unclasping while I sob uncontrollably in the silence of my car.

Why?

That simple question ravages my mind. There's no answer to it, nothing but anguish and sorrow.

Why did he have to land on my table? Why did I have to see his face? I never step past the drape. Never. But this time, I did. Why? Was it fate? I don't believe in it. Never have. Maybe tomorrow I will, considering what happened. Why me, out of all the cardiothoracic surgeons in this city?

Lively chatter drawing closer catches my attention. Two nurses I don't immediately recognize are approaching from the elevators. They might know me, they might see me falling apart in my car and tomorrow everyone in the hospital would hear about it, from the night janitors to M herself. I shift into gear and drive out of there before they can see my tear-streaked face.

Stopping at the parking garage exit to yield to traffic, I wipe my eyes with the back of my hand as I wait. It's raining and windy, weather throwing a tantrum that sends large droplets of water against my windshield with fury. The second day of March is only a spring picture on calendars; astronomically, it isn't going to be spring for almost three more weeks. This vengeful weather behaves like it wants us to remember who's in charge.

I catch a break in the traffic and turn, windshield wipers moving rhythmically in a hypnotizing pattern. Tears blur my vision, and raindrops against headlights blur it more. Yet I keep going, knowing home is minutes away. The heater is turned to the max, but I still can't feel the warmth. It's as if the sight of Caleb's unshaven face has frozen my blood for all eternity.

His heart should've restarted on its own, but it didn't. Why?

I should've been spared the decision I made. I wasn't. It doesn't seem fair, but life seldom is.

That doesn't change the fact that a perfectly good heart refused to beat after an apparently successful procedure.

I'm thorough; I know I am. I don't cut corners. I don't rush through my procedures, even if my fingers are stiff from sewing or if my back hurts from standing hunched over the operating table for hours on end.

I did more than that... I checked my work, right before they took Caleb Donaghy's body to the morgue. There was no visible reason why that heart stayed still once it was warmed up with saline and the blood flow restored. Most of the time that's enough. The heart warms up, fills with blood, and starts doing its job. It beats. It's written in its DNA.

Not this one. It didn't even flutter, no hint of v-fib even. Nothing. Perfect stillness, as if it were still paralyzed by the cold potassium solution. But I'd flushed it with warm saline until the temperature was up to the normal range required for sinus rhythm. Until it was warm enough to beat.

So, obsessively again, why?

My patient wasn't diabetic. I ran the entire pre-op blood panel twice. The last time was yesterday, checking carefully for any changes from a few days ago. His blood screening put him in a low-risk category for this surgery.

Yes, he was a drinker, and his liver was showing some signs of abuse, but his heart was okay, except for the aneurysm I took out and a slightly enlarged aortic valve. No history of arrhythmia, no syncope, nothing to give the slightest warning that his heart would simply refuse to beat.

As I drive, I go over the surgery in my mind, step by step, for the fourth or fifth time since it ended. I could do this fifty times more and I'd still have the same result. There was no warning sign. Nothing went wrong during the procedure.

Not until I stepped behind that drape and recognized him. Then everything changed.

But no one must ever find out who Caleb Donaghy was to me.

I take one last turn, and my house comes into view. It's my mother's house, really, but it's the home I always knew and loved. I could live anywhere I wanted, and probably my husband would be happier about it, but I can't bring myself to leave. Not with so many memories locked inside those red brick walls. Not while I still hear Melanie's laughter every time I step out into the backyard and the sun shines just right.

The house is large, my late father's vision of a comfortable home for his entire family, built back when he was a rising-star surgeon at the same hospital where I work today. He used to daydream of filling that house with grandchildren, and even great grandkids if he was lucky enough to live that long. He wasn't. He died when I was about to start my first year of med school. Sometimes, when I miss him really badly, I touch the glass of the living room window, where he used to rest his forehead and look outside. I swear I can feel his spirit touch mine somehow, through the walls, through that glass, as if he were still there, by my side.

The house is a straight shoot from the Lincoln Park Conservatory, three levels on a narrow lot, probably one of the last available lots in the Mid-North District of Dad's youth. A rare feature for the neighborhood, it has a double car garage that opens its door with the touch of a button.

I ease into the garage, then press the button again after I cut the engine. Darkness settles in gradually with the silently descending door. I could keep the lights on and fight it, I could leave the garage door open, but I welcome that darkness and the silence it brings, for it matches my mood. I close my eyes and invite darkness into my mind, to mute the day's horrible memories, to erase them into oblivion.

I'm home. I'm safe.

For now.

Until they come after me for what I've done.

A tear rolls down my cheek, then another, effortlessly. Somewhere, only a few miles south of here, a man's body lies on a morgue slab.

Did I put him there?

FIVE
HOTEL ROOM

The man loved to be straddled.

A little unusual for a power-hungry mayoral candidate. Paula had expected him to be a control freak of sorts, maybe even a bit brutal or overpowering, but he preferred to lie on his back with his hands interlocked under his head and let her use his body as she saw fit.

He wasn't disengaged or unparticipating. Not in the slightest. He watched her through half-closed eyes, with a hint of a loaded smile on his lips, his blue irises following every move she made with unshielded arousal. And he was patient, the future mayor of Chicago, in a selfless kind of way she struggled not to find endearing. He waited for her to be ready, followed her lead, perfectly timing his release to match hers.

Almost too good to be true. And in some ways, it was.

The simple gold band on his finger reminded her of the stark reality of their relationship. That he wasn't hers to have and to hold; he belonged to someone else.

For now.

She pushed the nagging thought aside and started moving faster and faster, resting her hands against his sculpted chest. If the citizens of Chicago could see him naked, they'd vote for him in a heartbeat. Most of them, anyway.

She dug her fingernails into his flesh and moaned. He stiffened underneath her, all his muscles tense, yearning. Seconds later, she landed by his side out of breath, panting with her mouth open and smiling. "You're good, Mr. Mayor, really good." She laughed. He placed a soft, satisfied kiss on her lips and wrapped her in his arms. He seemed ready to doze off, but she had different plans.

For just thirty seconds or so she allowed herself to be immersed in a blissful state of semiconsciousness, pretending it was real, believing it could become real. To wake up like that every morning... must be something.

Then she shifted in his arms, looked at his face. A firm jaw, salt-and-pepper hair a bit on the pepper side still, and perfectly blue eyes that reminded her of the Pacific Ocean before dusk. A firm nose, straight and classy, and sensual lips that seeded the tiniest dimples in his cheeks when he smiled. He had promise. For the both of them.

Reaching over him to the bottle in the ice bucket dripping water on the night table, she rubbed against his body slowly, biting her lower lip. "I'm thirsty," she whispered, although she couldn't bear the thought of drinking more champagne. "How about you?"

Grinning, he pushed himself up against the pillows and retrieved the two almost empty glasses from the table, then filled them up with Veuve Clicquot Brut. The liquid sizzled in the glasses. "It's your celebration, Ms. State's Attorney. You're calling the shots."

She took the glass from his hand and raised it a couple of inches until it met his with a cheerful clink. "Yeah, it is! Congratulations to me." She laughed, and he joined her. "I have more power now," she added, licking her lips. The champagne was exquisite, but a little on the stronger side. Or maybe she'd had too much bubbly already. "I'll know every single criminal case arrest, when it happens, and where." She took another sip and abandoned the glass on the night table. "And if I know, you'll know." She punctuated her statement with an index finger touching his chest, then starting to trace the lines of his muscles down to where the satin sheets blocked her path.

"Interesting," he replied, setting his empty glass next to hers and folding his hands under his head with expectation written in his blue eyes. "And why should I care?" he teased her in a slow, sultry voice.

She mock punched him in the shoulder and let herself fall back on the pillows. "Just think what we could do together." Her voice was all business now, maybe a little harsher than she would've wanted. "I can make sure you're there for all high-profile arrests, ready to speak to the press about your strong stance on crime in this city. After all, crime is the biggest concern for your voters."

"Aren't they your voters too?"

She laughed. "Not yet, they aren't. They will be, after a few years as head of criminal prosecutions. But then you'll be mayor, and you can endorse me for the state's attorney role the next election cycle."

"You've thought it all through, haven't you?" He was still smiling, but a hint of a frown was digging vertical lines at the root of his nose.

"And you haven't?"

He didn't answer immediately. She gave him time, knowing how important it was not to pressure him, to let him believe all the great ideas were his, not hers. Maybe some of them were: that was the value of their collaboration, after all. It was an alliance she was forging, not a love affair, she kept reminding herself, whenever she started to feel something for the unbelievably attractive man lying in bed by her side. She couldn't be sure she wasn't lying to herself, though. It would be so easy to let herself fall in love with him. So easy. Maybe she'd already fallen, just a tiny bit. Love was messy, though, and she couldn't deal with messy.

Absent-mindedly drawing little circles on his chest with soft, manicured fingers, Paula looked around, taking in the luxurious hotel room. She could get used to this.

The floor-to-ceiling window opened to what must've been a breathtaking view of Lake Michigan and the Chicago River in the daytime. Even now, she could see a glimpse of the city's nightscape with its myriad lights and the red and white trails of dense, downtown car traffic on the roads nine stories below their feet. By the window was a leather lounge chair she ached to sit in and read a book, although she knew she wouldn't have the time. The bed was an experience in itself with cool satin sheets, a weightless duvet, and soft down pillows.

She felt tempted to walk to the window naked and stand there, in plain view of anyone in the skyscraper across the street, to look at the restless traffic below and feel the curtains against her heated skin. Maybe one day she'd get a room for herself and let herself enjoy it. Or, in a few short years, she could replace Michael Hobbs as the state's attorney for Cook County and become the person with a standing reservation at the Travelle and one waiter's sole focus. Maybe it would still be Willie. Maybe he'd still remember her.

"You know, there's a story behind this champagne." His voice startled her back to reality. He sensed it and wrapped his arm around her, drawing her closer and caressing her back under the sheets. "I chose it for a reason." He chuckled. "I didn't just ask for expensive champagne to impress you."

She grinned, doubting what he'd said. "What was it, then? To show off your impeccable taste in French wine?"

He chuckled, visibly flattered. "Well, seems there was this French vineyard, if I remember correctly what I read, and the wine was okay, nothing great, because the owner had a textile business and some others that kept him busy. The name of the winemaker was—you guessed it—Clicquot. His son took it over after he got married, and set the wine business on a track to become what it is today. Then he abruptly died of some fever—I don't remember exactly what it was. He was really young. So, everyone thought the wine business would be sold, but his widow held on to it. She innovated the way the company was run, becoming one of the first women to lead an international business. In the eighteen hundreds—can you imagine?" He whistled in admiration. "She wasn't even thirty years old when her husband died. *Veuve* means 'widow' in French, and this is the brand that made her famous for centuries."

He picked up her glass and filled it again, then offered it to her. She took it, pulling herself up against the pillows.

"An homage to a powerful young woman on her way up," he said, raising his glass and looking straight at her. "You have the world at your feet, Paula. It's yours for the taking."

Impressed, she took a thoughtful sip of the sparkling wine and let it sit against her palate for a moment before swallowing. It was refined, exquisite. "Thank you. You never cease to amaze me, Mr. Mayor. You make such incredible pillow talk." For a brief moment, she fell into the trap of wanting him to stay, of wishing their alliance would become more.

"What's your favorite champagne?" he asked, thankfully scattering all the forbidden, nonsensical ideas from her mind. "Did I hit the spot?"

She laughed, relieved to be saved from herself. "No, and neither did my boss, with the Krug Grande Cuvée."

"Ah, well, of course he has one hell of an expense account," he quipped. "So, which is it?"

"Promise you won't laugh?"

He nodded, while tiny dimples appeared on his cheeks again. "Cross my heart."

"It's a cheap sparkling wine called Martini Asti. It goes for about twelve or fifteen bucks at the local grocery store. It's sweeter than these fancy ones, lighter. I like to call it champagne, though, just for the heck of it, even if I know it isn't."

He stared at her with eyes round with surprise. "Really?"

She gathered the sheet around her body to cover her breasts and lowered her gaze for a moment, feeling embarrassed. Maybe she shouldn't have shared that. "I grew up poor, what can I say? But it's really not bad. You should try it."

"Okay, let's try it," he replied, reaching for the phone. "I bet they have it here, or they could run a quick errand and get it for me."

She reached up and placed a long kiss on his lips. "Not today. I've just had all the champagne I can handle in one day. But next time, it's a date."

A hint of regret washed over his face, and she felt tempted to change her mind. She couldn't go down that path: once she started changing her plans to make him happy, their alliance was at risk of turning into something else. Why mess with perfection?

They met a couple of times a week, always in hotels, always in a different one, keeping a low profile for both their sakes. She couldn't be seen having an affair either, now that her career was taking off and she might get media attention. Her new role would enable her to choose the best, career-making cases for herself, and leave the routine ones for other ASAs, just as she'd done for her boss, SA Mitchell Hobbs.

Mitch. But not now, only from May onward. The memory of that comment made her chuckle. The man was a bit strange.

"I wonder what Hobbs is thinking."

Paula frowned at his question. It was as if he'd been reading her mind.

"Is he terminally ill or something? Suicidal, from a career point of view?"

"Why do you ask?"

"If he likes his job as state's attorney for Cook County, he should've buried you under a mountain of paperwork and never let you see the light of day. He must know you'll be gunning for it."

"He's fine with it," she replied, at the same time wondering if that statement was true. "At least that's what he said."

"I'd be wary of him if I were you." He moved to pour the rest of the champagne, but Paula declined with a wave of her hand. "In case it's a 'keep your enemies closer' kind of deal."

"Yeah, but why promote me, then? He's essentially opening the door to that path." She thought for a few moments. "No, I believe him. He might be gunning for governor and wants someone he can trust in the SA chair."

He hesitated for a split second before speaking. "Either way, I personally thank him, and I know you'll make one hell of a state's attorney one day soon. I'll be proud to support you on your way there. As mayor of our fine city."

She shook her head. "Quid pro quo, right?"

"Quid pro quo, Madam State's Attorney," he replied in a smooth voice, sliding slowly down the pillows and pulling the sheets off his body. "Let's seal the deal."

Resisting him was getting harder. "Would love to, but I have to run." She pulled herself away, keeping her back turned, afraid she'd cave if he insisted. Then she quickly walked into the bathroom, not taking a single moment to appreciate the gleaming white marble floors and the inviting rainfall shower.

His lovemaking was addictive, dangerous. She needed to escape before it was too late.

A splash of cold water against her face helped her regain control of her torrid senses. She sat on the edge of the bathtub until she could think clearly again, until she remembered what was really important.

A few moments later, she was fully dressed, getting ready to leave. He lingered in bed, the thin sheets hiding nothing of his body.

"Are you sure you won't change your mind?" His voice was riddled with desire, hot, urgent.

She slipped on her high-heeled pumps. "Can't. I'll text you."

He looked at her with curiosity as she adjusted her jacket. "I think I've seen you wear that before, haven't I?"

Of course, he'd remember. "The night we first met, at the fundraiser." She walked over to his side of the bed and leaned over until her lips touched his.

The silk bow collar of her blouse brushed against his skin. He moaned into her kiss. "I was memorable, wasn't I?" His hands landed firmly on her hips.

She wriggled free and walked toward the door, grabbing her purse on her way out. "Text me," she said, right before the door closed behind her.

Always leave them wanting more. That was the rule. It applied to everything and everyone, from courtroom jurors to bosses to lovers. She wasn't going to break it, but *damn.*

SIX
HOME

When the car door opens, it startles me aware. Not awake, because I wasn't sleeping. I'd let myself slide into comfortable numbness, dissociating from a reality I'm not yet able to handle.

It's still dark in the garage, with only a faint light coming from the door to the laundry room, now ajar. I don't know how much time has passed since I arrived home. I don't remember. I don't want to.

"Oh, sweetie," my mother says, crouching by my side and reaching for my hand. She's squeezing it tightly. Her skin is warm and dry, the kindness and love in her heart seeping through her touch. "You're frozen." She rubs my hand between hers, then tugs gently. "Come on, let's get you inside."

I don't want to go, but I do it for her sake. She's almost seventy years old and struggling with arthritis. She can barely put her weight on her left foot after a hip replacement surgery that she didn't fully recover from. Crouching in the cold and damp just to hold my hand isn't something she should be doing.

I offer her my arm, and she walks slowly across the garage, then climbs the two steps into the laundry room holding on to the doorjamb. I need to speak with Derreck about having some safety handrails installed. Here, and maybe in her bathroom too. The thought of my mother aging, needing grab bars, is heartbreaking. A sob climbs into my throat, choking me.

She senses that and gives me a quick look. "I'm so sorry, honey," she whispers as we cross the kitchen. She's still holding on to my arm, and leads me to my favorite spot on the sofa by the fireplace.

A lively fire is burning in the hearth. The logs have been there for a while, from a few nights ago when my husband Derreck and I were going to spend a nice, cozy Sunday at home, before one of my patients went into cardiac arrest and I had to drop everything and head back to the hospital.

Unlike Caleb Donaghy, that patient lived.

The logs were left in the fireplace, untouched until today. It's not like Mom to light a fire only for herself. The sad kindness in her eyes tells me she knows about my day.

"I'm sorry, baby," she repeats. "Ginny called me." She answers my question without me asking it. "She told me you lost a patient today. Here, sit down, and I'll make you a nice cup of tea."

I kick off my shoes and curl up on the sofa, leaning against the armrest, still feeling cold and shaky. I should've realized Ginny was going to call Mom. My surgical nurse, the one who's just survived a bad divorce, used to work on the same team as my mother before she retired. Mom used to be a surgical nurse too; that's how she met my dad. They made one hell of a team together, in work and even more so in life.

Ginny was one of Mom's protégés. I knew they kept in touch. When I was younger, I used to wonder if they were talking about me, about how I did my job. It felt as if I went to camp with one of my parents... humiliating. Like many young doctors fresh out of med school, I was insecure. That went away quickly in the first year of residency, when I became too busy to care about any of that nonsense.

Still, today it feels different, a pang of the old anxiety resur-
facing. "What did she tell you?" I ask, lifting my head off the
armrest just enough to see her face.

"Just that you lost a patient, and you are very upset about it.
So, I started a fire. I didn't know what else to do." She stirs some
honey into my tea, then brings it over on a small saucer.

My chest swells with love for my mother. I'm lucky to have
her. I've always known just how fortunate I was to have parents
like her and Dad growing up. I take the cup and wrap my
fingers around it, relishing the heat. "Thank you."

She sits by my side with a quiet groan. The cold Chicago
winter is tough on her joints. We watch the fire in silence as I
sip my tea. The hot chamomile burns my tongue and throat, but
I'm eager to feel that warmth spread from my stomach into the
rest of my body.

"People die, Anne. Hearts refuse to start again. You know
the odds." She speaks softly, her hand gently squeezing my
forearm.

"It shouldn't've happened, Mom. And you don't know the
half of it. This patient, this man was—" I stop, my throat
constricted, choking on the words I can't bring myself to say.
How can I tell my mother?

Her eyes search mine, a hint of worry coloring her loving
gaze. "You've been doing open heart surgery for years, and
haven't lost anyone yet. It's a miracle, a statistical fluke. What's
the operative mortality rate for aortic aneurysms these days?
Still fifteen percent?" I stare at her in stunned disbelief. "When
I was still working, that's what it was. Your father obsessed over
those numbers worse than you do. 'Every single number means
someone's child isn't coming home,' he used to say."

Speechless, I sip some more chamomile tea. I thought she'd
distanced herself from the hospital, from work, in the six years
she'd been retired. I've never known her to be interested in
statistics much.

I give her knotty fingers a concerned look. Maybe we should move someplace warm, where she'd be more comfortable. The idea, weakened by the thought of leaving all this behind, the house, my job, Derreck's too, dies before I voice it.

She traces the direction of my glance and rubs her hands together, her fingers visibly stiff. "It's what the OR will do to you if you let it," she says, with a touch of sadness. "Take good care of your hands, Anne. Keep them warm."

I have to tell her what I've done. If I don't get it off my chest, it will crush me. It will change who I am. It already has. But talking about my patient means talking about Melanie, and that will open deep wounds. I take a deep breath. "Mom, I—"

"It was bound to happen, sooner or later," she says, checking her hair as if getting ready to receive guests or go out. She wears it long still, colored blonde. She's a natural brunette, but her hair is almost completely white, and she likes wearing it blonde. It lightens her complexion, makes her look younger. "You have a natural talent, you know. Surgery was meant for you since the day you were born." She smiles as if at a fond memory and her gaze drifts away from my face. "Do you remember what you did with that big doll I got you for your birthday, when you turned six?"

The memories rush in and I smile, unable to resist. "The tall one with curly brown hair?"

"Yes, the princess." She laughs and slaps her knee. "She was so beautiful."

My smile wanes. "Some patients are." I meant my comment as a joke, but it sounds strange coming off my lips. I think of Caleb Donaghy again. Of Melanie.

Mom stares at me inquisitively for a brief moment as if she knows something's off. She's uncanny like that. "You cut her open, do you remember?"

I lower my head, hiding the anguish I'm feeling. "In my defense, I don't remember that." I look at her briefly, then take the last sip of tea. "I do remember trying to sew her back up. That should count for something." I place the empty cup on the table and sigh. She won't let me tell her what I've done. She's a veritable expert at changing the subject at the right time.

She's laughing so hard she has tears in her eyes. As if she knows what I want to say and just won't let me say it, so it won't become real. As if she wants her laughter and the fond memories we share to wipe out all the horrors of my day.

"Of course, you'd remember that. We came home from the hospital and found your fingers bloody from the needle, blood smeared all over your face and your clothes. Your nanny was horrified. You'd tried to stitch the princess's belly with my sewing kit."

My chin trembles as I struggle to hold back tears. "But then Dad—"

She covered her mouth briefly, to stifle a sob maybe. We both miss him so much. I'd heard the story many times, told at dinner parties and family reunions. And yet, each time she tells it, it feels different. "He went downstairs, brought back his suture kit, and showed you how to stitch that rubber belly properly."

The memory warms my heart. "Too bad I can't remember what was wrong with the princess to begin with."

"Oh, I do!" She squeezes my arm fondly. "Something was rattling inside, the device that made her cry and say 'Momma' and whatnot. You wanted to fix her."

"Great," I acknowledge with a hint of sarcasm, relishing the memory of that carefree time when I thought everything was possible. "She was the only doll I opened up, right?"

"Yeah. You lost interest in dolls the second your dad showed you how to stitch real skin, and that was a few weeks later, on—"

"On Thanksgiving," I say at the same time she does. "I remember that."

Her laughter fills the room again. For a brief moment, it

feels inappropriate, so soon after Caleb Donaghy. As if I should be mourning him.

But I never will.

"Can you imagine? I came downstairs that Thanksgiving morning, ready for endless hours of cooking, because we had guests. Your cousins were flying in from Seattle, and Dr. Seldon with his wife, and who else..." She frowns, trying to remember. "It doesn't come to mind right now. But everything had to be perfect."

I listen as if I've never heard the story before. Her face lights up as she tells it, as always happens when she talks about Dad. Or me.

"And there you were, the both of you, elbows deep in my turkey, stitching away. Muscle, ligament, skin... he showed you everything, and you were learning quickly. His med kit was on the table, and you were wielding that needle driver like a pro."

She stares for a moment at the flames, transported, as if my father's face was coming to life in the hearth he built almost fifty years ago. He loved sitting by the fire, right where I sit now. The smell of burning pinewood triggers so many memories of him, of us together. Of all four of us.

"I wanted to remove all the sutures before roasting that bird. I remember swearing—yes, I swore some that day and I never do that. I threatened your father that if he didn't get me a brand-new turkey, he'd be spending Thanksgiving alone. He didn't budge. He said the high temperatures in the oven would simulate the healing process, attaching the edges of the wounds, and once the bird was done, he could inspect the stitches and see if they were executed properly. You were so proud, it was a joy for me to look at you. And he... was beaming." She shakes her head and wipes a tear from the corner of her eye. "I couldn't fight that. Not after realizing what I felt in that very moment: pure, immense happiness. Never mind the embarrassment at the thought of serving a butchered turkey, or offering scissors to people to remove sutures from their holiday meal. All that didn't matter in the end. But my girl learning the trade from the most talented surgeon I'd ever met, that was pure happiness."

A thought rips through my heart. *What would Dad say if he knew about today?* Would he be ashamed of me? If he were still alive, would he want to look me in the eye? Or would he be deeply disappointed in me, regretting the day he taught me how to stitch turkey skin and muscle and sinew?

I can't breathe for a moment, not until I will myself to with all my strength. I can't bear the thought of Dad finding out what I've done.

For the first time in my life, I'm grateful he's gone.

Mom throws me another worried look, but doesn't ask. She just keeps on telling the story I've heard so many times. "Your Aunt Millie didn't touch her turkey. She always hated shop talk at the table, remember?"

I nod and smile, realizing what Mom is doing. She's reminding me who I am, of my heritage, the strength I have coursing through my blood. She's speaking of family and warmth and love, so I won't forget under the burden of my sorrow.

"I love you, Mom." I squeeze her hand and sink deeper into the sofa cushions, closing my eyes for one minute, so I can be alone with my monsters without her catching a glimpse.

Even if Caleb Donaghy's heart refused to restart on its own, even if it failed to restart after the first fifteen minutes of resuscitation efforts, his death was my doing. I could've kept on going. He was on pump; I could've kept on going for hours. I could've given him more epinephrine, a shot directly into his heart. There are other ways I could've kept on fighting for his life, ways I ignored.

Deliberately. After I saw his face.

All the contempt Dr. Bolger spewed for giving up so soon

was justified. And I'm willing to bet he didn't stay quiet about it.

The piercing sound of an approaching police siren rips through the stillness of the living room. Startled, I jump to my feet and rush to the window. My heart is thumping in my chest as blood drains from my face, symptoms of the paralyzing fear I'm feeling. I'm waiting for the police cruiser to screech to a stop in front of my house. I'm expecting cops to haul me away in handcuffs. Holding my breath, I stare at the empty street while I wait for the inevitable.

Mom watches me warily but doesn't say a word. The siren grows in intensity but then fades away, the police cruiser going on its way without even turning onto our street. Weary to the bone, I return to the sofa and lie down.

Soon they'll come for me. It didn't happen this time, but it *will* happen. Soon.

Because I killed a man.

SEVEN
CONFESSION

It's just three people to be seated at the dining table. The empty chairs haunt me tonight more than ever as I set the table. Mom's making roasted chicken with mashed potatoes, one of my favorite comfort meals, with gravy and all, as if today weren't a school night.

No school-age children have been seated around this table for many years, but we still call it that.

Mom tries her best with the meal, and I'm of little help. The mouthwatering smell of herb-encrusted roast fills my nostrils the moment she opens the oven, weaving through the air unseen, seeding hunger. That sensation immediately evolves into something else, more urgent. I rush into the bathroom and empty my stomach, holding on to the edge of the toilet bowl. I'm dry heaving when Mom arrives, pulling back my hair and placing her warm hand against my forehead, like she used to do when I was a child.

She doesn't say a word after that, just brews me another cup of chamomile tea and places it on the coffee table by my side, adding a few saltine crackers on the saucer. A few minutes later, they're gone, and my stomach is settled, at least for a while.

I help Mom finish setting the table, still dizzy and weak but knowing it's good for me to move, to immerse myself in the mundane. We aren't rushing; my husband is still not home.

Derreck.

The thought of facing him brings a stab of anxiety to my gut. What will I tell him? What *should* I tell him?

I didn't marry a doctor, like my parents had anticipated I would, like most doctors do. I fell in love with a young law student who visited our campus for a frat party when I was a sophomore. He was a senior. I still can't believe he passed his bar exam. He's nothing I'd imagined a lawyer would be. He doesn't have that innate aggression attorneys need to argue all day long in court, to cross-examine hostile witnesses until they break down on the stand. He's not "criminal attorney aggressive," but he's no softie either. His determination and willingness to succeed have different targets and different methods. For a while, he played with the idea of going into environmental law; he wanted to fight on the side of the good guys, because he's ultimately a good guy. To the core.

But it wasn't his brain that caught my attention the night of that frat party. His intoxicating smile and the sparks in his eyes lured me close, making me want to get to know him better. I was more than a bit disappointed to hear he was studying law instead of medicine, but a couple of slow dances later I was hooked, already falling in love, amazed it could happen to me and happen that fast.

I'd always been clinical about love, cynical even, knowing what lay behind the mechanism—the hormones and the genetic urge to ensure the survival of the species through reproduction. I could go on forever about what triggers chemistry, an addiction to each other like the one we had.

None of that mattered after I met him.

I was euphoric, the scientific term for being totally high on dopamine and oxytocin, unable to think about anything and anyone else but Derreck. For months, I dove right into the new romance knowing it would end soon. It wasn't supposed to last: it was too good to be true, right?

Six months down the road when he proposed, I flat-out said no. Doctors have very demanding careers. They're never home, doing seventy-two-hour shifts until they learn to sleep while walking and lose all interest in anything except their jobs. I would end up breaking his heart, because I'd never be there for him the way he deserved his wife to be. He accepted my answer with sadness in his eyes and a resigned nod, then he left.

I cried all night, thinking it was over. It wasn't.

Our romance resumed without a glitch the following day. When I asked Derreck why he wasn't leaving me after I'd rejected him, he said simply, "I love you, Anne. That didn't change because you can't bring yourself to believe in us. I'll just demonstrate to you that your three-day shifts go just fine with my eighty-hour work weeks." He kissed my lips and added, "We'll need a housekeeper, though. I have someone lined up." Then he offered me the key to his apartment.

Three days later, he was moving in with me and Mom. That was the ultimate test, agreeing to live with my mother and actually fitting in. I can't think of many men who would, even if Mom was always sweet and welcoming. Most men would value their privacy more than anything else, not willing to compromise, not finding a reason why they should.

We shared the guest room downstairs, reluctant to move upstairs. I was a bit anxious about the thin walls of our house and didn't feel too good about us making love only a few feet away from Mom's bedroom. That sense of uneasiness went away quickly as Derreck settled in as if he'd always belonged, and Mom started loving him like a son. We still sleep downstairs, though; in the sixteen years we've been together it never crossed my mind to move upstairs into the master bedroom.

That will always be my parents' room, even if Mom offered countless times.

The downstairs guest suite has many benefits on top of privacy. It's large enough, has its own bathroom with a shower and a jacuzzi, and comes with his and hers closets. It's close to the living room, a handy feature if I get insomnia and I want to watch TV, which happens sometimes. I can also sneak out quietly if a hospital emergency drags me out of bed in the middle of the night.

I am slicing bread on the table when I hear the sound of his Beemer on the short driveway. I drop the knife and go to the window, where I watch him grab his jacket and briefcase from the back seat. I wave at him when he looks at me, a routine we have—tiny little gestures of affection that have become engrained in the fabric of our life together.

This time, a sliver of anxiety cuts through me. *I'll have to tell him what I've done.*

I meet him by the door and raise my lips to meet his. He wraps his arms around me for a brief moment, then whispers in my ear, "Hey, baby." I could stay in those arms forever. He smells of deodorant and shower gel, seeming fresh as if he hadn't been in those same clothes since seven in the morning.

"Hey." I smile as I pull away. "Wash your hands, dinner's ready." And so, routine kicks in. He undoes his tie and abandons it on the back of the sofa, on top of his suit jacket. He rolls up his sleeves and washes his hands at the kitchen sink, while Mom waits patiently for her turn. Then he rinses bowls for her, making small talk.

I help Mom put soup in the bowls, then set them on the table. When I finally sit down, it feels like I haven't sat in ages. My long sigh gets Derreck's attention.

"What's wrong?"

I shake my head. "Just... nothing. I'm very tired. It's been a long day. Enjoy your soup." A frown flickers on his brow. Short phrases are not my thing; he knows something's off. I break eye contact and finish my soup, then help Mom serve the roast, while Derreck uncorks a bottle of Pinot Gris.

Memories swirl in my head, some good, like our wedding, about a year and a half after Derreck moved in with us. Other memories are painful, so painful I flinch, a million miles away from the low-key chatter at the table. I push pieces of chicken around my plate, knowing I won't be able to eat much. I take a bit of mashed potato and dip it in gravy, then let it melt in my mouth. To my right, Derreck eats like a champion after a big game, with hungry, enthusiastic gulps and carefree conversation. Without realizing, I stare into the empty space across from me, where Melanie used to sit.

Melanie.

I push my chair out and stand, a little dizzy still. "You guys carry on," I whisper. "I'll be right back." My voice breaks, and I turn away in time to hide my tears.

I head upstairs, holding on to the gleaming oak handrail, and climb the steps slowly, pressing my hand on my chest. It's amazing how we feel things in our hearts. But do we, really? The heart is just muscle, a pump doing a job of moving blood. I've held many hearts in my hand and that's all they are, muscle and sinew and fibrous tissue, and electrical impulses to tell them when and how to beat. We know pain takes place in our brains, but our hearts are blamed for it, because that's where we *feel* pain. There's a scientific explanation for it, to do with adrenaline and cortisol and norepinephrine and how these hormones impact the function of the heart, but it's not what anyone wants to hear when they grieve. They don't care *why* their heart is breaking; they just feel that it is.

I don't want to hear that either.

Instead, I want to hear that the pain will end. But it never will. I'll just learn to live with it a little better. That's all I can hope for.

I reach the second floor and walk slowly to the second bedroom on the right. The massive oak door is closed. I touch the lacquered wood with my hand while a sob emerges from my chest. I close my eyes and listen intently until I can hear Melanie's laughter coming from behind the door. It's not real; it's just a memory I brought back to life with effort and willpower.

I'm lying to myself. Melanie will never laugh again.

The pain ripping through my chest leaves room for anger in its wake. It's strange how all these years have passed, and I'm still grappling with that stage of my grief. Knowing what this is and how it works doesn't make it any easier.

Melanie was just a little girl who never got to grow up, to fall in love, to live. My sweet little sister.

I grab the doorknob and try to turn it, but my hand refuses to comply. I can't get it to squeeze that handle. I still can't go in there. Not even today, when I need it so badly. In a fit of rage triggered by my own weakness, I slam my open hand against the wood. *Damn it to hell.*

"You okay up there?" Derreck calls from the dining room.

I push air into my lungs. "Yeah, I'll be right down." I wipe my eyes with my sleeve and head back downstairs. Then I take my seat at the table, staring at my plate. I pick up the fork and take a lump of mashed potatoes and dip it in gravy, just like before. I can't touch the chicken breast meat. It reminds me of the Thanksgiving turkey when I was little, of my father, of the first piece of real skin I stitched. Of open chests and split breast-bones. Of Caleb Donaghy.

My mother throws me an inquisitive look I sense more than I see, but she doesn't ask anything. She knows where I've been and what I tried to do, just as she knows I failed again. There will be no words spoken about this, not tonight, not ever.

She gets up from the table, and Derreck also stands.

"I'll load the dishwasher," Derreck says, kissing her hand like a medieval knight. "Thank you for a wonderful dinner."

She smiles weakly at him, then, in passing, she caresses my hair and my cheek. I lean into her hand and close my eyes. A tear rolls down my face. Then she walks away to the stairs she climbs with difficulty.

"Okay, what's going on?" Derreck asks the moment we hear her bedroom door close. He pulls his chair to the side to look at me and grabs my hand. The chair legs screech in protest on the tiles, but the sound is so distant it doesn't seem real. "Anne? What happened?" His thumb wipes off a tear from my face with a tender gesture.

How do I even start? "I lost a patient today. I—um, he was —" I choke, unable to breathe, to say the words.

"I'm so sorry," he whispers, squeezing my hands between his. "I'm sure you've heard this enough already, but people die, Anne. The type of surgeries you do, they come with a risk. You know this."

I shake my head weakly, wishing he'd let me speak. "You don't understand, Derreck. This was no ordinary patient. This man was... I knew him."

His eyebrows draw together. "What do you mean? Was he, like, a friend? I thought surgeons never operated on people they know."

"Yes, that's true," I rush to explain, grabbing his rolled-up shirt sleeve as if to hold him still. "I didn't know who he was, not at first anyway. Then, when I saw, it was too late. Maybe... I don't know."

He stares at me for a moment, visibly confused. I'm not making much sense. Words fall out of my mouth in a frenzied rhythm, my secrets eager to break free. I want to tell him, but I'm so afraid at the same time. Petrified it might change who we are forever, that it might damage his love for me. But if there was ever a time to tell him it's now, not when the police start pounding on the door to arrest me.

He drinks some Pinot, then looks at me reassuringly. "Okay, so you lost a patient, right?"

I nod, unable to say anything. My throat is completely dry. My hands shake so badly I don't trust them with a glass.

"Did you do anything wrong?"

"Well, that's—" I shake my head again, lowering it until a few loose strands of long hair fall over my face. Then I look up at him with an unspoken plea. "I don't know, Derreck. His heart didn't start, not after surgery, not even after intense resuscitation efforts."

He tilts his head, seemingly relieved. "Sounds to me it wasn't anything you did. Doesn't matter who he was—"

"I called time of death early. I rushed to call it, I admit that, but his heart wouldn't start to begin with. But I stopped trying... after I recognized him."

He pulls away slightly, every inch of distance chilling the blood in my veins. "Are you saying you could've saved this man and didn't?"

Yes.

I want to scream the word, but I can't. My mouth gapes open but only a bitter sob comes out. He buries my head into his chest and holds me tight while I cry, gently caressing my hair. My tears aren't for Caleb Donaghy. They are for Melanie, and for our life that won't ever be the same after today.

After a while, when I can breathe again, I pull away, painfully aware I didn't tell him everything. But something in the way Derreck looks at me tells me he already knows. He must've figured it out on his own. Otherwise, he'd ask me why. He's shocked. I can see it in his widened eyes, in the tense, lowered corners of his mouth. Knowing I disappointed him hurts like hell.

"This could end us both. Our careers, our life as we know it.

Who else knows about this?" His voice is low, yet cold, factual, an attorney's version of clinical. A shudder rattles me to the core.

I shake my head vigorously. "No one."

"How about the people you operate with? They're not idiots... Do they suspect anything?"

My hand flies to my mouth, covering it briefly before I speak. I think of the anesthesiologist, Dr. Bolger, and his seething hatred for me. "There might be questions, b—but I have—" I stutter again pitifully. "My record is spotless."

"But you said you knew this man, your patient?" His voice is harsh, professional, as if I'm sitting through a deposition prep session. I'm grateful for that, for his lucidity. "Can anyone trace that connection?"

"No."

"Good." He stands and starts pacing the room. "Keep it that way. No unburdening your soul to anyone. No casual comments in the hospital cafeteria. No answering anyone's questions, unless you're in court with an attorney by your side." He paces for another minute while I hold my breath, apprehensive of what's to come. Then he stops behind my chair and puts his hands on my aching shoulders, giving them a rub. Warmth seeps from his hands into my body.

"Come to bed, baby."

EIGHT
SIX

Derreck gives good advice. Totally impractical when it comes to life in a hospital, but good.

At least I'll be better prepared for Monday when I go back to work. It's not like I can simply refuse to discuss the case should anyone want to. Hospitals aren't police precincts, where you can decline to answer any questions before your attorney joins you in the dreary, smelly, ten-by-ten room with scratched walls and crooked, stained furniture.

I've never visited a police precinct myself; just seen it on TV. I really hope I never do. My mind knits monsters and night-mares out of my fears as I sit on the sofa, watching the dying flames in the fireplace and waiting for Derreck to finish loading the dishwasher.

The sound of rattling dishes is grating, annoying, but I can't say a word to him about it. I feel nothing but gratitude for my husband's love and understanding, but I so wish he'd be done already with the ruckus, or let me do it instead. Maybe if I control the noise, it will bother me less.

I stand up and walk over to the kitchen, barefoot on the cold tile floor. "Let me do this, please." I look at him briefly, then shift my eyes, still afraid to face him, the hurt I've caused, the damage I've done.

"Nah, I'm almost done," he replies, placing a kiss on my forehead. "Why don't you go ahead and take a shower? Make it a long one, or maybe run yourself a bath while I finish here. Huh? What do you say?"

I reach for the glass of wine I abandoned on the table. It still has about an inch left in the bottom. I down that. It feels cold. It tastes funny, bitter, sour. Why do people drink this swill? Until yesterday, I used to like Pinot Gris. Maybe this bottle's different. "You go first," I whisper, painfully aware I can't argue with him and wishing that he won't insist. He doesn't. After a moment of silence disturbed only by clattering cutlery loaded unceremoniously into the dishwasher, I breathe with a bit more ease and head back toward the sofa.

I stop in front of the fireplace, yearning for the heat to touch my frozen skin. The flames have died, leaving smoldering cinders in the hearth, the embers throwing orange hues against the floor, the white walls, and my hands when I hold them close.

There's no wood left by the hearth. There's some out in the garage, but I don't feel up to it, and I don't want to ask Derreck. I don't want him to have to do anything for me today. I grab the poker from the stand and stir the embers until a small flame erupts, then another. I curl up on the sofa and enjoy the sound of the dishwasher drawing water with a satisfied sigh.

Soon it will be silence.

"Don't stay long, okay?" Derreck says, heading for the bedroom. He throws me a loving smile, but the tension remains there, in the two vertical lines flanking his nose, in the firmness of his jaw and the stiffness of his shoulders. I hope the shower will wash some of that tension away. Time will probably help some too.

Why did I have to tell him? I felt good for a minute or two, having a shoulder to cry on and feeling supported and loved, but at what cost?

I reassure him with a nod and a moment's eye contact, then I continue to stare at the tiny flames. Funny how they keep on burning, fragile yet persistent, a mere inch or less, when there's nothing left for them to burn. This fire still holds on, crackling and hissing and giving heat. Maybe it wasn't people who invented hope and endurance. Perhaps fire discovered that long before we mortals did.

I've let everyone down. My family. My team. My patients— those who I was supposed to operate on today, and tomorrow, when I'm staying home, per M's specific orders. The ones I operated on yesterday and the day before, and who I am supposed to care for during their recovery. What will they all think? That I've abandoned them at their most vulnerable. And yet it's better they think that and hate me for it, than be reminded that people can die on my table, under my knife. I was just reminded of that, and I still can't deal with it. Even more, I'm dreading the time when it won't seem so devastating, when I'll get used to it, like Dr. Seldon had said I would, after ten, fifteen more years as a surgeon. How can I imagine a world where I can grow accustomed to people dying? To delivering bad news to devastated families, shattering their hopes with one word? I hope it never gets better, not for me. Death can never become a statistic. Not on my table.

Because today was a special circumstance. That's what we call cases that don't fit the norm, that don't follow the rules; cases that defy logic and patterns and expectations. Death laughing in my face to remind me who's boss. How quickly I can change sides.

I hear the bathroom door open in the guest bedroom suite, then the sheets rustling. Derreck left the bedroom door ajar, and a warm light comes from inside, the promise of warmth and comfort and peace.

And yet, I'm not ready for any of that. Restless and tense, my jaw clenched to the point where it hurts, I walk into the bedroom, then straight into the bathroom, without saying a word. In passing, I catch a glimpse of Derreck, his broad chest naked above the comforter, his thin-rimmed reading glasses low on his nose. He's propped up against the pillows, reading a magazine with a scowl on his face. I don't stop to ask what reporter has offended him and how. I rush inside the steamy bathroom and close the door behind me, then lean against it for a while. Just breathing.

Tears flood my eyes, and a sob rips through my chest. Pressing my hand against my open mouth, I manage to keep it silent, then I turn on the shower for good measure. In a state nearing shock, my shoulders heave, and my frozen hands tremble as I let my clothes drop to the floor before I enter the shower. Under the flowing jets, no one can tell sweet from salty, water from tears.

I welcome the burning sensation on my skin, hoping it will cleanse my mind just as it does my body, but it doesn't work. Tension builds up, fierce, loaded with feelings I can't name. Against my closed eyelids, I see snippets of Melanie, of her face, laughing at me and sticking her tongue out. Of her thin, frail body shaking and cowering that day in the park. Of the bruises and barely healed cuts. Of her tearful, frightened shame.

As if executing a hard labor sentence, I wash myself with quick yet feeble movements, hoping I can finish before all my energy drains out. I'm still shaking as I come out of the shower.

I look at myself in the mirror as I would a stranger. The naked body I see in the fogged-up reflection doesn't feel like it belongs to me. It feels distant, foreign, numb. I wrap it in a large towel while I keep staring, then start drying my hair.

When I emerge from the bathroom a few minutes later, my teeth are brushed, my hair is dry and loosely braided for the night, and a white silk, strappy nightie is the only thing I'm wearing. I'm tense still, the heat from the shower quickly disappearing, leaving me weak.

I stop at the foot of the bed and look at Derreck. He barely acknowledges me. The comforter covers his body up to his lean abdomen, his legs crossed at the ankles underneath. He holds the magazine upright in his lap, his fingers fanned out against the cover. He's reading this month's edition of *TIME,* and he's clearly still not too pleased with the content.

"I wonder whose ass you need to kiss to get on the cover of this," he says morosely, flicking his fingernail against the red-framed cover.

I'm briefly grateful his mind is in a different place than mine. I remain standing by the foot of the bed, waiting, not really sure for what. The tension in my body starts unfurling, demanding, yearning. Slowly, unsure, and with trembling fingers, I push the strap of my nightie off my right shoulder.

Probably intrigued by the silence, Derreck looks up at me. A flicker of something indecipherable glints in his pupils. The magazine lands on the floor with a soft rustle, and his glasses rest on the night table.

The second strap slides off my left shoulder, pushed slowly to the side, while I look into my husband's eyes, ready to stop if he doesn't want me. But he doesn't hesitate. He waits for me patiently, his eyes burning with desire. The silk nightie falls to my feet while I continue to stand, naked, perfectly still and silent. I need this badly. I need to feel alive, immersed in the moment, to take a break from my dark thoughts and just live.

He tilts his head slightly and pushes over the sheets, inviting me to join him in bed. I shake my head slowly, looking at the floor, at my feet, at the white bundle of crumpled silk. I can tell he's frowning, even without looking at him, because by now he must know what I need.

I look at the chair where he left his clothes. My eyes linger on the belt looped on his pants, the elegant silver buckle hanging to the side. How can I ask him, the kindest man I ever met, to do what I need him to? How can I tell him I bought that belt for him, knowing a day would come when I'd want it cutting through my flesh and bruising my thighs? It's what I need, the intense pain, the feeling of being overpowered, so I can never forget what that could feel like. Today, more than ever.

I swallow hard, then take the belt hesitantly, pulling it free and folding it in my hand. Then I lay it gently down by his side, and walk backward to the foot of the bed. I wait, the tension gripping my body, unbearable.

Something dark washes over his eyes. He doesn't ask why, and I know he doesn't like what I ask of him, but he does it, nevertheless. When he eventually grabs the belt, I take a deep breath and draw closer, anxious and eager and craving what's to come.

"How many?" he whispers.

"Six."

NINE
VISIT

I've been back to work for a couple of days now. From Monday morning, I was immediately pulled back into the merciless rhythm of hospital life. It doesn't give me too much time to think, and I'm grateful for that.

The nightmares remain though, the flinching with every police car that crosses my path, the sense of impending doom I can't seem to shake. At first, I struggled to keep my mind clear about what happened, found myself obsessing over Caleb Donaghy's death. While that was happening, M, the hospital administrator, had me play second fiddle on a number of surgeries, "to get back in the game," in her own words. She paired me with Dr. Seldon for a couple of bypasses, and with the cardiothoracic surgery department chief of staff, Dr. Fitzpatrick, for a mitral valve repair.

Strangely enough, both doctors were willing to step aside and let me perform the surgeries. I believe I was being supervised; in fact, both senior surgeons probably asked to check my readiness to resume a normal schedule after the Caleb Donaghy incident.

The incident... that's what everyone's calling it. It wasn't an incident, that's for sure. An incident is when someone has a heart attack during a movie at the local theater. An incident is when the power goes off during a storm. I don't correct them, though; it would make little sense and would be uncalled for, a strategic mistake. It might give everything away.

Both doctors must've signed off on my post-incident professional readiness, because today, Wednesday morning at almost eight o'clock, Madison is bringing me a hot cup of coffee and the day's schedule for review, and it has a surgery on it.

I take the cup from her hand with a grateful glance and set it on the desk, on a keep-warm coaster that's always plugged in. "Thanks, Maddie." She looks a bit tired, her makeup seeming rushed, failing to cover her pallor. I don't ask; she shouldn't feel she needs to share what she doesn't necessarily want to.

Instead, I focus my attention on the colorful printouts she fans out in front of me.

"There wasn't any time to do much prep yesterday, so today you only have one procedure: a coronary stent on a forty-year-old nonsmoker. He's Dr. Seldon's patient. That's at two. Three consults one after another starting at nine, then you have prep sessions with the team for tomorrow's surgeries."

I frown, recognizing the names on the schedule printout. I met both patients yesterday. One of them needs the same procedure as Caleb Donaghy.

"Tomorrow, we have Mrs. Heimbach for the mitral valve replacement," she continues, unfazed, her schedule review with me the starting point of every day. "Then Mr. Molinari for the triple A."

Ah. I glance at her quickly and she smiles awkwardly. She didn't call it an ascending aortic aneurysm... now it's a *triple A*. But I'm being oversensitive, still raw, overthinking this. I'm willing to bet a lot of money she's used the acronym before. We all must have, even if I can't remember it for sure right now. It's shorter, easier.

"I need thirty minutes longer to prep the triple A with the team, considering what happened the last time around. We should discuss everyone's concerns if they have them." I take a sip of coffee, glad it's so strong and bitter, packing a good punch. "Who's the anesthesiologist?"

I cringe, while she rummages through her papers to find the information.

"Dr. Barrymore."

I'm so relieved I could hug her. She smiles, as always uncanny in her ability to read my mind. But then her timid smile vanishes, leaving room for a look of concern. "I probably shouldn't tell you this, but rumor has it that Dr. Bolger went to M and requested he never be your anesthesiologist again."

Did he, now? I was expecting nothing short of that from Bolger. And still, the news has me rattled, anxious again, the sense of doom stoked inside me like a drywood bonfire. Who knows what he told M? I breathe deeply and slowly, willing myself calm, reminding myself I didn't like working with him either, so there might be a small win in all this ugliness.

"Sorry, Anne," Madison whispers, shooting a quick glance at the open office door. "You know what a prick he can be, without even trying."

I smile nervously. "I'm fine. Don't worry about me." I bite my lower lip, thinking hard, feeling rushed to make a decision, desperately wanting to make the right one. "Maybe I could call Dr. Seldon and see if he can take Mr. Molinari tomorrow. Maybe it's too soon for the team to work another aortic aneurysm so soon after—" The words I want to say get caught in my throat.

Madison touches my forearm. "Let's not waste a favor," she says, lowering her voice. My office door is still open, and the corridor is only a few feet away. "Why don't I call his assistant, see if it's possible before we ask? Then she and I can work the schedules together."

She's wonderful, Madison. She has more wisdom that I thought possible for a thirty-four-year-old to possess.

"You do that, all right?" I glance at the digital wall clock. Almost forty minutes left before I have to start the first consult. "Where's... um... Caleb Donaghy? Was he picked up?"

She frowns at me and presses her lips together disapprovingly, probably unhappy with my growing obsession that she doesn't understand. "Not yet," she replies with a long, pained sigh. "He's still at the morgue. I heard they're going to do an autopsy."

I stand, looking at the clock again, considering what I'm about to do. I know it's wrong, but I can't stop myself. I have to see him again, to make sure I saw what I saw. Just one more time. "I'll be downstairs."

"Anne—"

I rush past her fast enough to discourage any comment, because I already know what she'd say if given a chance. To make it worse, she'd probably be right about every single word.

Once in the elevator, I press the button for the basement. It takes me there after stopping a couple of times and loading other people, then unloading them all in the lobby. I keep my face turned away in case I see someone I know, but they're complete strangers. *Small miracles.*

The basement is shrouded in silence and dimly lit. I've always wondered why basements seem to have weaker lights than all the other floors, when in fact they need it more. Probably it has something to do with budgets and the cost of lightbulbs.

The morgue is almost completely empty, the only exception a young assistant busy cleaning test tubes in the back wall sink. The air is cold and dry, and the whirring of multiple refrigeration units is loud enough to obscure the sound of the running water. Yet the assistant senses me entering the morgue through the swinging doors and pivots to look at me.

He turns off the faucet and dries his hands quickly on a small towel hanging from the wall. Then he takes a few steps toward me, smiling hesitantly, while I realize how unprepared I am for this. What will I say? How can I explain what I came here to do?

"Ah, it's you," he eventually says. "'The heart girl.'" He's making air quotes and beaming.

His comment throws me off. "What?"

He grins widely, showing crooked teeth that could use a retainer, and fishes his phone out of his pocket. "Here, I'll show you." He flips through several images then shows me the screen, holding it a little too close to my face for comfort. "The highway billboard. You seen this?"

Of course, I have. I used to be proud of it, thrilled that I, a then thirty-nine-year-old surgeon, had been chosen to be the face of the prestigious hospital on billboards advertising the cardiothoracic surgery department. I felt flattered and humbled at the same time. Dr. Seldon or even Dr. Fitzpatrick, the chief of staff, deserved it more than I did, and still, I was the person they selected. *Maybe because I'm a woman*, I told myself at the time, *and times are changing*. Derreck had said, "From cars to donuts to surgery, sex sells." I remember mock punching him in the side for that comment, while I stubbornly chose to believe it was only my professional acumen that had earned me the honor. I even asked M about it, that's how sure I was of myself. She had stared at me over the rims of her glasses, probably wondering how an idiot like me could make a half-decent surgeon, and said, "Your impeccable record contributes in no small measure to the success of this organization. And it doesn't hurt at all that you're also a beautiful blonde with long, wavy hair, blue eyes, prominent cheekbones, and a figure to die for." I don't recall how I reacted to that, only that I signed the deal the next day in a daze. Afterward, Derreck had said a few times how he told me so, but then encouraged me to see the good in it, the recognition, the value. The opportunity.

The billboards went up about a year and a half ago. There are five of them, really large, visible from the busiest highways and the interstate. They depict a smiling male patient with white hair, lying on a hospital bed and hooked up to monitors, while I stand by his side, smiling also and wearing a white, crisp lab coat, making the hand heart gesture over my chest. The slogan in blue, bold lettering below says, "Life. From our heart to yours." Underneath, in a smaller font, "Meet Dr. Anne Wiley, cardiothoracic surgeon at Joseph Lister University Hospital."

After a year of having them out there, the advertising agency reviewed the results and decided to keep the billboards unchanged for at least another year. Seemed that people responded favorably to them, to my image, to the message itself. I'd lie if I didn't admit I was tickled. I was a star... thrilled for a little while longer, then forgetting all about it.

But I never heard anyone call me "the heart girl" before. *Not to my face. That's new.*

I smile at the morgue attendant and take a step back. "Of course, I just forgot about it, that's all."

"I'm going to tell everyone I met you in person!" He's pacing around excitedly. "What can I do for you?"

My smile wanes. Plunging my hands deep into my pockets, I draw closer to the refrigerated storage shelves, where the bodies are kept. "I had a patient die on the table last week. I was hoping I could see—"

"Say no more," he announces cheerfully, his enthusiasm ill-fitting for the place we are in. He opens a door without hesitation and pulls out the shelf, then squints at the name tag. "Caleb Donaghy, right?" He must know where every one of his guests is lodged by heart, without checking. Or maybe his hotel is almost empty.

I nod, approaching slowly as he peels the sheet from Donaghy's head and torso. I shudder when I see the face I know, discolored by livor mortis, his port-wine stain even more striking than I remember.

"I'll give you some time," he says, walking backward to the sink. "But don't feel bad. It's not your fault. You're our heart girl and we love you." He taps his chest twice with his open hand and chuckles awkwardly, then resumes cleaning the test tubes under a jet of hot water that puts a faint trace of steam in the air.

I wait until I see he's immersed enough to stop paying attention to me, then I take out my phone and snap a picture of the man's face. The light is poor, and my hand trembles slightly, but I manage after two or three botched attempts to get a decent shot. Donaghy won't be stored in the morgue forever, available to visit whenever I start doubting my sanity. Or my memory.

I slip my phone back into my pocket and come closer, studying the shape of his birthmark. Yes, it's the same I saw that day in the park. I'm 100 percent sure. The face I stare at starts shifting into a memory from when I was fourteen years old, walking my little sister of only nine through Lincoln Park, heading for the zoo. I was so proud of her, and so happy, it seems surreal now. I still recall staring at passersby, trying to see if they noticed just how beautiful Melanie was, how pretty in her pink ruffle dress and blue ponytail ribbons. She was singing out loud and off-key a childish zoo song, excited, laughing. She'd never been to the zoo before. And I was beside myself with pride for being trusted to take her by myself, like an adult.

We were almost at the gates when her voice faltered, and her hand squeezed mine desperately hard. A whimper climbed from her chest as she hid behind my legs, grabbing the fabric of my jeans with her other hand and clutching it fiercely. I turned around, trying to look at her face, calling her name, trying to make sense of what had happened. Had she twisted her ankle? But she hid her face, pleading and sobbing.

"Let's go home," she cried, her face buried against my leg, only moments after bellowing improvised lyrics to "Let's Go to the Zoo." Naturally, I protested. Was she suddenly afraid of the zoo animals she hadn't seen yet? I would take care of her, keep her safe.

I crouched by her side and hugged her. Her thin body was shaking in my arms, her eyes wide open in fear, staring at a man who sat on a park bench about ten, fifteen yards away. His sweaty forehead showed a stain of something red I didn't know back then was a birthmark, partly obscured by his hair, right at the limit of his receding hairline. The red stain was memorable, so unusual and recognizable it burned its shape in my memory forever. The man was about thirty-five years old, reading a newspaper, unaware of our presence. He wore work-stained jeans and a checkered shirt, the top two buttons undone, showing a bit of hairy chest.

"Don't let him hurt me again," Melanie whispered through whimpers and tears. "Please don't let him take me."

I promised her I wouldn't let him near her again, and we rushed home—one of the hardest things I ever had to do. I still remember how much I wanted to go to that man and punch him straight in the face—me, the delusional yet recklessly bold teenager—and ask him what he'd done to my sweet little sister.

But I already knew... I'd seen the signs on her body, the day she first came home.

I no longer need to ask him what he did to Melanie. I just need to tell him.

"You killed her, you sick son of a bitch," I whisper through clenched teeth near his ear, unable to restrain myself. "And now you'll pay for it. I hope you rot in hell."

"I talk to them too, you know." The attendant's voice startles me. I step away from the corpse and look straight at him. He seems as jovial as when I first came in and stands a good few feet away, probably out of earshot. "Not all the time, but sometimes, when I'm bored..." He shrugs and smiles crookedly. "Need him out any longer? We have to keep them cool, you know."

I shake my head, ready to bolt out of there. My heart thumps in my chest angrily, torn, aching, still reliving painful snippets of that day at the park.

What I should've done instead of just going home. What I should've said.

Maybe she'd still be alive today.

TEN
QUESTIONS

The three consults scheduled for the morning take longer than anticipated. Two of them are elderly patients struggling with crippling fear on top of their respective heart symptoms. The third consult, a younger male with a more serious issue, is a cynical denier, poking fun at all things death and reassuring me he's lived long enough, anyway.

Yet there he was, waiting more than an hour for the consult he bravely maintained he didn't really need.

When I get back to my office, I find a cup of chamomile tea on the warm coaster. Next to it is the file I asked Madison to put together, neatly laid on my desk, but no Post-It note affixed to it like normal, with details about the patient, like surgery date and room number. This time, I don't need one.

I sit and open the red folder, knowing what to expect. I asked her to put together everything we have on Caleb Donaghy. Test results, imaging, evaluations, the whole file. I want a copy for myself, something I can review again when things quiet down a little bit. One thing is missing though. I take out my phone and choose the best of the pictures I snapped in the morgue, then send it to the color printer with one tap.

Madison gets to the printer before I do. She grabs the sheet from the tray and looks at it briefly, then at me with a quizzical, disapproving look on her face. I can't explain anything to her. I'm better off if she thinks I'm overreacting to the patient's death.

As I return to take my seat, she places the printout on top of the open file. Then she leans against my desk with her hands propped firmly on it and looks me straight in the eye. "It happens to everyone, Anne. Why can't you let it go? It's not healthy."

I stare down at his face, and a shudder courses through my veins. *Donaghy is dead. What's done is done.* Slowly, I close the red folder, leaving the photo on top of the test results.

Madison holds out a hand, waiting for the file folder. It's her job to archive them after the patients have been discharged, or, in this case, after their deaths.

But I can't let go. Not yet.

I place my hand on top of the file as if protecting it. "I'll need this for the formal review."

She looks at me with a raised eyebrow, stopping short of calling bullshit. Instead, she props her hands on her hips and sighs. "You have living patients to worry about. You're going back into the OR at two, with barely enough time to grab some lunch and get ready for the procedure." She stares at the red folder with disdain. "Need I say more?"

I don't need lunch, and I'm ready to step into that OR when I'm scheduled. A hint of rage riles up my heart rate. All I need is some peace, not to be spoken to like I'm five.

She senses she's overstayed her welcome and steps outside. Relieved yet still a little angered by her endless fussing, I open the file again and indulge my obsessive need to stare at the man's face, barely noticing the phone ringing in the distance.

A moment later, Madison returns, briefly announced by a tap at the glass door that separates her office from mine.

I barely have time to close the folder. The rushed, clandestine gesture itself angers me worse than before. Why am I hiding from her? Or is it my own subconscious mind telling me I shouldn't be looking at Caleb's dead face anymore? I steeple my hands above the red folder and look at her sternly. "Yes, Madison?"

"M wants to see you."

Of course. I grit my teeth, despite knowing damn well this was bound to happen. "When?"

"Right now. She just called." Without another word, she returns to her office. I throw the red folder a quick look, wondering if I should take it with me, but decide against it. When I walk out past her desk, she's typing case notes at her usual fifty-words-per-minute speed.

At lunch time, the hospital is abuzz with activity. It's nothing like eight in the morning, when the start of the day brings hordes of new patients in through the revolving doors, but the corridors are still usually heavy with traffic at noon. I weave my way through people and wait for an elevator for a few minutes, then take it down to the second floor, where M's office is housed next to the billing department.

Unlike earlier, I walk with my head up straight and my hands casually plunged into my lab coat pockets.

M's management suite is labeled simply, "Administrator." A much larger version than mine yet similar in layout, I have to pass by her assistant's desk before I can enter M's office. The assistant waves me right in, but I stop for a brief moment, looking inside M's office through glass walls covered in open, wood-colored blinds.

M is standing and gesticulating, having a heated conversation with Dr. Fitzpatrick, the chief of staff for the cardiothoracic surgery department. He's, essentially, my boss. He's responsible for all the medical staff in our department. If I'm reading his body language correctly, he's apologizing to M for something. And M seems on fire. She's pacing around her office in high-heeled pumps and a tight business suit, the jacket buttoned up just enough to show some cleavage, but not too much. Her dark, curly hair bounces off her shoulders, her moves energetic and fueled by that zest that has made her famous.

The glass walls are thick, and I can't catch a single word of what's being said. Knowing M's assistant is probably looking at me, I knock twice, then open the door and enter the office.

"You wanted to see me?"

"Yes," she replies, turning to me instantly. "Come on in, join the party." She gestures to a coffee table surrounded by several small armchairs, then leads the way by taking a seat and crossing her legs. Her left foot bounces in the air slightly, the only sign of impatience she's showing.

Dr. Fitzpatrick gives me a quick look, then takes his seat. I choose to sit across from M, feeling a strong uneasiness unfurling in my gut.

"There's going to be a formal hearing for the Donaghy case," M says. Her voice is harsh but not unusually so. Her words are spoken quickly and passionately, in a rush to be said. "I'm sure you were expecting that, Dr. Wiley."

"Yes." I keep my answers short, the way I do when I'm unsure of myself. The way Derreck taught me to.

"It's just routine," M adds, reassuringly. That puts more fear into me than if she had started to yell at me. "You know the drill." I frown, a little confused, unwilling to assume anything when it comes to M. Her foot bounces in the air impatiently. "Or maybe you don't, since this is the first patient you lost."

She makes it sound as if it's a bad thing I'm not well-versed in losing people. I ignore that and patiently wait.

"Let me refresh your memory," she says. "Don't speak with anyone about this case. Not the press, not any family members, no one except the people in this room." She keeps her hands in her lap and counts on her fingers as she speaks. "Direct anyone with questions to the hospital counsel."

I nod my agreement, thinking it's the last thing I need: the hospital counsel drilling me with questions I don't want to answer. "Understood."

"All right, that's it," she says, standing up abruptly. Dr. Fitzpatrick follows suit, and so do I. He smiles at me weakly, reassuringly. The fact that he thinks I need it is terrifying.

What are they not telling me?

What has Dr. Bolger told them? Madison said he spoke with M, requesting not to work with me again. That has to have done some damage to my career. It's definitely not what a chief of staff or a hospital administrator wants to hear about one of their surgeons: that a reputable anesthesiologist won't work with them again. *But how bad is it?*

In a second, all my fears are rekindled. I spent the weekend building my self-confidence, in no small measure reassured by Derreck that everything was going to be okay if I played my cards right and kept my mouth shut. But now, I don't know anymore. Maybe they told me about the review to keep me busy and calm until they figure out what to do with me. How to get rid of me. Or... if they should report the "incident" to the authorities. How to have me arrested without damaging the hospital's reputation in the process.

Because that's what M cares about: her hospital. I've heard her say it several times. Doctors come and go, patients come and go, but her hospital will be the best there is, and anyone who screws with that will wish they chose a career in flipping burgers.

"Any questions, Dr. Wiley?" she asks me.

I didn't realize I was frozen in place, processing my angst. "N—no," I manage to articulate, then walk briskly out of her office, forcing my head high and an expression of calm on my face, although I'm crumbling inside.

Before leaving the suite, I look over my shoulder and see the animated conversation between my boss and his boss continuing as if I were never there.

The walk to my office takes forever, or so it seems, although I keep my pace brisk, rushing through the lunch-hour crowds and muttering "Excuse me" every now and then. When I reach my office, my knees are weak and I want nothing more than a bit of peace, to gather my thoughts and reassure myself again that everything's going to be all right.

But what I want doesn't always matter. A woman is waiting to see me, seated on one of the two visitor chairs Madison keeps for that purpose in her office, by the glass wall facing the corridor. She's about forty years old, dressed sharply in a charcoal pantsuit with a white silk shirt and black kid leather pumps. When I enter the office, she stands quickly, holding a briefcase in her left hand, and follows me into my office before Madison can stop her.

"Paula Fuselier, from the State's Attorney Office," she announces herself. Her business card materializes on my desk.

She's an assistant state's attorney.

A prosecutor.

My blood turns to ice. It's starting, and I'm not ready.

I turn to face her, shoving my hands into my pockets where she can't see them tremble.

"What can I do for you, Ms. Fuselier?" My voice sounds strong and the right amount of rushed. I'm channeling M the best I can.

Without waiting for an invitation, she takes a seat in front of my desk and places her briefcase in her lap, popping the locks. She doesn't open it, though. "We have a few questions about a patient of yours, a Mr. Caleb Donaghy."

I remain standing, hoping she'll see it as an indication she's not welcome, and she'll leave. "What questions?"

"What can you tell us about his death?"

I frown. Derreck's advice zooms through my mind, followed closely by M's request to not speak to anyone.

But I can't just not speak, not without raising suspicions.

"For all patient deaths during surgery or immediately after, there's a formal review process that will examine what went wrong, and if the death could've been prevented or anticipated," I recite calmly, thankful for having had to train residents for the past few years. The information I'm giving doesn't pertain to Caleb Donaghy at all and cannot be used against me, in a court of law or elsewhere. Because I'd rather not bring the hospital counsel in on this.

A crooked smile flickers on the woman's lips. "You're dodging my question, Doctor."

I take one step closer to the door. "I'm afraid I don't have time for this right now. I'm due in surgery." I hold the door open for her. Madison waits on the other side of the glass door, ready to escort her out. Her eyebrows are ruffled, and her tense mouth promises nothing good.

Slowly, the prosecutor locks her briefcase and stands. Before reaching the door, she stops and looks straight at me. "Had you met Mr. Donaghy before last Thursday?"

I nearly choke. "Yes." My voice somehow sounds calm, decisive. "I met him twice, actually. The initial consult, and then the pre-op visit." I smile impatiently. "Please, you'll have to excuse me. I'm running late."

"I still have questions, Dr. Wiley." Her gaze lingers on my face for a long, tense moment, probing, hunting for the tiniest flinch.

"We can't exactly keep critical patients under sedation in favor of people who don't like making appointments. So, sorry." My eyes drill into hers mercilessly. What I see in them scares me.

Determination. Hatred.

She moves at last. "My office will be in touch," she throws over her shoulder as she leaves.

I let the door go. It swings to a close, silencing the world around me, but not my racing thoughts. I grab the edge of my desk for support, feeling too weak and shaky to stand.

Then Madison barges in, shooting sideway glances to the busy corridor where Paula Fuselier has vanished from sight. "What the hell was that about?"

ELEVEN
LESSONS

I can't answer Madison's question. If I knew the answer, I'd probably share. For the life of me, I can't begin to understand why the State's Attorney Office is looking into the death of a gravely ill patient who died during surgery. It doesn't make any sense. All surgeries have some degree of risk, of operative mortality, and I can't think of a single time when the State's Attorney Office became involved.

I refrain from calling Derreck to see if he can explain: if the State's Attorney Office is asking questions, who knows what else they might be doing? Maybe my office is bugged.

I'm losing my mind. I expected the cops to come after me with questions. But a prosecutor?

Then I look at the digital wall clock and freeze. In less than thirty minutes, I should be scrubbed in, ready to perform the coronary stent procedure on Dr. Seldon's patient. There's no way I can pull that off... my hands are shaking badly. Reluctantly, I let go of the desk and examine my hand as if I've never seen it before. The spike in adrenaline is giving my fingers a slight, unmistakable tremble. The weakness in my muscles urges me to sit, but I can't. There's no time.

"Check the schedule for Dr. Seldon and text me his location," I tell Madison as I run out of my office. I'll try his office first. Thankfully, it's on the same floor as mine.

His assistant tells me he's getting scrubbed in and I can find him in OR5. At the same time, my phone chimes with a message from Madison, indicating the same location. I run at a light jog through endless corridors to the cardiothoracic operating rooms and catch him still scrubbing at the sink, flanked by two assistants.

Standing there looking at him, out of breath and sweaty, I'm at a loss for words. The stent procedure was sent to me from Dr. Seldon himself. He'd asked me for a favor, which he rarely does, and which I agreed to do. Now I can't begin to think of how to ask him to bail me out again.

His scrubbing slows down when he sees me. I must be some sight... all flushed, and with loose hair falling on my face and sweat beads covering my forehead. He looks at me critically, yet there's a hint of empathy in his gaze. Then his focus shifts to his fingernails and the energetic scrubbing resumes.

He knows what I came there to ask.

"Jeez, Anne..." He rinses his hands under the water jet then pats them dry with sterile towels handed to him by his nurse. "Okay, I'll do the stent right after this. Shouldn't be later than four."

He looks at me again and I choke with embarrassment. Tears burn my eyes and I lower my head to hide them. "Thank you," I whisper.

He turns to enter the operating room, but then stops and turns to me again. This time, there's sadness in his eyes, and that hurts the most. "You're letting one stubborn, weary heart ruin your career. Our patients need us to be reliable. To be diligent and responsible and strong when they need us the most. That's what being a good surgeon means. A steady hand and a clear head under the direst of circumstances. What if you were operating under enemy fire or after a natural disaster?"

Ashamed, I watch him enter the OR and regret coming. He's right. I should've pulled myself together and done my job, instead of running to my mentor for help. Because I know I *am* that surgeon, the strong one who prevails, unwavering, regardless of what's going on. All those people who believed in me, Dr. Seldon included, can't be wrong.

I'm also deeply damaged, broken inside, and it's starting to show.

Dr. Seldon's assistant looks at me with a trace of contempt in her eyes, tapping on a tablet. "So, we're shifting your two o'clock to Dr. Seldon's team for the four p.m. slot, right?" Her voice is professional but cold.

Through the glass doors, I look at Dr. Seldon's back, hunched over the chest of his patient. He taught me better than this.

"No," I reply, calmly, looking at the time with a frown. "I'll do it. Please thank Dr. Seldon for me, will you?"

She smiles. No one likes long hours and unexpected changes in surgery scheduling. "You got it."

I send a message to Madison while walking briskly back to my office to confirm my team should be scrubbing in as scheduled. She immediately acknowledges.

But when I turn the corner and my office comes into sight, I freeze in place, petrified. A cop is waiting across from my door, leaning against the wall, checking his phone. He's wearing the Chicago PD uniform, weapon included.

Seems I won't be doing the stent procedure after all. My time has run out.

I'm not going to stand there staring even if I feel like I'm about to faint. I'll tackle this head-on, with dignity.

With a steady, determined gait, I close the distance until I reach the cop.

He doesn't react until I'm less than three feet away. He's a muscular guy, heavy-set, clean shaven—and that includes his scalp. His shirt sleeves are stretched taut on his biceps. The radio attached to his collar garbles occasional static.

"I'm Dr. Wiley," I say, my voice a bit strangled. "Are you looking for me?"

He looks up from his phone and frowns. "I've been told to wait here for news about my partner. Double GSW to the chest?"

I stare at him, confused, failing to understand what gunshot wound he's talking about, my mind stuck on what *I* have done, not someone else. But then I realize he's not here for me, and a wave of relief washes over me.

I clear my throat and ask, "I'm not his surgeon, am I?" *What an idiotic question.*

His raised eyebrows agree with my assessment. "N-no, it's Dr. Fitz—something."

"Dr. Fitzpatrick. My assistant can check on his status if you'd like."

He follows me into Madison's office with a grateful smile. A minute later, he's gone, after Madison points him in the right direction. His partner is fighting for his life in OR3.

The stent procedure is a success, and finishes more quickly than expected. I'm ashamed to admit to myself just how relieved I feel, as if I were still a first-year resident.

A bit over an hour later, I'm back in my office with a tall cup of coffee on my warmer, and Madison obsessing over my skipped lunch.

While she's gone to the cafeteria to address that, I get a call from M on my cell. In less than thirty seconds, she rips me a new one for not getting my shit together already.

Someone on Dr. Seldon's team ratted me out.

"You can't be indecisive about procedures, Dr. Wiley," she tells me in her habitual machine-gun rhythm. "You either do your job as well as we've all come to expect of you, or you don't come in to work until you're ready for it. These patients are not game pieces you get to throw to someone else if you don't feel like playing."

"I understand," I manage to say, when she pauses to draw breath.

"Take more time off if you need it, but when you walk through that main door, your mind should be in the game, one hundred percent. Is that clear?" I don't get a chance to answer. "Good," she says, then hangs up.

I deserved that. All of it.

I can't stop thinking of everything that's happened since I laid eyes on Caleb Donaghy's port-wine birthmark. I sit behind my desk and take a sip of coffee. It lands hot and bitter at the bottom of an empty stomach, churning. But I'm not paying attention, my eyes drawn to the red folder containing Donaghy's medical records.

I open it slowly and stare at the man's discolored face. I feel nothing. No regret and no remorse. Donaghy was a monster who deserved to die. But did that make a difference when I was holding the scalpel near his heart? Did I somehow sense who he was?

Madison brings a small Caesar salad and a cellophane-wrapped fork. I thank her without lifting my eyes from the folder. The patient number from one of his test results is the key to finding the surgery video recordings on our server. Moments later, I munch salad absently while watching the procedure recorded from multiple angles and synchronized with patient vitals.

I followed protocol. I know I did. I did everything by the book, until I saw his face and recognized him.

Could he have lived? Had he been operated on by a

different surgeon, would Caleb Donaghy be alive today? I watch the video, over and over: the part after I stepped in front of the screen and until I called time of death. I'm looking for answers. There aren't any clear ones to be found. Or perhaps I don't want to admit there are.

Maybe he could've lived. Another surgeon would've given him epi delivered straight into his heart, and restored it to normal sinus rhythm. They would've kept massaging and zapping it for a while longer, eliminating all possibility of doubt.

Then a monster would've been allowed to live.

Once I learned who he was, I couldn't take that chance.

I'm not sorry for what I've done. I'm at peace with it, albeit petrified of what that makes me.

A killer.

What drives me crazy is why his heart didn't start in the first place. Why I was able to call time of death at all. It shouldn't've happened. Everything was done well, and still, the heart refused to beat. *Before* I stepped in front of the screen and saw who he was. *Before* I realized that heart belonged to a sick, disturbed animal who didn't deserve to draw breath anymore.

Why?

Madison's voice draws me back into reality. She's bringing Lee Chen with her into my office, and he doesn't seem too thrilled about it.

"Tell her what you told just me," she says, not letting go of his arm, as if she had to drag him in there.

Lee is hesitant, his eyes squirrely, his face pale. I smile at him, encouraging him to speak. He licks his lips and fidgets in place for a moment. "I just, um, thought you should know there's a state's attorney out there, trolling the corridors, asking all sorts of questions. She seems to know a lot of stuff. I didn't say a word, I swear."

TWELVE
ROOM SERVICE

"Ooh, Mr. Mayor, you remembered," Paula whispered, reaching for the glass of so-called champagne offered to her.

The bottle, now abandoned on the black marble table top, was her favorite brand: Martini Asti.

"Of course I did." Their glasses clinked in midair, then she reached up and placed a long kiss on the man's lips. "I'm no stranger to cheap wine, you know." He laughed.

She pulled away and gave him a long, mock-bemused look. "Do I even know you, Mr. Mayor? I thought you came from money. Lots of it." She'd done her research and knew his background, but he didn't have to know about it.

He definitely didn't skimp on hotels for their afternoons together. This time, it was the LondonHouse, top floor, with a stunning view of the river and its many bridges. She liked nothing more than to stand naked by the window, only a fine white veil between her body and the hundreds of windows in the towers across the river. That was her vision of a wedding gown... just perfectly white sheer, with nothing else underneath. But she didn't crave marriage like other young women did. She'd had her chances; a couple of them had been good ones. At thirty-nine, Paula didn't regret having said no. She was still the master of her own game, free to chase her career goals and have affairs and do whatever the hell she wanted. She would've liked a daughter, but she didn't see herself bringing a vulnerable soul into the world, knowing too well it only took one glitch of fate, one stupid accident or unforeseen disease to leave her all alone, at the mercy of strangers. That was not a risk she was willing to take.

She took another sip of her favorite sparkling wine. "Don't tell me you've had this before. I thought you only enjoyed the grand cuvées of the world."

He shrugged, an uncomfortable smile on his lips that didn't touch his eyes. "I'm not as wealthy as I'd like to be." A shadow darkened his eyes. "Yes, I've had Asti before, and it's not that bad." He joined her by the window, seemingly unconcerned with his nakedness exposed in the floor-to-ceiling window. "This city could be ours," he said, wrapping his arms around her body.

"This city *will* be ours, Mr. Mayor." When she said it like that, with him by her side, and looking down at the river, it sounded true. Possible. Achievable.

"Want some more?" he whispered, nibbling on her ear.

She held her glass out, pretending she didn't understand the real meaning of his question. He loved their double entendre games. "Sure, top me up."

His hands locked around her waist. "Gladly." He grinned, scooping her up and carrying her to the bed. Her empty glass fell to the floor, rolling soundlessly on thick, plush carpet.

She looked at him, head to toe, and licked her lips. "I'm famished." Then she reached for his champagne glass and filled it with the rest of the sparkling wine in the bottle. "Thirsty too."

"You drive me crazy, woman," he whispered, looking at her naked body sprawled on the satin sheets with unmistakable lust. "I can't get enough of you."

She took a sip of champagne and smiled with just the right amount of sadness in her eyes. "Too bad I can't stay much longer." She held out the glass for him, but he shook his head. The earlier shadow over his eyes had returned. "Why don't you leave her?" she asked, thinking the question had to be asked sooner rather than later. She wanted him to leave his wife. No... she *needed* him to. Maybe now was the right time, when he was staring at what he was about to say goodbye to without having his fill.

Her question made him jolt away from her. "You know I can't. It would completely kill my chances as mayor. A divorce or a scandal would land me on the unemployment lines." His voice sounded weak, unconvinced. There had to be something else holding him back.

"Are you being honest with me, Derreck?" she whispered.

He glanced at her briefly before looking away. "After the election is won, I'm all yours, Paula. If you'll have me. I'll be free to do anything I want."

Liar.

She knew one when she heard one speak. Derreck wasn't any better than the hordes of perpetrators and murder suspects she'd interrogated on the stand. All guilty men lie the same way.

He moved his hand to pull the sheet over his midsection and a ray of the setting sun glinted on his wedding band. She touched it briefly; he pulled away.

He wore the damn thing in bed with her.

"I've always wondered how you ended up living in your wife's childhood home, with her mother. It can't be easy."

"You had me investigated, huh?" He frowned. "Can't say I blame you." Turning to face her, he put his hand on her leg and squeezed gently. "Trust me, it wasn't my first choice. We live there because Anne is attached to that house, to her mother. It's just easier that way. It's close to the hospital, to my office. But why are we talking about her?" His hand traveled north slowly, seeding heat in her abdomen.

"Because I don't want to sleep alone tonight," she replied coldly, her voice a subdued whisper, a hint threatening. "You don't seem to care." She shifted her eyes to the picture window, where dusk was starting to shroud the city in myriad lights. "I've got to go." She sat on the side of the bed, facing away from him.

"I can stay late today." His words came out quickly, his voice tinted with urgency. "Anne's had some issues at the hospital. She won't be home for a while."

She let a few seconds of silence deliver a stern message, then asked, "Why? What happened?"

A frustrated sigh left his chest. "I already told you about it. She lost a patient. Some guy died on the table. Nothing for you to worry about."

"It won't impact your career, whatever this is that your wife's going through? If the media—"

He was looking at his hands. "No... it's nothing like that. Surgeons have a hard time when their patients die, that's all. But it happens all the time."

At that moment, a thought rushed through Paula's mind. That was probably why he'd never leave his wife. She must've been the wealthy one, following in her rich daddy's footsteps. Derreck didn't earn his wealth; he'd married into it. That's why he was used to cheap wine. That's why he was willing to live with his mother-in-law.

"Who was this patient?" Paula asked casually, although she knew very well already. "Was he someone she knew, or...?"

A one-sided shrug warned Paula that he was about to lie again. "Just some patient, I don't know. But I can stay if you'd like. We have the room until tomorrow."

That statement deserved a smile. She pulled closer to him and trailed her fingernail on his chest. "Can you stay until tomorrow?" Her voice was loaded with promise.

He clasped her hand and ended its downward voyage, lifting it to his lips. "I can stay until tonight, eleven at the latest. I have a tough day tomorrow."

"Ah." She stood and went into the bathroom, wrapped in a silky sheet. When she closed the door and looked into the mirror, her smile faded away as the sheet fell rustling to the black, hexagonal tile floor. "Damn that bitch," she muttered, looking at herself in the mirror. Thinking of her lover's wife made her blood boil. She was always there, between them, even when they were lying naked in bed. The power she still held over him fueled her rage, and that rage spilled over to engulf him as well. "You, Mr. Mayor, ain't getting any more of *this* tonight. Not until you learn your priorities."

She splashed cold water on her face and then drank from the faucet, relishing the cooling, refreshing sensation after the champagne. It was bad enough she wanted to run back to bed and screw the man's brains out. It was even worse he was still loyal to his wife, despite lounging naked in expensive hotel beds with her at least once a week. *Some loyalty...* Well, he was a politician. What could she expect?

But most people—including politicians—can be trained, and Derreck Bourke was no exception, despite his charisma and blue eyes and famous success with women. He could be taught to be faithful and true to the right person, even if that required a few cracks of the whip.

When she came out of the bathroom, she trailed the sheet on the floor with a playful glint in her eyes, swaying her hips as she walked. She found him lying on the bed, his hands under his head, ready for her. Pretending she didn't notice his arousal, she wrapped herself in the sheet and took the armchair by the window, looking outside. "Get us some hors d'oeuvres, will you? I can't stay long."

Derreck sat on the side of the bed, visibly disappointed, and called the front desk on speaker.

"And another bottle of champagne," she asked, just as reception was picking up the call. She listened to him giving detailed instructions about the champagne.

He hung up, grinning. "Happy?"

She licked her lips. "Uh-huh." The Rooftop Lounge was bringing them a selection of their best appetizers: blackened scallops and grilled octopus salad. Derreck loved his seafood a little too much for a landlocked-city mayoral wannabe.

He reached for his clothes, but she waved her finger. "Nope. Not yet. Unless you want me to get dressed too."

"We have room service coming."

She shrugged indifferently. "So let them come. I'm willing to bet they've seen naked people before."

He chuckled and came toward her. She turned her gaze to the panoramic view of the cityscape. "I have issues at work too," she said, speaking softly, slowly, waiting for him to engage.

"What happened?" He sat on the floor at her feet, on the crumpled sheet, leaning against her legs and resting his head in her lap. She hated him for doing that. It made everything seem possible, domestic. As if he really loved her. As if he wasn't going back to his wife tonight.

She pushed aside the thought of Dr. Anne Wiley, the stunning surgeon she'd just met. Just being in the same room with her had made Paula feel small and insignificant, ugly, meaningless. She had everything. The looks, the wealth, the husband, the power. *Damn that bitch.*

Then she found herself wondering why Anne Wiley had not taken Derreck's last name, Bourke. It was probably because the name "Wiley" still meant something in the medical landscape of the city, and she was milking that heritage for all it had.

"I'm really torn about something," she eventually said. "There's an eleven-year-old boy who witnessed a shooting downtown. I need him to testify. But his father won't allow it."

She paused for a while, caressing Derreck's hair slowly. "He's a single dad, scared out of his mind. I can understand why."

"Will you let it slide?"

"What? And let the killer walk? I can't do that. Wish I could, though. I've always been passionate about protecting the rights of the underprivileged. That's why this case is tearing me up inside."

"I know this," Derreck said, looking up at her. "You're involved in so many community outreach and legal aid programs. I've always wondered why you cared so much. Is it personal?" He grinned like a cat watching a blue jay coming in to land. "Does it have to do with your preference for cheap champagne?"

Damn... He asked too many questions. And he knew too much.

A quick rap on the door, and a male voice announced, "Room service."

"Oh, shit," Derreck muttered, springing to his feet and looking for something to cover himself with. He reached for the comforter, but it was too bulky.

She laughed, seeing him flustered. "In the bathroom."

He disappeared in there for a moment, then emerged wrapped in a terrycloth bathrobe embroidered with the hotel logo. Then he opened the door and signed for the delivery.

By the time he brought the food over and set it on the desk, his unwelcome question was already forgotten.

She took a scallop and placed it in her mouth, slowly chewing it, savoring its exquisite taste and texture. "That's my dilemma," she said, continuing her earlier trail of thought unabated. "Should I let this slide, even if that means putting a murderer back on the streets? Or should I press on and force this kid to testify, consequences be damned?" She waited for Derreck to open the new bottle and fill the two glasses that came with it. "What would you do, Mr. Mayor? What's in the best interest of your citizens?"

He poured the liquid slowly, careful not to spill. "The law is clear in this kind of situation. The witness must testify. You can put him in WitSec if you have concerns for his safety. As he's a minor, his father would go with him. You have no real option here. If you refuse to do it, the SA will reassign the case."

She stabbed a piece of octopus with her fork and tasted it. It was unexpectedly flavorful, the mayonnaise sauce delicious with herbs and spices, a symphony of taste and zest. "I guess not. It sucks to feel torn like that over something you don't really control." She shot him a quick glance. "I wonder if Anne is struggling with the same kind of thing."

He seemed confused, and visibly unhappy she'd mentioned his wife again.

"You know, with the patient she lost?"

THIRTEEN
SAFE

The house is quiet and dim. I usually prefer it like that, whenever I find myself shying away from light and refusing brightness in my life. Today is different, as if I'm inviting shadows to start creeping up on me, oozing from memory and the fabric of time in a slow, terrifying invasion. While in the office, I kept the blinds closed, even if that raised Madison's eyebrows. Now, at home, when it's dark outside, all I have to do is not fight the darkness that prevails at the end of each day.

It's Wednesday, Mother's weekly bridge game day, and she's out for the evening at her best friend's house. She wanted to cancel and spend time with me, but I reassured her I'd be working late.

I didn't.

I just wanted the house to myself. Derreck works late most days, rarely home before seven. Today he texted and said there's a special election committee meeting he needs to attend. That usually lasts until nine or even later, if they can't see eye to eye and have to debate every single action item on the agenda. I honestly can't figure out how he can endure something like that.

For a while, I wander aimlessly through the living room, considering dinner. My stomach is not in sync with my dark mood, demanding sustenance after a day of being ignored. But making dinner requires effort, the kind of effort I'm not willing to put into something so inconsequential. Food is fuel, and all I need is a pitstop, not a fancy event.

A few saltine crackers smeared with peanut butter fit that bill, eaten standing between the kitchen island and the fridge. It doesn't take much to replace the gnawing sensation of hunger in my stomach with nausea. I screw the peanut butter jar cap back on, noticing in passing the loud sound it makes, echoing and reverberating against the walls. I place the jar back in the fridge, and snatch an opened bottle of wine from the door shelf. It's Pinot Gris, one of my favorite wines. Maybe it will work its usual magic and release the knot in my throat. I pour the remaining liquid into a glass, frowning when I see it's only about a third full.

The first sip seems bitter and much too cold. Nevertheless, I take the glass with me as I head into the den. It's a small room decorated sternly with an old, walnut desk and matching bookcase that belonged to my father. The Persian rug in deep shades of burgundy and red is a little worn, its tassels frayed in places. Everything in that room was chosen by him, touched by him. Only the laptop is mine, and the white shawl on the back of the twentieth-century studded Dutch leather chair.

I run my hand over the desk surface, knowing he touched it so many times. He used to sit in this chair every night, working, reviewing patient case files, learning, teaching. His presence is still intense, humbling, heartwarming. How I wish I'd taken the time to ask him everything I wanted to, when he was still here, with us.

We always assume we have time.

There's never any time. Every day we're alive is borrowed against the unforeseen.

So many questions left unanswered. About Melanie. About the day we brought her home. About what I did the day she died. He'd know what to tell me. No matter how searing, his words would heal the wound in my heart. He'd probably forgive me, even if I can't forgive myself.

I place the glass of wine on the windowsill and look outside for a while. Our street is a small cul-de-sac, with very little evening traffic. In the distance, the bustling city lives and thrives around the clock, but from where I'm standing, all I can see is the cloudy night sky reflecting the downtown lights; all I can hear is the occasional police siren that still sends shivers down my spine, against the low hum of heavy traffic muted by the distance.

The last sip of wine seems to taste better and warms me up a little. I abandon the empty glass on the windowsill and walk over to the bookcase. I crouch in front of it and grab the bottom row of books with both hands, pulling it to the side as I would a cabinet door. It's a sliding cover for my personal safe, disguised as two rows of book spines.

I stare at the safe for a while, knowing perfectly well what's in it, and still needing to see it again. The combination is the day Melanie came home to us.

The safe door swings open and a faint, musty odor fills the room. Some safes get moisture inside, and all the papers stored for a long time have to be sealed in waterproof envelopes. One such translucid waterproof envelope sits underneath everything else I have stashed in there—the house deed and the little jewelry I possess. It's light blue in color and the surface is smooth and damp to the touch as I pull it out. A few moments later, it's laid out on the desk, and my laptop is pushed to the side to make room.

Memories rush to my mind as I take a seat in the old Dutch chair, making it groan in protest when I drag it closer to the desk. The blue envelope is still sealed, and I hesitate. I was in the first year of my residency at Joseph Lister when I finally got the courage together to start looking for Melanie's records. The thought of finding answers had crossed my mind the first day I got my own credentials on the hospital's computer system, but something held me back for a few months. Whatever I found, she would still be gone, and nothing would ever bring her back. It almost felt disrespectful to her memory, to my father's, to let my curiosity prevail, but I had needed to know. I had to be sure...

Everything I knew about Melanie's life before she came to us was speculation or inference. I needed certainties like I needed air.

After waiting a few months—torn between what I felt I had to do and my conscience—I started looking, digging through archived medical records whenever I caught a bit of time of unsupervised computer access. I found very little. Vaccination records mostly, under the name Melanie Wiley. Nothing else. Which wasn't surprising, considering my father was a doctor and had cared for us at home whenever we were sick.

But what had been her name before she came to us?

I never knew.

I still recall the day we brought her home. She had been nine years old. I was fourteen, and excited out of my mind at the thought of having a sister. Without much warning, my parents took me one day to meet her and take her home. I'm guessing it was an orphanage, the place we visited, because there were other children there, not just Melanie. The building was decrepit and smelled of mold. The yard was barren, only traces of grass here and there, uneven and muddy. The smell of mac and cheese and cooking oil gone bad came through a window equipped with a fan. It was nauseating.

She'd been returned to the system after running away from her foster home. Twice. Melanie was a skittish little girl, her long, brown hair clumped, her face and hands dirty. She had big, round eyes that pierced the soul somehow, because I instantly understood what she wanted, what she feared. I chatted with her and played with her a little bit, while my parents were busy talking with other adults, finalizing adoption paperwork, I assume.

When we were getting ready to leave, Melanie started crying hysterically, trying to break free from my father's hand, begging him to let her go. I took her other hand, and she stopped crying, clutching my fingers with unusual strength, but looking back at the yard full of children as if she didn't want to leave that horrid place. She whimpered quietly the entire drive home, still clasping my hand tightly in the back seat of my father's car. Every now and then she'd wipe her eyes with the hem of her polka dot gathered skirt, one of the ugliest garments I'd ever seen. It was stained and soiled with street dirt and spilled food, and her off-white shirt wasn't any cleaner. Both items looked as if they were hand-me-downs, too frayed and used to have belonged only to one child. I didn't care, though; I knew my parents would dote on her just as they'd done on me, making sure my new sister had everything she needed.

When we got home, she started to sob again because I briefly let go of her hand to open the car door. She clutched my forearm with both her hands, begging me to stay with her. I did, in my infinite naivete, happy she had bonded with me, not understanding what was really happening. I took her hand in mine, looked straight into those big, tearful eyes, and promised her I would never, ever leave her. I swore on my life.

She believed me.

Quiet and subdued, she followed me out of the car. Her ruffled skirt got entangled in the seat belt buckle, exposing her legs. I stared at them, then looked at my mother. Her smile was gone; she was white as a sheet. My father was muttering an oath, a thing he rarely did. Then Mom took her hand from mine and crouched by her side, welcoming her to our family and our home with a few heartfelt words. She promised the little girl she'd always be safe, and nothing bad would ever happen to her. Then she took my little sister to give her a bath.

At first, I had thought her legs were dirty, but later I learned they were badly bruised. As if someone had beaten her in places that didn't show, underneath her clothing.

Later that day, we showed Melanie her new room. She was thrilled at first, touching everything, the smooth sheets, the stuffed animals I'd scattered everywhere, the cheerful curtains hanging at her window. She sunk her face into the bed linens and inhaled, then said they smelled of fairy tale princesses.

Then she learned she'd sleep alone in that room, and broke down in tears again. I didn't understand back then; now I do. Instinctively, I knew what to do. I showed her my room, right next door to hers, and asked her if she'd like to sleep with her new sister for a while. She still seemed scared, but agreed with enthusiasm.

That night, we slept together in my room. Melanie wanted her beautiful new bed to be left untouched as long as possible. She was funny like that, always reluctant to touch beautiful things—as if she didn't deserve them. As if her touch would soil or degrade them irreparably.

The telling signs of a badly damaged child.

She'd fallen fast asleep, curled up against me, when I started hearing my mother's sobs through the adjacent wall.

Until that night, I'd never heard my mother cry, except when Grandma died. I was terrified. Her hushed sobs were mixed in with tense whispering, both her and Dad discussing something that broke her heart. They weren't arguing... their voices weren't raised or angry. But something terrible was going on and I didn't know what.

In my juvenile ignorance, I was scared that Mom didn't like Melanie and they wanted to take her back to that dreadful place. Instead of speaking with them about it, I clammed up and lived in ridiculous fear for a while. In retrospect, for my fourteen years at the time, I was very naïve. My parents had done their best to protect me from the horrors of this world, but in doing so, they left me unprepared to understand what was going on with my new sister.

Now I know more of the horrors of this world. Too little, too late.

I unseal the plastic envelope on the desk, then extract the thin file and open it. The topmost page is titled AUTOPSY REPORT.

In my first year of residency, when I finally searched the hospital for Melanie's records, I didn't find anything relevant, but I didn't stop there. By that time, they were both gone—Melanie and my father. I couldn't bring myself to open Mom's wounds by talking about it, by voicing my questions. Melanie's adoption records were sealed: another dead end.

I looked elsewhere for answers.

My first break came in the second year as a resident, during my general surgery rotation, when a Chicago PD detective landed on my emergency room table with a deep laceration on his arm following a difficult arrest involving a machete-wielding methhead. As I was stitching away, I asked if family members had access to autopsy records. He said the records were technically public, but it could take a while if I filed a formal request. He offered to make a call to the Cook County medical examiner, and I begged him to. He made the call right there, from the gurney, while I was dressing his wound.

A few days later, a courier dropped off a copy of Melanie's autopsy records.

I couldn't read it immediately. I had to wait until I was

home alone, unwilling to upset Mom. My hands trembled the first time I read it, just as they tremble now, when I turn over page after page. Every word typed in those pages is forever etched in my memory, and yet I sometimes revisit it as I would Melanie's grave, with breath caught in my chest and tearful eyes.

Old fracture of her ribs. Old spiral fracture of right wrist. Marked myositis ossificans traumatica at both thighs—bone tissue developed in soft tissue after repeated traumatic injury. Old, healed, small, stab wounds on her thighs and abdomen. Scarring of older vaginal lacerations.

In a tightly typed page, the story of an innocent girl's torture and abuse at the hands of the man I put in the morgue, Caleb Donaghy.

It still feels too little, too late. He should've suffered more.

A tear falls and stains the last page of the autopsy report. I rush to wipe it off, although it's not the first one. That page is barely legible after the many tears I've shed reading it.

I don't know how much time I spend staring at those pages, as if they could somehow change and make reality different than it is. When Mom's car shines its headlights against the den window, I scurry to seal the autopsy report back into its plastic envelope, then slide it inside the safe. A push of the button with a silent beep and the safe is locked. While Mom opens the laundry door and walks into the kitchen, I slide the fake rows of book spines to hide it and rush to greet her.

I've known for some time what she and Dad were whispering about that night. Well, I'm assuming... I don't really know, because she hasn't told me, and I've never asked. But when I see her, I hug her really tight and don't want to let go. I wish I could tell her what I've done.

"Hey, Mom," I whisper, my face buried in her hair, the scent of her perfume filling my nostrils with warmth and love and belonging.

She eventually pulls away and studies me warily. "Hey, sweetie, is everything okay?"

I fall silent, unable to answer her simple question.

Melanie was only nine years old when she became my little sister.

Five years later, she was gone.

FOURTEEN
PROBLEM

There's something stuck in my mind as I start doing my morning rounds. I left the empty wineglass on the den windowsill last night. For some reason, this irrelevant little fact refuses to be forgotten, as if it matters somehow. Its persistence is probably a stress response.

I'm tired and yes, I feel stressed, my nerves taut, stretched to breaking point.

I spent a restless night, tossing and turning in bed, unable to fall asleep until Derreck made it home. It was well after midnight when he finally arrived. He tiptoed his way into the bedroom, then placed the lightest kiss on my cheek and covered me with the comforter as you'd tuck in a child. I love it when he does that. I pretended to be asleep, knowing he'd do just that, until he started getting undressed. Then I said hello and turned on the table lamp, so he could see. That gesture earned me another kiss. He smelled fresh, unbelievably so after such a long day. How does he manage that? I'll ask him one day. There was a whiff of wine on his breath, but that's no surprise. Those endless meetings often include dinners and drinks at the candidate's expense.

I should've asked him last night. I woke up at four, unable to sleep, wondering about it. I'm sure it's something really basic, like carrying a solid deodorant in his briefcase to use when needed. His favorite brand is Old Spice. That's what he smelled of last night: wine and Old Spice. But I didn't try to banish the senseless worry from my head. It was better to stay awake obsessing over Derreck's deodorant instead of Caleb Donaghy's vile heart.

It's been precisely one week since I called time of death on that monster. And it's the first day since then with a full schedule. My rounds are light, though. I've been off the normal workload schedule for a while, and yesterday there was only one procedure—the coronary stent on Dr. Seldon's patient. Today I have a mitral valve replacement I've reserved the bulk of my time for. Not that many patients to visit in the morning.

I find Dr. Seldon in the coronary stent patient's room, listening to his heart with his digital stethoscope, while looking at the screen of his phone for a visualization of rhythm. I stop in the doorway, a little unsure, before entering. "Good morning," I say, cheerfully. The expression "Fake it until you make it" comes to mind when I hear myself speak. I don't blame Dr. Seldon for taking over his patient after yesterday's conversation. I wouldn't trust myself, either.

"Ah, Dr. Wiley," Dr. Seldon says, taking the stethoscope earpieces out of his ears and folding the tubing until it can fit into his pocket. "We were just talking about you." The patient grins and nods. "You did one hell of a job with this young man. He'll live long enough to bury us both." Dr. Seldon has a way with words to encourage patients, a bit over the top, but it works. If they believe they will live a long and healthy life, there's no harm in that.

I spend a few minutes talking with the patient and listening to his heartbeat. His chest tingling is gone, his breathing has normalized. I shake his hand and leave, but Dr. Seldon catches up with me before I enter Mrs. Heimbach's room.

He pulls me to the side, by the window, away from the constant pedestrian traffic. Then he lowers his head, speaking barely above a whisper. "Off the record, Anne, I've lost more patients than I'd care to admit. It's a sad reality that comes with our jobs. But I've never been investigated for it. Not internally, and not by the State's Attorney Office. Just the usual formal review."

Hearing his words, blood freezes in my veins. I can't breathe and I feel I'm about to faint, even if my heart is pumping force-fully, driven by panic. What could possibly be the explanation for the investigation, if it never happens to other surgeons? I stare at Dr. Seldon, my mouth agape, speechless.

"Just hang in there, and it will pass. But be very careful. I don't know what this is about, but it feels like you're being targeted by someone." He looks left and right, as if to make sure no one can hear us talking, then he continues. "Someone powerful and motivated. Do your job well and don't give people reasons to add more fuel to the fire." He squeezes my hand to encourage me. "Like the request yesterday, for the stent proce-dure—?" He nods his head toward the patient's door as if I didn't know what he was referring to. "By the way, I'm happy you changed your mind about him. The one thing you need more than anything else right now is success. That'll build you back up, revitalize you. Okay?"

I nod, still speechless, horrified at the thought of the entire hospital talking about me, about the State's Attorney Office investigation. About Caleb Donaghy. I thought no one else knew about the ASA's visit yesterday except my team. Turns out, I was wrong.

Dr. Seldon pats me on the shoulder, then starts walking toward the operating rooms, his back a bit hunched, his gait a little crooked. He has an early procedure; I saw it on his schedule.

I need a few minutes before seeing Mrs. Heimbach, to regain my cool. Then I spend more time with her than anticipated. Until two hours before her procedure, she didn't think of having an advance directive drawn up, and reserved all her questions for me. I happen to be a fierce supporter of advance directives. In a for-profit health system, it's people's only chance to control what happens to them in a worst-case scenario.

Madison comes to the rescue with a form to fill, and serves as her witness when she signs it, only minutes before Mrs. Heimbach is taken for her last scans and pre-op prep.

When I leave her room, I almost bump into M. My boss is wearing a light gray pantsuit so tight around her waist I wonder how she moves so quickly in it. She is, as usual, incredibly direct and focused.

"How are you feeling? Are you up to resuming your full workload?" Her right hand is propped on her thigh; her left holds a small stack of cardiology patient charts. I recognize them by the color coding.

"Yes, one hundred percent," I say without blinking, hoping it will become the truth soon.

"Anything else I need to know about?"

"No," I say, calmly. Short answers, per Derreck's advice.

"Good," she replies, immediately resuming her rushed bounce through the endless, busy corridors. I finally breathe with ease when she's about twenty feet away, although I've known her to change her mind and come back from greater distances.

I'm relieved she doesn't seem to know anything about the State's Attorney Office interest in my dead patient. She might be the only one in the entire hospital, although that thought's just a product of my sarcastic mind. Probably very few people know about it other than my team, and now Dr. Seldon. Maybe it will stay that way.

Maybe pigs will fly, and we can all ride them to work.

But I can't stop wondering why this prosecutor has taken such a keen interest in me and my patient. Does she know something I don't? Is there something to know, something to worry about?

Several more turns and a short ride down on the elevator, and I'm back on my floor. I check the time and pick up my pace. There isn't too much time left until I have to scrub in.

Madison waits for me in front of my office, and starts walking briskly toward me when she sees me. She seems disconcerted, panicked even, shooting side glances toward my office with eyes rounded in fear underneath a deeply creased brow. "I'm so sorry, Anne, there was nothing I could do to stop her," she whispers, as we both walk toward my office.

I'm about to ask what she's talking about, when the glass wall of my office comes into view, and I see for myself. That assistant state's attorney is sitting behind my desk, installed comfortably and flipping through the pages of a surgery treatise. Underneath the six-hundred-page book, I can see the red folder I put together for Caleb Donaghy.

I gasp. What if she's opened it? Every bit of information about him is in that file.

The nerve of that woman.

I storm inside my office with Madison in tow. "What the hell gives you the right to barge in here?" I ask, keeping my voice low.

She closes the book slowly and stands, then walks around the desk until she's in front of me, barely two feet away. She's wearing a black pantsuit and heels, paired with a white silk blouse showing generous cleavage. Her matching black leather briefcase is open on the corner of my desk. She's like a younger, more beautiful version of M. I shudder at the thought the resemblance might go beyond appearances.

A smile flutters on her lips, dipped in contempt. "So, you think you have the right to privacy here, Dr. Wiley? The hospital didn't think so when they gave you glass walls to your office."

Madison takes one step forward, angry as hell, hands propped on her hips. "People here have manners. That's not—"

"It's okay," I whisper and stop Madison's rant. She's right, but that's irrelevant. Derreck always maintains that what's right doesn't matter in the justice system. Only what the law says, and the caliber of the attorney who wields it as a weapon. "What can I do for you, Ms.—?" I pretend to have forgotten her name. I haven't. Not when it's been haunting my every thought since I met her.

"Fuselier," she says calmly, her smile crooked now, her eyes riveted on mine, pupils wide. It must be too dark in my office, or she could be reacting to something else—a strong emotion, perhaps. Fear doesn't make sense... Anger maybe? It's definitely an adrenaline response. But why?

"Ms. Fuselier, yes," I say gracefully, while I step sideways to the light switch on the wall and turn it on. It's not much brighter. She shifts her eyes briefly in reaction to the light, but then looks at me again. Her pupils are still dilated. It's as if I'm staring into the eyes of a venomous predator. "What can I do for you?"

A flicker of contempt tugs at the corner of her mouth. "Were you always this entitled, Dr. Wiley?" She chuckles when Madison gasps. "I bet you were. Born into a rich family, a surgeon for a father, no care in the world." She's shaking her head slowly as if all that is shameful or wrong somehow. "You don't even care about your patients, do you, Dr. Wiley?"

I can't wrap my head around what motivates her. She's fishing, obviously. If she had anything concrete, she'd come right out and say it. She'd arrest me and drag me out of here in hand-cuffs. Instead, she's just provoking me. *Well, I can play that game just as well.* "Who was Caleb Donaghy to you?" I ask with unfeigned curiosity.

She takes a step forward. I can sense her breath on my face. I raise my hands in the air instead of taking a step back. "Please, maintain your distance or wear a mask. We're in a hospital."

"The question is who he was to you, and why you let him die," she whispers, ignoring my request. "Let's focus on that instead, Dr. Wiley."

"I'm calling security," Madison says, but I grab her sleeve and stop her.

"Ms. Fuselier is no threat, Maddie. She's an officer of the law. A government employee." All this time I hold her gaze, stubbornly refusing to let myself blink. "She wouldn't overstep the boundaries of her official function. That would be a career killer."

I see the flicker of rage in her eyes. It tells me what she cares about. What she's after. A high-profile case to elevate herself within her office or who knows where. Bringing down "the heart girl" would probably fit that bill. The case would have instant visibility and media attention. I can see the headlines in my mind.

"Can I offer you a mask?" I ask. Madison disappears for a moment, then returns with a sterile mask. The woman doesn't take it. Instead, she takes a small step back, her eyes throwing daggers at me.

I've won the first round. Hopefully it won't cost me more than I can pay.

"Why did Caleb Donaghy die?" she asks, coldly. "Was it a mistake? Everyone makes mistakes; it's understandable."

She must think I'm a complete idiot.

"I'm sure a mistake is what you made when you harassed my team with your questions."

"I was doing my job. You might not be familiar with the concept. You inherited this job, right? All that 'stepping into the father's footsteps' nonsense, nothing but an excuse for cutting corners and landing jobs you're not qualified for. You know what I mean, right?"

I passed the point where I was insulted a long time ago. Now I'm just plain scared. If she's here, talking that way to me in front of witnesses, she must know something I don't. She must have some blank check from someone.

Dr. Seldon was right. This feels personal, beyond a witch hunt, almost like an execution.

I check the time and frown. I should be scrubbing in right now. She probably knows it. "If you have a legitimate question, I'll do my best to answer it. You have thirty seconds. After that, I'm due in surgery." I step aside and gesture toward the office door, inviting her to leave.

"Why did your patient die? What went wrong?" Her voice is threatening.

Madison takes a step back and shoots me a worried glance.

"For all patient deaths during surgery or immediately after, there's a formal review process that will examine what went wrong, and if the death could've been prevented or anticipated." I recite the same words I said to her yesterday. "A report will be issued. I suggest you contact the hospital's legal department to request a copy." I open the door for her. "Now, if you'll excuse me, I have work to do."

"You're not going to get away with this," she says, collecting her briefcase from my desk.

"And I'd appreciate it if you stop interviewing my team without the hospital counsel present. I'm pretty sure it's illegal, but if you'd like me to, I can make a few calls and find out."

My second threat hits the mark.

She leaves my office without another word, shooting me another venomous glance before she disappears from view.

Madison sighs loudly. "Unbelievable, that woman! Good thing she's gone."

I look at her sternly. "She's not gone, Maddie. She's just starting."

"Starting what? Nothing was wrong with that surgery. The patient died, okay, but we didn't do anything wrong." She paces my office in a state of agitation—the last thing I want from her before a valve replacement surgery. Or from myself. I feel it too, the anxiety, the feeling of being hunted, trapped, only I hide it better. I hope.

After a long, tense moment of considering my options, I pick up my desk phone and call M. She answers immediately.

"What's going on?" she asks, instead of the usual greeting.

I fill my lungs with air. "We might have a serious problem."

FIFTEEN
TESTIMONY

The drive to the Cook County State's Attorney Office building was a short one, too short to give Paula the time to stop fuming. A couple of blocks before her destination, she pulled over and stopped. She needed a few more minutes to find the composure she'd lost within seconds after leaving the hospital.

Why did some people get all the shots in life? Anne Wiley was self-assured and unflinching, the kind of courageous that strong people are innately. Those raised in good families, surrounded by love and money and possibilities. Those people didn't know fear. They didn't know struggle the way impoverished families did. They had no idea what it meant to be completely alone in the world, vulnerable and broke and desperate; just like that kid, Kestner, whom she'd discussed with her boss last week, over lunch, whose stolen car had almost made him jump off a bridge.

People like Anne Wiley made phone calls when they were bothered with questions by the likes of Paula Fuselier. She would bet a steak dinner that, within moments after she left the arrogant surgeon's office, Anne had picked up the phone and called someone.

Damn her to hell and back. Life was so unfair. She had everything. A good job, an excellent reputation, her face on bloody billboards all over town. And Derreck. She could've married an abusive drunk but, no, she had to marry a smart, ambitious lawyer with a golden future and manners like he'd been raised in Europe by a French nanny, not in Joliet, on the wrong side of the tracks right next to the old prison.

Some people just had it all.

Life was random. That didn't make it right.

Thinking of Anne Wiley, with her tall slim figure, her calm demeanor, and her beautiful face, made Paula want to break something, to rip something to shreds. She looked around in the car, but there was nothing she could tear to bits. Frustrated, she let out a long sigh loaded with oaths.

Derreck would never leave her; he'd be crazy to. Paula wasn't delusional. No matter how many promises she made to him or how much she pushed his career forward, Derreck would never divorce his wife. She'd always be the mistress, the other woman, fending for herself as she'd aways done, alone in this world, with no one to call hers and no phone call to make in case of trouble.

She *hated* Anne Wiley. She reminded her of everything that was wrong with her own life, of how hard she'd had to work to put herself through law school, of every ass she had to kiss and every opinion she had to swallow to get ahead. The attorneys, like the self-assured surgeon, had trumped her many times in life, in school, in the SA's office, always getting ahead faster, cutting in front of her without even looking, as if she didn't exist.

Now the famous Dr. Anne Wiley had finally made a mistake. A patient had died on her table. Paula had been waiting for months for that to happen. Hunting season was finally open for entitled, rich bitches with medical degrees. When she was done with her, Derreck would drop her like a hot potato, glad she never took his name legally, eager to have his divorce expedited.

She started the engine and peeled off into traffic, wondering nonsensically if Anne was good in bed. Maybe med school taught secrets of the human body that law school has no reason to. *Nah...* she was probably just as ice cold in bed as she was in her professional life. Measured, calculated, procedural, calm. Not a fiery, lusting, hot-blooded woman like herself.

At some point, Derreck had to realize he deserved better than Dr. Icicle.

The thought made her laugh, the nickname one that would probably stick in her mind for a while, because it fitted her well. Too bad she couldn't share it with anyone.

Pulling into the office parking lot, she smiled tensely, imagining herself breaking Anne's body into tiny pieces as if it were actually made of ice.

Back in her office, she skirted the boxes she'd already stacked by the door, even though more than seven weeks were left until she moved to the fifth floor. Half her stuff was packed up—the items she didn't use on a daily basis, mostly law books and old case files she kept for her personal archives. But packing made it all real. She was ready for the new office, the new job, the new life.

Her investigator, Adam Costilla, wasn't in his office. She knew exactly where to find him. He was a permanent fixture of the cafeteria when he wasn't out in the field or typing a report, and she'd seen his car in the parking lot.

In the downstairs cafeteria, Adam was seated at his usual table, blowing into a fresh, tall cup of coffee.

She pulled out a chair, taking a seat across from him at the small melamine table, frowning slightly. "Adam," she said, looking at him with a hint of concern. He was overweight and struggled to breathe most of the time. His skin was blotched with splashes of deep red, probably a sign of high blood pressure, yet he was mainlining caffeine like it was his last day on earth. At this rate, it soon would be. "Don't tell me, it's your first fix for the day?"

He laughed wholeheartedly, his jowls bouncing like a bulldog's. "More like the fifth, boss. You keep me busy. I have to make do."

She wanted to say he should slow down, but knew she'd be wasting her time. "I've got a case for you," she said instead.

He pulled out a small notepad from his pocket, the kind cops use. A click on the end of his pen, and he was ready. "Shoot."

"Joseph Lister University Hospital has a Dr. Anne Wiley on staff, a cardiothoracic surgeon."

"I know her," he announced, cheerfully. "It's the super-hot blondie on those heart billboards, right?"

Paula closed her eyes for a moment to hide the anger glinting in them. "Yeah. I need you to run a full background on her. Everything you can. Malpractice suits, complaints, deceased patients, personal history, the works. Search under every boulder, if you know what I mean."

He looked at her with a raised eyebrow. "What's going on?"

"Her patient died under suspicious circumstances last week."

"Which precinct is looking into it? Streeterville?"

"They're not looking into it, we are. Got a problem with that?"

He put two fingers to his temple in a mock military salute and grinned. His teeth were stained with tobacco. "No, ma'am! I go where I'm told."

"Smart man," Paula said, pushing herself away from the table with a grating sound of metal against concrete. "Thanks... and take it easy with that coffee, Adam. There's this concept called moderation. Look it up. It might save your life."

He rolled his eyes and groaned. "I don't plan to live forever, you know." He took a rushed sip of coffee as if Paula was about to snatch the cup out of his hands. "Don't go away yet. Moses Degnan is here to see you. He brought his son. I stashed them in the small conference room on third."

"Ah, crap," she muttered.

"Have you made up your mind about it? He's just a kid, Paula."

She shook her head slowly, still thinking. She couldn't afford to read the tea leaves wrong on this one. It would be better to get some inkling of direction from her boss. "Is Hobbs in?"

"Uh-huh, he's upstairs. They just finished a hairy leadership meeting. I heard he was in a foul mood."

Great. Just what she needed. "All right," she said, "I'll see what I can do."

Simon Degnan was the eleven-year-old boy she was feeling torn about. He had witnessed a shooting in his projects building. His neighbor, Vicente Espinoza, in a drunken fit of rage, had shot his pregnant wife, accusing her so loudly of cheating that the entire neighborhood heard the insults and threats. Simon saw the shooting from only a few yards away, from his balcony. He called the cops, and waited for them downstairs to tell them what he saw. The boy's father, a widowed mill worker named Moses, had later refused to let his son testify, citing concerns for his safety.

She could force the kid to testify, and make sure the case was a sure and easy win. Or she could let him off the hook, and use forensics and the shooter's prior record to speak for the prosecution.

Not an easy decision to make. Unlike the Anne Wileys of this world, the Degnans didn't have people to call to get them out of life's messes. No one cared if an eleven-year-old Black kid from the 'hood was found shot one day in some alley. Except her. She genuinely cared about the boy.

The question was, did she care more about him than her career? Could she protect one without endangering the other?

She took the elevator to the fifth floor and walked quickly to Mitchell Hobbs's office. His assistant had her wait for a couple of minutes until he finished a call, then opened the door for her.

"Ah, my favorite ASA," Hobbs greeted her, leaning back in his chair and interlocking his fingers behind his head. He'd taken off his jacket and loosened his tie knot. He wore his white shirt with the sleeves rolled up to under the elbows.

His posture reminded her of Derreck and his favorite horizontal position in bed. For a split second, she saw herself straddling her boss. *Ew.*

She smiled, banishing the disturbing thought. "I need your input on the Espinoza case. The eleven-year-old witness—we don't really need him to win this, do we?"

"Are you having second thoughts?" Hobbs looked at her intently, his eyes half-closed.

"Second thoughts? No." She shifted her weight from one foot to the other, noticing he hadn't invited her to sit. "I'm concerned the boy's life might be at risk. A lot of people saw him talk to the police. By now, I'm sure Espinoza knows too."

"But you know who Espinoza is, right?" He was asking her questions as if she were a third grader in front of the class, her homework not done.

"We liked him last year for the Kravitz murder, the elderly man whose head was bashed in during a robbery. Same building, different floor. But there wasn't enough evidence to file charges."

Hobbs's hands remained intertwined behind his head. He leaned backward, his leather chair tilting under his weight. "Okay, so what's your level of confidence if you proceed without the Degnan testimony?"

She bit her lip before answering. She could see where this was going, but she had to be honest and conservative in her answers. "I'd say a good ninety percent chance to secure a guilty verdict."

He stood abruptly and walked to the window. "It's not one hundred percent, though, is it?" He wasn't looking at her anymore.

"No, it's not. With forensic evidence, we run the risk the jury might lose interest or could lack the understanding—"

"Do you know who works on this floor, Paula?"

She cringed, waiting for him to continue. He didn't. It wasn't a rhetorical question. "The best this office has to offer?"

"Nope. Want to try again?"

Her cheeks caught fire. "No, sir. I'd rather take this as a learning moment."

"Everyone on this floor is a one hundred percent guy. Or gal. Everyone here does whatever it takes to have an impeccable conviction rate. We don't hesitate, we don't go to court unprepared, we don't pull Hail Marys. We get the job done. And if we have legitimate concerns for witness safety, we call in Witness Protection. But we always win." He turned and looked at her with cold, determined eyes. "Clear enough?"

"Crystal, sir." She took two steps backward, getting ready to leave.

His gaze softened a little. "Let them move to Wyoming on the taxpayers' dough," he said, making a dismissive gesture with his hand. "It's not like they have a life here they can't leave behind, right? I bet they have burger-flipping jobs up there too."

She clenched her jaw but managed to keep her opinions to herself. His dismissive attitude grated on her badly. "Yes, sir."

"Now, make it happen."

Her meeting was over. She walked out of Hobbs's office and didn't stop until she reached the third-floor conference room, determined not to let this issue ruin her future. Hobbs was right, even if she hated to admit it. It wasn't as if the Degnans had a lot to lose if they moved.

When she entered the conference room, Moses Degnan sprang to his feet. "Finally," he said, stepping behind his son's chair and putting his hands on the boy's shoulders in a protective gesture. "I have a job, you know," he protested. "Waiting for you costs me money I don't have."

"I understand and I apologize. I was in court all morning." She pulled out a chair and sat, then crossed her legs. The air was stale and smelled of sweaty armpits and rancid fast-food oil. The table was littered with food wrappers. Seemed that someone had brought them lunch while they were waiting. "You have something to tell me?"

"Yes," he said, pressing his lips together for a moment as if to control the words that wanted to blurt out. "I won't let my boy testify, and that's final."

"I'm afraid you'll have to." Paula sighed, frowning. She would've preferred not to take a strong stance, but Hobbs had been perfectly clear about it. "The Cook County state's attorney has decided to subpoena your son. If we deem the threat to his life is viable, we'll place you both in WitSec."

"And leave my job?" He started pacing angrily between the table and the back wall. "Are you crazy? Do you know how hard it was for me to get this job? What am I gonna do? Start working for eight bucks an hour again and starve?"

"I'm really sorry, Mr. Degnan. There's nothing I can do." She meant every word.

He stopped his pacing right across from Paula and stared down at her, his fists clenched and pressed against the table, his knuckles white. "I got us a lawyer, and he told me you'd do this. He told me you prosecutors only care about throwing people in jail. He said we can get a competency hearing. Let a judge decide if my son here is able to testify. He's just a kid. He might not know what he's saying." He slammed both fists against the table. "From now on, you're only talking to my lawyer, okay?"

"Fine."

He pushed an attorney's business card across the table. "Here, take it. And I swear, if anything happens to my little boy, I'll come after you, 'cause I won't have anything left to lose, you hear me?"

SIXTEEN
ARTICLE

I sit at the dinner table, weary to the bone, content to let my engine idle for a change. Mom's setting the table, and Derreck is uncorking a bottle of red Bordeaux. For a moment, I'm grateful he's home for dinner, a rare occurrence lately. It's good to have him close.

Then my mind shifts and I'm miles away, reliving the day's events, processing the trauma of a complicated few hours. Paula Fuselier's visit left me a bundle of nerves. Mrs. Heimbach's surgery went well, but my hands had a faint tremor in them the entire time, a tremor I could barely control. All I could think was, *What if she dies too? What if I lose another patient on the table, just days after Caleb Donaghy?* That state's attorney would be out there, watching, waiting like a spider, ready to move in for the kill.

Thankfully, Mrs. Heimbach lived. The valve replacement was a success.

Paula Fuselier is turning me into a nervous wreck.

I wonder how she learned about Caleb Donaghy. Hospitals don't exactly publish lists of people who don't make it. There are privacy laws in place that prevent the disclosing of any information pertaining to patients' cases.

Caleb Donaghy didn't have a next of kin. Knowing who he was, I'm not surprised. He couldn't've done the horrible things he did to Melanie, and no doubt many other little girls, while his wife and kids watched TV in the other room. Or maybe he could have; who knows with people anymore?

But I checked in the hospital system before I left today, and there were no calls logged about him. As far as I know, his body is still in a refrigerated morgue cabinet. That can only mean one thing: no family member or loved one filed a complaint about his death or asked the State's Attorney Office to look into it.

So how does this ASA know about it, and why is she on my case?

Recalling the venomous words she spat in my face, I start trembling with anger again. I'm not entitled. I never was. I worked hard all my life to get to where I am. Yes, I was fortunate to have good parents, and I'll always be grateful for that. I know others aren't so fortunate. I definitely don't need this woman to remind me, after Melanie.

I honestly can't remember a single time when I felt or acted entitled. Maybe I'm wrong... but I can't find peace with her accusations. Yes, my father taught me how to stitch turkey skin and put the first needle driver in my young hand, and that gave me an edge. That edge was something I was always grateful for and paid forward. I followed in my father's footsteps, but in a different way than the ASA meant. I mentored residents, volunteered, and put in weekly hours at free clinics. I didn't rush home to party or get my hair done. And I've never, ever held a position or accessed something I didn't work hard for. For crying out loud... I was still in med school when my father died; it wasn't as if he picked up the phone all day long to call in favors with the hospitals and professors he knew to make sure I landed the job I wanted.

The problem with what Paula Fuselier said is that others will believe her. Even *I* believed her, and that's why I'm now agonizing, still arguing with her in my mind. The words she threw at me were loaded with such hatred they made me feel defensive, and that's unforgivable. I shouldn't doubt myself so much, just because someone out there attacked my integrity. I can't believe I'm such an idiot.

Or maybe that's her strategy. Make me doubt myself and do something stupid, to confirm her suspicions and seal my fate. But why would she—

"Want some wine?" Derreck's voice yanks me back to the present. The rim of the bottle is hovering above my glass. I nod and smile weakly.

They set the table and Mom fills our plates with deep-dish lasagna covered in a thick layer of molten cheese. Must be a thousand calories per bite, but my mouth is watering, awakening my senses.

"It's purely vegetarian," she rushes to clarify. "It's an adapted pasta primavera recipe, really, just topped with cheese and stuck in the oven." She looks at the plates with joy in her eyes, satisfied with the result.

She stopped serving meat last week, after I didn't eat the chicken the night after Caleb Donaghy's surgery.

I take a small bite of lasagna and chew it slowly. It's delicious.

"This is wonderful, Mom." She smiles, delighted. "It's okay to cook with meat, you know," I add, loading another piece on my fork.

She laughs. "I know, sweetie. Your father was just like that. He sometimes couldn't stand looking at the meat on his plate after a rough day in surgery." She drinks a sip of wine, then touches her lips with her napkin. "You know what else he did? He redecorated the bathroom with dark blue tiles. He couldn't stand the sight of white tiles. It made him see blood."

I look at her, frowning slightly.

"Back in the day, ORs were all white tiles, and lots of blood-soaked lap sponges landed on the floors."

Derreck laughs. "I can't believe I got used to this kind of conversation over a meal. Any other lawyer I know would push their plate aside and ask for a shot of something strong."

I reach over to him and squeeze his forearm. It's so good to hear him laughing. The house has been shrouded in silence for the past week. I look at his handsome face and can't believe how lucky I've been in my life, my family, my career.

I could lose everything in one blink of an eye.

Darkness descends over me like a loaded storm cloud.

They could still find out who Caleb Donaghy was, and what I've done. That case review meeting hasn't happened yet; it's not scheduled until next week, and things could go sideways from there, especially with Dr. Bolger testifying, which I'm sure will happen. What if I don't come home after that meeting? What if tonight is the last time we have a peaceful dinner together? How do people know when it's the last time for anything? The last time they make love? The last time they leave the house, or say hello to a loved one over the phone?

"What's wrong, sweetie?" Mom's hand finds mine.

I shake my head and realize tears are streaming down my face. "It's nothing, just a tough day, that's all." I sniffle and pat my eyes dry with my napkin. Both of them look at me intently, worried, expecting more. "There's an investigation into the death of my patient from last week."

Mom gasps and covers her mouth with her hand. It trembles slightly. I hate myself for making her anxious.

"I had no idea it had started already," she whispers.

"What investigation?" Derreck asks in a professional tone. "What are you talking about? Are you being sued?"

"No." I turn to face him. "There's no next of kin. I won't get sued. There's a state's attorney looking into the patient's death."

I've never seen Derreck so angry. His pupils dilate, his brow furrows, his jaw clenches. "What state's attorney?" he asks calmly, but it's the calm at the eye of the storm.

"Paula Fuselier. Do you know her?"

He swallows hard. "I know *of* her, yes. It's a small government." His teeth are grinding. I touch his forearm again, trying to soothe his rage. He doesn't pull away, but tenses even more under my touch. "Must be my run for mayor, stirring up all sorts of trouble."

That's something I didn't think of. It makes sense. It definitely would explain why someone has it in for me.

"Is this something Boyd Lampert would do?" I look at him with raised eyebrows. Somehow, I don't see the sitting mayor of Chicago conspiring to taint my professional reputation just to get Derreck's name off the ballot.

Derreck holds his wineglass but doesn't lift it off the table. He turns it in place, over and over, obsessively. "I don't know. Maybe. We lock horns often."

"Oh, dear," Mom whimpers. She pushes her plate aside and folds her hands in her lap. "This is terrible."

"But you know who else I know?" Derreck asks, with a strange glint in his eyes. "I know Mitchell Hobbs, the Cook County state's attorney. He's this woman's boss's boss. I'll make a call."

"No, don't." I grab his hand with both of mine. "It will make things worse. The hospital is already involved, they assigned counsel. It's an entire mess, and if you intervene—"

"Unbelievable," he mutters, pulling away and running his hand through his hair in a gesture of pure despair. "Fucking unbelievable."

"Please don't make that call," I insist. "Please, promise me." I stare at him until he lowers his gaze.

"Okay, Anne, I promise. For now." He empties his wineglass with two thirsty gulps, then reaches for the bottle and tops it off. "But watch your back. Don't talk to anyone. Don't be afraid to ask for your own attorney."

I look at him intently, nodding at everything he tells me to do. "But you know this patient was—"

His finger touches my lips, demanding silence. "He's just a patient, Anne. A random guy who happened to need heart surgery, and who, sadly, died during the procedure." He looks at me until I nod again. "Good." Then he lets air out of his lungs in a pained sigh.

"It was routine, his surgery, but it went badly. It's not like we have hearts readily available if one refuses to restart after the aneurysm repair." I find myself struggling to breathe as I try to rationalize everything. "There's a committee that looks at all patient deaths and audits the procedures. The hospital administrator brought forward the date of the hearing, to have the report ready in case the prosecutors keep digging. That could go very badly. They could say—"

"This is an attack, nothing else. We will weather it." He finds my hand and takes it to his lips. "I'm so sorry you have to be the target of this, Anne. It's so unfair. But politics is dirty, as dirty as it gets." He pauses for a moment, shooting a quick glance at my mother. "Unless you guys want me to quit the mayoral race."

Another tear rolls from the corner of my eye. I can't ask him to do that. It's the only big thing he's ever wanted for himself. I can cope with a little heat until November, if that's what it takes. It doesn't change what I've done in the operating room and why, but it changes how I feel about it. "No, baby, definitely not."

"Absolutely not." Mom replies almost at the same time as I do. "You're like my own son, Derreck, and I couldn't be prouder of you. The Wileys are strong women, in case you need me to remind you." She chuckles and looks away briefly. "Determined, fearless women you can count on."

"Don't let the bastards win," I whisper through tears,
thinking of Paula Fuselier sitting at my desk. "Give them hell.
You'll make a fine mayor come November."

He raises his glass and smiles. His rage is almost completely
gone. He's back to being the charismatic and upbeat man I'm
very much in love with. "To the future, my fine ladies," he
toasts. We raise our glasses too.

A moment of silence ensues, as each of us apparently delves
into our thoughts.

Mom fidgets in her seat, then eventually stands, abandoning
her napkin on the table. "Then I guess it's as good a time as any
to tell you what I saw in today's evening paper," she says, in a
shaky voice.

A sharp pang of anxiety rips through my abdomen, the
physical manifestation of stress hormones being released into
the bloodstream. I watch her walking slowly and stiffly to her
purse, then returning with a folded newspaper, which she lays
in the middle of the table between us.

"This." She taps a small article with the tip of her finger.
"They don't waste any damn time, do they?"

Derreck picks it up before I can. "What's this? 'Suspicious
Death of Cardiothoracic Surgery Patient Investigated,'" he
reads, his voice lower, more dismayed with each word. "That's
the title." I can see his eyes moving as he's reading fast,
mumbling to himself. "This is insane," he says, letting go of the
newspaper when I reach for it.

I read it with my breath caught in my lungs from the first
word that dances in front of my eyes. The article is searing,
speaking of the "wonder girl" of Joseph Lister University
Hospital's cardiothoracic surgery department losing her first
patient under what appears to be suspicious circumstances, and
how the patient's death will be investigated. The article makes

no mention of Derreck's run for mayor, which I find strange if he's the intended target. Toward the end, the article cites sources close to the State's Attorney Office.

Paula Fuselier.

Game, set, and match. She's destroyed me.

SEVENTEEN
WHIP

It was unlike Derreck to want to meet her early in the morning, in public no less. His texts were commanding and didn't offer an explanation for the urgency of his request, but she didn't need one. She had been expecting something like that to happen the moment Anne Wiley went home and cried bitter tears on her husband's shoulder about the State's Attorney Office investigation. The entire setup was a ticking bomb, and it had just blown up. Now all she could hope for was the maximum damage.

At a few minutes after seven, the Starbucks parking lot was almost empty, while the drive-through line was long enough to circle around the entire building. This worked well for her; she wasn't eager to have witnesses to what could end up being a heated conversation. There would come a time for the limelight, but not for a little while longer.

Derreck's car was parked right in front of the entrance. She pulled hers in two spots away from it, then walked briskly into the coffee shop. It was almost deserted, yet the baristas were hustling to serve the drive-through customers. The place smelled of freshly ground coffee beans, caramel, and warm cinnamon pastries.

She looked around the shop and saw Derreck seated at a table in the back with a tall coffee in front of him. Smiling as if nothing was wrong, she clacked her three-inch heels walking over there, just slightly swaying her hips. When she reached the table, she dropped her briefcase on one of the empty chairs.

"Good morning," she said, undoing the silky white scarf she wore around her neck and hanging it on the back of the chair. "I'll go get myself—"

"Sit the fuck down and shut up." Derreck's hand gripped her wrist mercilessly. He yanked it so hard she almost fell on the chair instead of sitting. "What kind of screwed-up game are you playing, Paula?"

He was glaring, just as enraged as she'd anticipated. Still smiling, she looked at him as if nothing was wrong. "That's no way to treat a lady, Mr. Mayor. Let go of me, then kindly wait until I get myself a coffee."

He released her wrist, then took his cup and slammed it down on the table in front of her, so hard a few droplets found their way out through the lid, landing on her blue jacket.

"Tsk, tsk," she said, still smiling. "I'll send you the cleaner's bill for that." She took the cup and sniffed it, then took a small sip. It was burning hot, and just plain, black java. Not a macchiato.

She stood up halfway, but he grabbed her arm again and slammed her back into the chair. "Sit down. You're not going anywhere until you tell me what kind of fucked-up agenda you have."

She didn't like the glint in his eyes. She might've pushed him too far. Her smile waned, but she kept her cool and pushed the coffee cup toward him. "I don't like this. I want something else."

"Tough shit," he hissed. "Why are you harassing Anne over the death of that patient?"

He was nothing if not direct, Mr. Mayor. She liked that in bed, liked it much less at seven a.m. in a coffee shop that was about to get busy. "Maybe I should tell her about you and me instead. What do you say? Should I drop my investigation, say, for personal reasons? Tell her we've been seeing each other for a few months?"

"You can't be serious," he replied, running his hands through his hair a couple of times as if it were falling over his forehead. It was too short for that; the gesture was self-soothing. "Why are you throwing everything down the drain?"

Her smile widened. The carrot she'd offered still had pull. Maybe he didn't care so much for the wifey after all. "You're doing that, not me. I promised I'd support your ascent to power. I never said I'd be derelict in my duties while I'm at it. Dr. Anne Wiley is being investigated by my office. I thought, under the circumstances of our agreement, it was best I took the case so I could control the damage."

He stared at her with his mouth agape for a moment. He wasn't buying it yet. "Controlling it? How? With newspaper articles? How is that supposed to boost my chances as mayor?"

She tilted her head and smiled crookedly, as if asking him to stop being an idiot. His jaw clenched. "I have a job to do, Derreck. It was published on page whatever, short and deeply buried, invisible enough to prevent any real damage to your career. It didn't name you, did it?"

"No," he admitted with visible reluctance. "It didn't."

"And, thankfully, your wife didn't take your name when you married her." She looked at him for a moment, trying to ascertain if she'd cracked the whip hard enough. Not even close. "People won't put two and two together. Not this time."

He wrung his hands, his head hung low, his lips pressed tightly together. For a moment, there was silence between them, heavy, foreboding. "How did you learn about Anne's dead patient? From me?"

She didn't reply, just looked at him, weighing her options.

"Answer me, damn it!" he bellowed. Two baristas turned their heads and looked at them. "Be honest with me for a change. Whatever it is, I can take it."

Paula chuckled, playing with a strand of her hair, twirling it around her fingers. "Typical narcissist, to think everything's about you." She paused for a moment, while he visibly held his breath. "No, Derreck, it wasn't you. Someone from the hospital called the State's Attorney Office with a complaint. A case was created based on that call, and I took it."

His anger turned into poorly masked surprise. "Someone called? Who?"

"You know I can't tell you that."

He muttered an oath under his breath. "You and I have long exceeded the boundaries of propriety, Paula. I'm sure you could bend the rules a little more and give me a hint."

There it was: his concern for his wife overshadowing every-thing else. She'd assumed, since they'd been together for so many years, that boredom might've distanced him from Anne, a crack in their bond large enough for her to drive a wedge through and then push.

"You shouldn't worry about that, my dear Mr. Mayor. You should focus on getting your side of the deal taken care of. When the time comes and my name is in the hat for the next Cook County state's attorney, I know you'll make good on your promise to me. Meanwhile, I'll make the right calls and put you in front of the media for each and every high-profile arrest. You will shine, Derreck. Do you have your speech ready for the first one?"

He stared at her as if he'd never seen her before, a hint of contempt in his eyes. She resented him for that.

"If I can't trust you, Paula, there's no deal to be made."

"You can't trust me?" she asked, speaking slowly, her voice filled with unspoken threats.

"No, I can't." He looked at her sternly, then drank a big gulp from the coffee cup she'd pushed aside. "If you had told me about the investigation before Anne did, before I read about it in the papers, then yes, maybe. But now, I don't know what game you're playing, and, honestly, I'm done with it." He stood and buttoned his jacket. "Goodbye, Paula."

He only took a step or two before Paula said, "I can still destroy you, just as easily as I can make you. Don't you dare walk away from me."

He froze in place, looking back at her for a moment.

Then, as if in a trance, he returned to the table and sat down. "Or what, Paula?" He smiled derisively. "Or you're going to be the cliché mistress who doesn't get the fine print? You'll tell my wife about us?" He leaned back in his chair and folded his hands in his lap. "Perhaps you're going to be the misguided ASA who ends her own career by harassing the wife of her secret lover. How's that headline for you?"

Her blood was boiling. She hadn't imagined Derreck would defy her like that, would bring her within an inch of pure madness. Everything she was trying to accomplish was disintegrating before her stunned eyes.

She couldn't let him get away. Not like this. Her first thought was to reach for the gun she carried in her briefcase, a small Glock, always loaded. But then she steadied herself. Shooting Derreck was pointless. Served no one. Achieved nothing.

She drew a long breath of air and exhaled slowly, calming her fraught nerves. Hot-blooded rage didn't mix well with her agenda. When she spoke, her voice was level and cold. "How about this headline instead: 'Promising mayoral candidate found with twenty grams of cocaine. Charges to follow.' Will that work better for you, Mr. Mayor?"

Slack-jawed, he stared at her in disbelief. "You wouldn't... Paula, you can't possibly be serious."

She stood and gathered her things, slowly wrapping her silk scarf around her neck, fussing for a moment over an elaborate bow. "I'm late for court, Derreck. It's nothing major—just a possession charge with intent. You know, over fifteen grams? I'm hoping to get the max, but he's a first-time offender. I'm sure I'll get him five years in a state prison. Easy-peasy." She winked and left, walking slowly toward the exit.

In the large window, she could see his reflection fading in the background. He was still seated, looking at her, his hand covering his mouth.

She'd cracked the whip hard enough this time. Now he'd follow her lead.

EIGHTEEN
MONDAY

We spent the rest of the week in wake-like silence, the tension in the house unbearable, waiting. Everyone had fears and questions, yet no one spoke of them. We all pretended to be fine. I'm sure Derreck wasn't fine as he spent the whole time researching a case. Mom didn't seem fine either. She spent most of Sunday by the window, staring outside, holding a folded newspaper in one hand and a pencil in the other, but never finishing the crossword puzzle. And I wasn't doing too well, run down by anxiety at the thought of today.

At two in the afternoon, I will appear in front of a committee that will examine Caleb Donaghy's case. By then, the committee members will have watched the video recordings of the procedure, will have reviewed Donaghy's medical records, and will be ready to hear testimony and ask questions. At stake: my life as I know it, my medical license, my freedom.

I was grateful for the weekend-long chance to breathe and think away from the hospital and gladly stayed indoors, pretending to work on something or other, when, in fact, I was preparing my testimony. Things I wanted to say. Things I wanted to make sure I didn't say. Things I wanted to use as a medical reason for calling time of death so quickly, when, in fact, the real reason was my patient's identity. Things I needed to ask Derreck about.

On Sunday, right before a dinner I couldn't eat, he prepped me, reminding me to keep my statements short, clear, and simple, even if testifying in front of other doctors. Lastly, he said to keep in mind the transcript of my testimony could end up being read in court or held against me, as if I'd been arrested and Mirandized.

That simple piece of advice kept me up all night.

But today I'm ready for what may come. I'm dressed sharply in a dark blue pantsuit with a longer jacket. I matched that with navy-blue pumps and an even darker blue silk blouse. I even applied makeup. It's Derreck's idea: in case something should throw me off and make me flush, the redness will be less notice-able under foundation. I popped a beta blocker last night, another this morning, and a third one waits in my purse for lunch. It will keep my hands from trembling and my voice from choking. The pills will dampen my fight-or-flight response to stress. Instead of either, I will stand my ground calmly and answer all questions like a professional who's done nothing wrong.

But first, I have rounds.

Madison just walked me through the day's schedule and the week's outlook. She didn't insist much on the scheduled consults and new admissions; I didn't let her. I want today to be over with, so I know one way or other before I make a week's worth of plans.

I have a couple of new patients waiting for me. Mrs. Orlowski was admitted this morning. She's a sixty-three-year-old woman scheduled for bypass surgery tomorrow morning. She's spending the day in the hospital, getting another round of bloodwork done and some more imaging. The second patient is an emergency room transfer from last night, a forty-three-year-old truck driver from out of state complaining of chest pains. His imaging shows mitral valve vegetation, very early stage, but they wanted me to take a look.

Both their charts are on my desk, above the red folder that's been sitting there since last Thursday. I grab the charts and take another sip of chamomile tea before heading out. No caffeine for me today, although I need it like air.

"You spoke with that prosecutor without counsel present?" M's raised voice startles me. I turn around and find her in the middle of my office, the glass door behind her still whooshing to a soft close. Her hands are on her hips, her eyebrows joined at a furious angle above her nose. "What are you, three? Or a complete idiot?" She stomps her foot and puts one hand on her nape, rubbing it forcefully. "If you do anything else to further jeopardize this hospital's reputation, you're gone faster than I can say fired."

My throat is dry, although I thought I was prepared for this. "All I told her was to contact the legal department to get the result of the committee review. That's all. Just like you instructed me."

"That's not what I asked you to say." She pivots in place as if looking for something that's not there. "When you called me last week and told me about her, you didn't find it necessary to tell me you'd already spoken with her? Twice? She didn't have to know about the damn committee meeting, did she?" She grabs the door handle, but doesn't leave, just holds on to it, her motion stopped halfway while her entire being vibrates with pressure like an overheated steam locomotive. "You were supposed to say absolutely nothing to her. Not a word. And that's not what I'm hearing you did. After I specifically warned you." She points a threatening finger at me.

Someone talked. Someone always talks. That's the rule. Of course, glass walls don't help much with keeping secrets.

"Really, I didn't say anything. There was nothing to say, and I didn't—"

"Save it for the committee, Dr. Wiley." She walks out without giving me another look.

I've never felt so ashamed in my entire life. And so afraid.

I could lose everything.

In a few hours, I'll have to stand before my peers and justify every decision I made that day, every action I took, even the unjustifiable ones.

After today's meeting, I could leave the boardroom and find police waiting for me, ready to take me away in cuffs. No matter how hard I try to steel myself for that scenario, I'm not able to. I can't even think of that, of what I'd do. I'd rather the earth opens and swallows me whole.

That rarely happens when people need it.

I was planning to see M before the meeting, to ask for an early look at the autopsy findings, to better prepare myself. Now that's out of the question. She'd probably throw me out of her office before I even opened my mouth.

When I feel I'm about to collapse, it soothes me to think of Melanie. What I did, I did for her and no one else. There was no agenda, and no other thought in my mind, just the memory of my little sister scared out of her mind when she saw Caleb Donaghy on that park bench. The bruises on her legs. The findings in her autopsy report revealing years of trauma and unspeakable abuse.

That's why my patient is in a morgue fridge now.

Because of what he'd done.

If delivering justice for Melanie when no one else could will end my life as I know it, at least I'll have that. The knowledge that I have avenged my little sister's suffering and death.

But still, the same question buzzes through my mind like an annoying little insect that won't settle. Why *did* his heart refuse to restart in the first place?

Madison reminds me to get on with the day. I'm already running behind.

By the time I start making my rounds, the truck driver has been reassigned to Dr. Fitzpatrick per M's request. *Now she's taking my patients away.* My eyes sting with tears as I leave his room, and move on to see Mrs. Orlowski, my bypass patient, half expecting her to be reassigned as well.

She isn't.

She's waiting for me, pale and monosyllabic, while Ginny takes her blood pressure. Some people act like that when they're afraid, as if opening their mouths and talking about what's on their minds will somehow diminish who they are. Unfortunately, such internalized stress heightens the risk of a procedure going badly. I make a note to myself to swing by after the committee hearing, to lift her spirits a little more.

Right now, I don't have the time, and my mind is stubbornly elsewhere.

"One-forty-five over ninety-seven, Doctor," Ginny announces.

I open the chart and look for her medication. She's already on two prescriptions for her blood pressure. "A little high for someone resting comfortably," I say, smiling encouragingly. "Nothing we can't handle, though." I scribble on the chart briefly, then hand it to Ginny.

"Test results are back," Ginny says, probably noticing I haven't reviewed them. She hands me back the chart, and I flip through the pages, looking for Mrs. Orlowski's labs. I find them, organized neatly and easy to review. The out-of-range values are listed at the top in bold font, easy to catch. Her cholesterol is higher than normal, but not insanely high. Triglycerides are high too. Nothing surprising there. Everything else is normal, especially values I'm looking at before surgery, like coagulation factors, blood sugar, and hemoglobin. This is not her first set of labs, and it's consistent with what I've seen before.

I like a visit with no surprises.

I close the chart and smile. "I'll be back in a couple of hours to chat a little bit more. I believe this stubborn blood pressure of yours could have something to do with stress." She stares at me without a word. "Maybe if we talk for a little while, we'll see it go down." I give her a few moments. Still nothing. A quick glance at my watch tells me I can't wait any longer. I nod and leave the room, closing the door gently before I head back to my office.

I'm almost done, stacking papers on top of the red Donaghy folder. I have everything I could think of, including a couple of peer-reviewed articles about calling time of death after cardioplegia. I printed those last night and highlighted the sections that supported my decision, even if remotely. Finding them was like the proverbial needle in a mountain of hay.

Then my phone rings loudly, startling me. I swear under my breath. I'm so tense I really don't know how I'm going to live through this review. It's Derreck's ring tone though, and I need his voice, his strength, right now.

"Hey," I say quietly, turning toward the window for privacy.

"Hey, back," he replies casually, but I can sense the tension in his voice. "Did you have lunch?"

I chuckle, remembering the beta blocker I was supposed to take. "We normally instruct patients to present for surgery with an empty stomach." My attempt at a joke sounds lame and contrived.

A moment of silence, then he asks, "Have you heard from that nosy ASA again?"

Paula Fuselier. The thought of her runs a blade through my gut. "Thankfully, I haven't. Last thing I need today. Why? Do you know anything?"

"Nothing," he replies, a little too fast. He must've made the damned call to the State's Attorney Office anyway. Damn men and their genetically coded need to protect women. If M hears about it, I'm toast. "Just wanted to check on you. I know you're going through a rough time," he adds, and I'm instantly sorry for my bitter thoughts.

"Thanks," I whisper on a long sigh. "It's time to cross your fingers for me. The review starts in ten minutes."

"Fingers and toes. Call me when you know something. I've freed my entire afternoon."

The end of the call fills the office with forbidding silence. I remember the beta blocker and take it, then head out with the stack of papers and the red Donaghy folder.

A few minutes later, I open the boardroom door and enter, looking around for faces I recognize. All the committee members are tenured surgeons and department leads, people whose professional opinions carry a lot of weight. I have some friends in there, like Dr. Seldon, but also some enemies, like Dr. Bolger, who grins wickedly when he sees me. He'll probably be the first to testify.

One person's presence fills me with dread. He's sitting by M's side, a heavily built man in a charcoal suit, white shirt, and blood-red tie. His squinty eyes look at me with curiosity and concern while he offers me a quick nod before looking away.

I've only met him a few times before. He's Aaron Timmer, the hospital's lead counsel.

This is no ordinary case review.

It's far worse than I thought.

NINETEEN
PROOF

Sometime in the past few months, she'd become too closely involved with Derreck.

The conclusion made her spring up from her desk chair and start pacing the small office, looking out the third-floor window at the busy downtown traffic. Monday mornings were the worst: constant honking of horns almost always ending in collisions. But today, the two dense lines of cars working their way past the corner streetlight seemed miles away, in a different life almost.

Her mind was on Derreck Bourke.

At first, Paula had believed she could use her body as a weapon to get what she wanted, especially after meeting Derreck and seeing he wasn't hard on the eyes one tiny bit. There was something about him that made her believe he could be the next mayor of Chicago, given the right circumstances. He had a calm, strong presence, enhanced by his broad shoulders and high forehead, or perhaps his deep blue eyes staring in the distance as if he was in search of a vision. He was smart and articulate, and debated any subject without becoming offensive, no matter how aggressive the opponent would get. He was White House material, even if he didn't know it.

For months, she believed she could stay disconnected emotionally, remain cold and factual and determined, a professional chasing a goal. She didn't have any problems with her conscience because she was sleeping with him with a personal agenda; many before her had done it and people didn't care, as long as they didn't read about it in the newspapers. Even for the hardest working of women, success was always believed to have come in exchange for sexual favors. Who did she sleep with to get that job, or part, or book deal, or whatever?: That was always the question. That was part of the stigma associated with being a woman, and it would probably stay like that for generations more to come.

But with vulnerability fueled by years of solitude, she'd slowly grown attached to Derreck. He was no longer just an entry in a calendar of appointments; he was the text message or phone call she waited for with excitement. He was the reason she visited high-end lingerie stores more often than ever before. Insidious and unescapable, her emotions had entangled things badly.

Was she falling in love with Derreck? Or had she fallen for him already?

She could kick herself. A perfect plan required perfect execution, and she was strong. If she couldn't believe in herself, how could she ask others to? Still, she'd turned into a disappointing cliché, the weak, infatuated female who can't help but fall for the wrong man.

She'd spent the entire weekend waiting for a sign from Derreck, anxiously pacing her apartment, unable to concentrate. Her phone stayed stubbornly quiet, and she didn't text him either. After the Starbucks meeting on Friday morning, it didn't take a rocket scientist to figure out he didn't want to have anything more to do with her. Probably their afternoon at the LondonHouse last week was the last time he'd hold her in his arms.

And there it was—deep, breath-shattering pain at the thought of having lost his love. When did that start to matter? Probably at the same time she stopped being able to tolerate hearing Anne Wiley's name on his lips without grinding her teeth.

She was lying to herself though, if she believed Derreck had ever loved her. Friday morning had made that abundantly clear. Derreck's first and foremost allegiance was to his wife. Paula had never been more than a passing fling, a few furtive evenings in snazzy hotel rooms with champagne and hors d'oeuvres and lots of crazy-hot, passionate sex.

Her entire plan was falling apart. Whatever pieces might've still clung together, she'd ripped apart on Friday morning, so eager to crack her imaginary whip and show him she had the power, not him. She thought she'd got what she wanted, there at the coffee shop. Then why did she feel like grieving still?

Because she'd fallen in love and didn't even realize it. *How stupid could someone get?*

Somewhere along the way, she should've revisited her priorities. What did she want from this relationship? How important were her goals? If Derreck meant more than just a means to an end, she should've seen it in time and acted like it.

She still knew how to press his buttons. Unlike her, Derreck's priorities seemed to have stayed the same. Running for mayor in November. Winning that race. She could still make a difference for him, and maybe that was the way back into his arms.

But to what end? He'd never leave his wife, not as long as she drew breath.

At last, a cold smile fluttered on Paula's lips. People could be finished, taken out in more ways than one. And men's minds could be changed; it wasn't that hard for a smart, motivated woman.

With that conclusion, she grinned widely. It was going to be an excellent week. She was due in court in a couple of hours, but she was well-prepared and didn't anticipate any issues before bringing home another win.

A quick rap against the door and it swung open. Adam Costilla, her investigator, always barged in like that, as if he were in full SWAT gear busting down a suspect's door. It made her jump out of her skin every time.

"Good morning, boss," he said, holding on to the door as if he'd decided not to come in. "What's the final say in the Degnan testimony?" He panted, out of breath, beads of sweat covering his forehead. He must've taken the stairs again.

"Hey, Adam," she replied, looking through a file folder. "Yeah, we have a subpoena for the boy's testimony." She handed him the sheet of paper.

He took two heavy steps inside her office and closed the door behind him. The floor creaked under his weight.

"You know, I don't understand you," he said, still breathing heavily. "I don't know who you are anymore. You used to care about these kids."

"The boss was very clear about this. He won't tolerate a loss, and we can't risk it. Everything we've worked for—"

"If this thug walks for his wife's shooting despite all the physical evidence we have stacked against him, we'll be on him like ducks on a June bug and nail his ass the moment he spits on the sidewalk." He rested his hands on his hips and sighed with bitterness. "But you don't put that kid's life in danger, Paula. It's not worth it."

She hated to admit he was right. A line should be drawn before the system got children involved in picking killers out of lineups and having eleven-year-olds testify in court.

"We don't have a choice. It's up to Hobbs, and he made the call. If we don't deliver, we get pulled off the case, and a new ASA gets assigned, someone who can get him what he wants.

I'm not going to risk it. It's career suicide, and for what? Simon Degnan will have to testify either way."

Adam stared at her as if she were a piece of crap. There was something inherently direct and uncompromising about him, a set of core values that held him on the straight and narrow, while a strong fire burned inside. He didn't pull any punches when anything came into conflict with that inner mantra, even if it was her.

She rubbed her hands together, feeling cold, her fingers frozen as if the chill of the windy Monday morning had seeped into her office, drowning the warm air coming from the vents. "The Degnans requested a competency hearing."

"Huh... I wonder who gave them that idea," Adam said, laughing, tilting his head to the left just a tiny bit.

"Jeez, Adam... Whose side are you on, anyway?"

His laughter died instantly. "You used to know that, Paula. Justice, that's all I care about. You and I used to share that belief."

She scoffed angrily, pacing the floor, scowling at her investigator. "Issuing a subpoena for a witness to testify in a murder case is perfectly legal."

"I said justice, Paula, not law. That's a difference you used to care about back in the day. Seems the air is getting pretty rarefied here, in this building, the higher up you get. It can cause lapses in judgment."

They locked eyes for a tense moment, then she looked away. He was right. When she was the next Cook County state's attorney, she'd make the calls and draw the line at kids. Until then, she had a boss, and his orders were the law.

"Make sure he's there next Monday, Adam, ready to testify. If the judge finds him competent, of course." She had to give it to Adam, he was resourceful. She closed the case file without sitting back down at her desk. Then she asked, "Where are you with the Caleb Donaghy case?"

He pressed his lips together for a while, then took out his notepad and flipped through the pages.

"I didn't have much time, and there's nothing to find, really. I looked at everything I could get my hands on, and there's no connection between the lady surgeon and the dead guy. This Donaghy fellow was a drunk and a piece of crap, did a couple of stints in jail for battery and assault in the past ten years. Nothing before that." He shrugged and closed his notepad.

"Did you talk to anyone who knew him? Family, friends, neighbors?"

"Has no family and no friends. I asked the bartender at the local watering hole, and he told me to go screw myself. I asked him why, and he said he'd tell Donaghy the same. I told him the guy was dead, and the bartender spat on the floor and said, 'Good riddance to hell.' That's the only character reference I was able to get."

Fabulous. "And the surgeon?"

"What about her?" He seemed genuinely confused and a tad worried, because a few fine ridges were lining his forehead.

"Financials?"

He laughed again, sounding unconvinced. "Hey, I only had a couple of days, all right?"

She smiled sheepishly. "And?"

He shook his head. "Only high level for now. There's nothing there. The surgeon lady is loaded."

"She married into it?"

"Uh-uh. The other way around. She holds the money, from family investments mostly, although she makes really nice dough cutting into people. Her mother's name is on the checks that paid for the husband's TV ad campaign. Your surgeon married a dude who had zero to his name."

There it was: the backup evidence to one of the main reasons why Derreck would never leave his wife. *Damn that woman...* Without even knowing, she won every time. "Right. Phone records?"

"Nothing yet. I need a subpoena first. Dr. Wiley isn't some street junkie whose rights I can trample all over. This woman's got pull and I'm not playing with fire."

"Then never mind the phone records. We don't have enough for a subpoena."

"That's what I was thinking. Why are we looking into this surgery thing? Did anyone complain?"

She considered her answer carefully for a moment. All official complaints were logged into a system Adam could easily access. It made no sense to lie to him, as she'd done to Derreck. "No, no one called anything in."

Another shrug. "Then?"

"I heard a rumor, okay? I was in the hospital for personal reasons, and I heard people talk. It's as if someone had filed a complaint, and that someone's me."

He whistled in disbelief. "That's nothing, Paula. You got nothing. People talk shit all day long. It's what people do."

"I still want to look into this, and it's my prerogative, okay?" Her voice cut like a knife. The temperature in the room dropped a few degrees. "Just tell me if I need to ask someone else to look into it for me."

"No need for that, boss. I'll do it. Like I always do what you need me to do."

"Then find out why Caleb Donaghy died, all right? Something happened, and I need to know what."

"Copy that," he replied, visibly more cautious. "By the way, I was at the hospital today, handkerchief in hand, balloons, waiting on the benches by your doc's office, to see what's what. There's a review meeting today at two. They're analyzing the Donaghy case internally."

"Today? It was supposed to be Wednesday!" She raised her voice, frustrated. She'd planned to show up at Anne's office right before that meeting, to throw her off balance. "Damn it to hell."

Adam's jaw slackened. "Why do you care? What's it to you when they have their review meetings? Those things are routine when a patient dies, aren't they?"

She willed herself to be calm. Adam was her friend, they went way back, but there would be a limit to his willingness to look the other way. "I was planning to speak with her before that review, that's all. I was hoping to get my hands on a copy of the Donaghy autopsy report."

Adam looked at her for a moment, curious. "Paula, there's a certain way our office investigates crime. This ain't it. We have procedures for a reason. We get warrants, we file requests for documents, and so on. Yeah, I might've snuck in there with a bunch of balloons in hand to hear what's what, but that's only because you and I are friends, and you asked me to."

She looked away for a moment, then straight at Adam, with a little more gratitude in her eyes. "Thanks, Adam, I appreciate it. You're the best." She clasped her hands together and walked behind her desk as if looking to put some distance between them. "Just trust me on this, okay? If you can't find anything in a couple of days, we'll forget all about it."

"Sure, whatever you say." He shifted his weight from one foot to another, seeming ready to leave. "Where do you want me to look next?"

"Those phone records would be great, if you could manage, you know, without a subpoena for now. If not, let's deep-dive into her financials. Look for offshore accounts, tax issues, cryptocurrency investments. Maybe she's selling fentanyl on the side."

He frowned and rubbed his chin for a moment. "I don't think so, but I'll look."

"Why do you say that?"

"Because she's a golden donor for Doctors Without Borders.

Every month, she donates a big chunk of her pay to that organization and a couple of others. She doesn't fit the drug-dealing profile." He paused, staring at Paula, but she ignored his curious gaze and looked at the case file in front of her, thinking intently.

"Okay, maybe she's not dealing fentanyl, I'll give you that, but something's not right about this woman. Find out, Adam. Dig through her social accounts, neighbors, friends, see what people have to say about her. Somewhere you'll find a lead you can follow."

And, hopefully, her entire world will unravel, she continued, in the privacy of her thoughts.

Adam's eyebrows rose, but he nodded. "Sure, boss. Whatever she did, if she jaywalked or littered some dark alley in the past twenty years, I'll find out for you."

Paula looked at him intently. "I know she killed Caleb Donaghy. She murdered him. I promise you that. Just get me some proof."

TWENTY
REVIEW

I take my seat in the large boardroom and look around. I don't see a friendly look or a smile of encouragement from anyone.

It's officially called a peer-review case analysis, but these people are not my peers. They are my bosses and their bosses, people with enough power to make or break careers in this hospital and the entire country. Most of them wear white lab coats over business formal attire, jackets replaced by the starched white hospital garb.

The room is flooded with filtered sunshine through half-open vertical blinds. The table is littered with files, spread in front of every seat, taken or not. That tells me a few people are yet to join us. A side counter with cabinets hosts two coffeepots, one marked decaf, and a third one with hot water for tea. Two stacks of plastic cups are set on the counter, next to a tray with chilled water and pop on ice.

I still have time to get some water before the meeting starts. I won't rush, a little afraid I might drink too much fluid due to stress and then have to use the restroom. Even in a medical environment, it would be embarrassing to ask for a brief recess.

The file in front of me is labeled with my deceased patient's name and his case number. I open it and flip through the pages. They're neatly separated by dividers. M's assistant has done a very good job, preparing these files with the rigor of board meeting presentations.

The first few sections are case history, labs, and imaging. Then there's a statement from Dr. Bolger that fills my chest with rage and my eyes with the threat of tears. He accuses me of gross negligence and demands that my medical license be revoked for incompetence. It takes all I have left in me to stay calm and not rush over to slap him across his smug face.

The last section in the file is the autopsy report. My breath gets caught in my chest when I turn the page and start reading. M brought in the Cook County medical examiner to conduct it, instead of using one of our own cardiologists like normal. Seeing his name and title stamped on the last page of the report confirms this is no routine case review.

It almost feels like I'm on trial for murder.

Perhaps I am.

I flip back to the beginning of the autopsy report and start reading. The medical examiner examined the aneurysm repair, the stitching, the Dacron graft, and found nothing wrong with the way the surgery was performed. He wrote two pages of findings, from an enlarged fatty liver with several cysts present to kidney stones and a small adrenal tumor, then summarized his findings in a single paragraph that exonerates me of all culpability.

I close my eyes for a moment of gratitude as relief washes over me. Then I go back to the previous page, where something caught my attention.

Higher concentration of potassium found in the chambers of the heart, most likely traces of the cardioplegia solution used during the procedure, but not abnormally high. Traces of saline solution.

I had flushed that heart thoroughly, rinsing it for a full two minutes with saline. There should've been no potassium left-overs to keep that heart from beating.

The room is spinning with me for a moment, while I try to remember.

I always do it the same way. After so many years performing procedures, patient resuscitation is routine, not something you could suddenly forget how to do correctly. I watched the surgery videos countless times and didn't catch anything out of the ordinary.

For a moment, I consider asking M about it, then imagine what Derreck would say to me if I did. Yes, I'd be an idiot. She has Aaron Timmer by her side, the head of legal, as if she wants to be sure she's covered, no matter what happens. Time for me to keep my concerns to myself, and just survive the review with my license, my freedom, and my life intact.

"Thank you all for joining me today," M announces, and the low-level chatter in the room dies, leaving a tense silence. I look straightforward, thankful that across the wide table from me, the seat is still empty. "You've all had time to review the case data and the video recordings of the procedure." M looks around the table as if to make sure no one disagrees with her. "All right, then, I'll proceed with the statements, then we'll ask Dr. Wiley to answer any questions from this group."

Another moment of silence, while most of my colleagues do their very best to avoid looking at me. Dr. Seldon is fussing over his cup of coffee. Dr. Fitzpatrick, my boss, is still flipping through the pages of the case file, jotting down notes with a green pen. Dr. Dean, the echocardiologist in my team, is fidgeting, visibly stressed out. Only Dr. Bolger is smiling.

Damn it.

Out of the blue, I wonder how much damage that assistant state's attorney has already done. What if Paula Fuselier has spoken with Dr. Bolger? What if he's the one who called her? If he told her what he wrote in his statement, no wonder the woman wants to throw me in jail for murder. A whirlwind of panic sweeps over me. I look over my shoulder at the cabinet counter where the water and pop are, regretting I didn't stock up when I had the chance.

"Dr. Bolger," M says, "you have the floor."

He stands and shoots me a disapproving glare before clearing his throat and adjusting his tie.

"I have worked with Dr. Wiley and her team many times before this case. Too many, perhaps. Over the years, I have approached the hospital leadership with concerns about Dr. Wiley's performance and warned them this would eventually happen. Dr. Wiley is too relaxed to lead to good surgical outcomes. Her so-called team is constantly chatting and playing music, probably too distracted to pay much attention to key minutia that can make the difference between life and death in the operating room. Not unlike many other female surgeons, Dr. Wiley is simply not physically equipped to respond appropriately. She lacks... gumption," he says, clenching his fist in the air. "She simply gave up on Caleb Donaghy after only twenty-three minutes of resuscitation efforts. Why? That's the question you all need to ask yourselves. Yes, the surgery was performed well. Yes, her stitching was perfect, her technique impeccable. For centuries, women's fine fingers have wielded needle and thread far better than men. But when it comes to the willpower, the force, and the determination needed to carry on resuscitation efforts for as long as it's necessary to save a life, Dr. Wiley comes short. Terribly so." He breathes and looks around the table. "This is just her first of many victims to come." He nods coldly and sits.

M stares at him for a moment longer than her usual norm. "Thank you, Dr. Bolger." Then she turns to her left. "Dr. Seldon?"

My mentor stands and runs his hands down his tie as if making sure it's perfectly smooth, then buttons up his lab coat.

He doesn't make eye contact with me, not even for a split second. "Thank you, Dr. Meriwether, I'll keep it very short."

Great. That son of a bitch Bolger took his sweet time, but the only friend I have here today is in a hurry.

That very moment, I notice M's file is the same color as the rest of ours, but about an inch thicker. What the hell could she have in there that I don't? This is not a day when I'm open to surprises.

"Fifteen percent," Dr. Seldon says. "That's the average intraoperative mortality rate for our cardiothoracic surgery department, and we're in the best five in the entire country. You," he points at Fitzpatrick and at a younger surgeon, "and I, we all score somewhere around that number. We lose people. It happens. But not to Dr. Wiley, not until this one." He taps his finger against the case file cover. "Caleb Donaghy was her first patient to die on the table." A moment of silence. "I don't know about you, but I envy the kind of numbers she has." There is light, subdued laughter around the table. "I have asked her many times how she pulls it off." He finally looks at me and nods, smiling. "She told me she keeps death at bay with hard work and team spirit and music and jokes and an environment where everyone can speak freely about any concern. Other than that, she didn't know what else to say." Another moment of silence, so deep and so tense I can hear Bolger's teeth grinding. "Is her incredible success rate a fluke? Maybe. I don't know for sure, although I was her mentor. But I know that someone who has such a low mortality rate deserves my trust when she calls time of death. I'm not going to question that." He looks at Bolger and his kind, tired eyes turn to steel, cold and sharp. "Even if she's a woman."

He sits and whispers a thank you to M. Then looks at me and I smile with gratitude. He nods, a silent encouragement.

"Anyone else willing to make a statement?" M asks, then waits in silence for about fifteen seconds before proceeding.

"Dr. Wiley, the committee has some questions, based on their review of the case file and the recordings of the procedure."

I stand and clear my throat. It's parchment dry and constricted, but I'm ready. As I'll ever be.

"Dr. Wiley, the hospital pulled your surgical stats and noticed that in three other cases, when hearts wouldn't restart after surgery, you spent an average of forty-three minutes to establish normal sinus rhythm. In one case, you worked on the patient's heart for almost two hours. Is that correct?"

"Yes." I think so. I don't recall exactly but it's not the time nor the place to say that. M wouldn't lie about a thing like that.

"Then the question is, why did you give up so soon in Caleb Donaghy's case? What was different about him?"

The question brings a bitter scoff to my lips, but I manage to keep it quiet, undetected. *Maybe my other patients weren't monsters who deserved to die.* But I obviously can't say that.

"His heart," I answer, calmly. Derreck would be proud of me. "In most cases, flushing the heart with warm saline and filling the chambers with blood is all we need to do to get the heart to beat again. Yes, maybe we'll get some fibrillation, but then we use paddles and reestablish NSR. This heart was different."

"In which way?"

"I flushed with warm saline for almost two minutes." I check my notes as I speak. "That's on the recording, if you'd like to check." M nods. "Then I released the clamp and filled the heart with blood, and nothing happened. Not even a slight tremor. Absolutely nothing." I look around the table. There's curiosity, some vague sympathy, and some very obvious hatred from Dr. Bolger. The attorney is whispering something in M's ear and she's whispering back.

"Has this ever happened before?" M asks.

"No, never. For lack of a better way to put it, the heart was dead already."

The moment I say the words, I want to roll my eyes at myself. Such an idiotic statement, albeit true. Derreck would pounce right back and ask, "Oh, yeah? Then, who killed it, if not you?"

Thankfully, M doesn't. "But you still engaged in resuscitation efforts?"

"Of course. During the entire time I worked on the heart, either with paddles or massage, I didn't detect a single flicker of movement, not even the tiniest of fibrillations. Nothing. That's why I called time of death."

"The patient was on pump, was he not?" M asks. "You could've continued resuscitation efforts virtually for hours. Yet you decided to call it quits after twenty-three minutes. Why?"

I fill my lungs with air, hoping I find the right thing to say to the question I can't really answer. Did I rush to call time of death after I'd seen his face? Yes, I did. Was I eager to see him gone, rolled downstairs to the morgue, and locked up in a box?

I was more than eager. I was afraid he'd come back to life through some screwed-up twist of fate and force me to close that chest and let him live again after everything he'd done. I couldn't let it happen. I just couldn't.

"Dr. Wiley?" M prompts.

I realize tears are pooling in my eyes. I breathe them away and gather my thoughts. "The answer is in the heart muscle's temperature," I say, hesitant at first, then gaining momentum as I explain. "Cardioplegia protects the heart by lowering the temperature to near freezing. Once normal temperature has been restored, the heart is no longer protected. Yes, technically you can say that we can continue resuscitation forever while on pump, but in reality, a heart so damaged it didn't even fibrillate under resuscitation efforts and multiple shots of epi would only continue to deteriorate."

M looks around the table, but no one raises their hand. Dr. Seldon is nodding slowly. Dr. Fitzpatrick's lips are tightly sealed, but he's not grim; his expression is one of shame, for a reason I fail to understand. Dr. Bolger's arms are crossed at his chest; he's fuming.

"One more question, before we let you go," M says. "To your knowledge, how did the State's Attorney Office become involved in this patient's case?"

I shake my head. "I'm sorry. I don't know." It feels good to tell the truth again. Dr. Bolger probably called them, but that's speculation, and I won't point fingers unless I have some proof.

"All right, Dr. Wiley," M says. "We have enough information to formulate our conclusions."

Sheets of paper start to circulate from hand to hand toward M. From what I can see, they are identical, simple one-question forms with multiple-choice answers. Several of them have scribbled notes below the typed question-and-answer options.

M reviews the sheets quickly, sharing some of the answers with the counsel. One of them causes a bout of heated whispering that lasts a good two minutes, while my heart races faster than on my morning jogs.

Finally, she pats the sheets of paper to stack them neatly together and folds her hands over them. "This committee finds no fault for Dr. Anne Wiley in the death of Caleb Donaghy."

I breathe, fully filling my starved lungs with air. Attendees start shuffling their papers and pushing away from the table.

"There's one more finding I must share," M announces, raising her voice a little to cover the noise. Silence falls thick and immediate. "The peer review committee found the behavior of Dr. Bolger to be contemptible and severely inappropriate, both during the videotaped surgical procedure and during this committee's statement session."

Dr. Bolger gasps and stands. "You can't be serious! This is insane."

Dr. Fitzpatrick, seated next to him, grabs his sleeve and tugs downward, trying to get him to sit.

"Therefore," M continues unfazed, "based on several requests from the members of this committee, Dr. Bolger will be placed on administrative leave, pending an investigation into his professional conduct." M pauses for a second, staring Dr. Bolger into shutting up. "This committee thanks you for your participation. You are dismissed."

Among the wave of chatter stirred up by M's final comments, I thank them and leave first, feeling their eyes on my back as I exit the boardroom. Dr. Bolger is livid and enraged, but I don't care anymore. Out in the corridor, the air is colder, fresher, and I can breathe with ease. I rush toward my office, eager to be by myself for a few minutes.

I made it.

There are no police waiting to arrest me. Paula Fuselier isn't there either; just Madison, whose expression is one of tense determination. She looks at me with an unspoken question, then hugs me.

"It's okay, Maddie," I say, fighting back tears. "We were cleared. Let the team know."

She disappears to make me a cup of tea, but I call after her and ask for coffee instead.

Then I sit at my desk, infinitely tired. My eyes wander until they land on Melanie's photo, framed on my desk. It's an old one, taken a few days after my parents adopted her. We were both playing in the backyard. She'd been laughing with her head tilted backward that day, sunshine on her face, spinning and twirling as if she'd never had a worry in her entire life. Until she finally wore herself out and landed by my side on the bench, holding my hand tightly. That's when the picture was taken; by Mom, if I'm not mistaken.

Next to the picture, I keep a lacquered pine cone she gave me for my birthday that year. She'd picked it up from the backyard and Dad helped her turn it into a gift. They varnished it together using tiny brushes that reached between the seed scales. Then she offered the cone to me tied neatly with a green bow, singing "Happy Birthday" off-key but with a beaming, wide grin that had made my day.

I brush my fingers against the pine cone scales, then pick up the photo and run my fingers over her sweet face. But I only feel the cold glass underneath my fingertips and the tears running down my cheeks. Her eyes speak to me, though, as if she were still alive, still with me.

Caleb Donaghy deserved to die for what he did to my little sister.

I've made peace with what I've done.

Two questions still haunt me, though. Why did his heart refuse to start? And why has the State's Attorney Office made Donaghy's heart into a case worth investigating?

TWENTY-ONE
FORMAL

I don't get much time to wallow in my tearful relief after the peer review, thinking of Melanie, because my office is soon filled with everyone on my team. I barely have time to send text messages to Mom and Derreck with the outcome of the committee, before Dr. Seldon stops by to congratulate me. Lee Chen, usually taciturn, is unexpectedly cheerful, and Ginny hugs me every two or three minutes.

I'm humbled by their affection.

After a while, I raise my hand, asking for attention. "Yes, today we were cleared in the death of a patient. Mostly, *I* was cleared, because calling time of death and the surgery overall are my responsibilities. But still, we lost a patient. I promise you I'll continue to look into the details until I find out what made his heart refuse to beat."

"Of course you will." Madison laughs and gives me a side hug. "So, I take it I can't shred that red file today?"

"Nope, not just yet."

"Spoken like a true leader," Dr. Seldon says, shaking my hand vigorously. "Don't obsess over it, though. Sometimes these mysteries remain unsolved. It's biology, not engineering. Not all light bulbs turn on when you flip the switch, for no apparent reason."

His comments raise laughter. Someone I can't see because of the crowd plays with the light switch on the wall, turning it off and on a few times, and more laughter ensues. It's the relief after the deadly storm.

"We have an entire backlog of patients to work through. This department needs you, Dr. Wiley," Dr. Seldon adds.

I smile and nod. "Thank you," I whisper, my voice a little choked. "For everything."

He makes his apologies and leaves. He has a four p.m. surgery scheduled—a triple bypass if I'm not mistaken.

Madison suggests we all reconvene here for cake in a couple of hours, after work. While everyone scatters, I get called into M's office.

I walk quickly along the almost deserted corridors, my palms sweating, my heart pumping hard. I've had more than my share of stress for the day. Although the committee just cleared me, I have a bad feeling about this. Although I don't believe in premonitions.

I have good reasons not to.

When I get to M's office, I look through the glass doors before knocking. She's with Aaron Timmer, the hospital head counsel, and another man. He looks familiar. I believe I saw him last week waiting for someone with a bunch of balloons in his hand. He must be one of my patients' loved ones.

Feeling a pang of dread, I hope no one else has died. The timing would be really awful. Then I knock on the doorjamb and get invited inside with a rushed wave of M's hand.

"Dr. Wiley, thanks for coming over so quickly. This man is Adam Costilla, an investigator with the State's Attorney Office."

Blood drains from my face. I can feel it, just as I can feel my hands turn ice cold and my heart thump desperately against my rib cage.

The investigator offers me a hand that I choose to ignore. "Dr. Wiley, we have several questions regarding the death of your patient, Caleb Donaghy, while under your care."

I look at M briefly, but she doesn't get the chance to intervene. Aaron Timmer is faster.

"I would like to know why this particular death is of such interest to the State's Attorney Office," he asks calmly. He steps closer to the investigator, almost pushing me out of the way. I don't mind.

Timmer's question throws the investigator off course. He takes a step back and shoves his hands into the pockets of his long, black trench coat. He's a massive guy, soon to become some cardiologist's emergency patient based on the blotches of purplish red staining his face and neck. I have to stop myself from offering to take his blood pressure. With anyone else, I wouldn't hesitate.

"I will ask my office to prepare a statement if the hospital demands it. But I only have a few simple questions at this time—"

"I also have a question," I blurt out.

"Dr. Wiley," M says in a low, commanding voice I barely notice. "This is not the time."

"I'd like to know, weren't you here last week?" I ask, despite the voice of reason screaming inside my head to shut the hell up. It screams louder than M's hushed orders, yet I still ignore it. "Lurking in the corridor outside my office with balloons in hand, pretending to be someone you aren't?"

"What?" M promptly takes position in front of the man, her hands propped firmly on her hips. "Is that true?"

The man grins nervously. "It's not illegal. I'm conducting an investigation. It's called a stakeout. Maybe you've heard the term before?" He scratches his forehead, though. He's embarrassed. He probably didn't expect me to notice.

They were staking me out? What the hell is going on? His

words reverberate throughout my entire being, weakening my knees. Maybe they've bugged my office, my phone; who knows what else they've done? They might know what I talked with Derreck about and that Donaghy was no stranger to me. *Oh, no. Please, don't let it be true.*

The nightmarish vision of cops dragging me out of here in cuffs comes back with gale force. I feel dizzy and faint.

M whispers something quickly in Timmer's ear. He whispers something back, very short, probably a word or two. He then turns to the investigator and says, "Mr. Costilla, we'd like a formal statement from the State's Attorney Office regarding this so-called investigation you're conducting. Just so we're clear, I'd like that statement to include the case number and the state's attorney's signature."

Costilla's chin trembles with anger. He doesn't say anything, just stands there glaring at Timmer for a moment.

Timmer takes a step forward. "Don't make me call Mitch Hobbs. We were classmates in law school. If you have a valid reason to be here asking questions, show me the paperwork."

When the investigator turns around and leaves without a word, the oversized tails of his trench coat flutter around him like a cape, but he's no superhero.

He's the harbinger of bad news to come.

TWENTY-TWO

CRIME SCENE

A few more days had passed and still no word from Derreck. Paula checked her phone for the fifth time since she woke up that morning. Wednesdays had become their usual day to meet at some hotel for an afternoon of sex and making ambitious plans for their future together.

Was there still a chance for a future together? She'd texted him twice since the weekend, and the messages were not responded to. She was being ghosted and she hated it. With a passion.

Yet she didn't blame Derreck. She was the one who had made threats and forced him to cave under her pressure. How could she expect love after that?

Love.

What a loaded word. Until last Friday, she hadn't even acknowledged love was something she'd been expecting. She would've probably played her cards a bit differently if she had. Now, that seemed off the table completely, rendered impossible by her own endless hatred of Anne Wiley.

He had to leave her. He absolutely had to.

She still waited for a sign from Derreck, for a text message with a hotel name and room number, getting ready to be surprised again by his choice of venue, like a child on Christmas morning. Life had been financially tight for her: she hadn't had people lavishing her with the finer things in life, not until Derreck, and she'd managed to ruin that, possibly forever. Even if he did invite her for an afternoon together, what would that be like? How would a man, after the way she had threatened him, take her to bed? Would he be rough? Or disgusted with her, filled with hatred, unable to bear the sight of her?

He was probably right to keep his distance for a while. Then, maybe he'd slowly start missing her more than hating her for what she'd threatened to do to him. She clung to that irrational hope, while at the same time obsessing over Anne Wiley's dead patient. If there was a way to what she wanted, this was her best chance. Who knew how many years it would take until she'd have the same opportunity, especially if Derreck won the election without her help? Then the two of them would live happily ever after like Paula never existed. She'd be left behind, forgotten faster than a one-night drunken mistake.

She really couldn't deal with abandonment. Being left behind, ghosted, discarded like an old shoe. It filled her with unspeakable, red-hot rage that burned everything in its path, making her feel irrelevant and cheap.

She was on the verge with Derreck, almost ready to let herself go and give in to her burning desire to exact vengeance.

Did she really need Derreck to make state's attorney? The thought of depending on him, of needing him—or anyone for that matter—made her nauseated. People lied, betrayed, and generally couldn't be trusted. She had a better shot at the top prosecutor role on her own. If she played all her cards right.

She checked her phone again. Still nothing. Repressing a bitter, frustrated sigh, she headed into her office, nodding in passing to greetings from her coworkers.

"Good morning," Marie said, as Paula passed by her desk.

"You're requested at a crime scene," she added, just as Paula was entering her office.

She turned around and walked back to her assistant's desk.

Marie looked at her paperwork with a little too much interest, seemingly avoiding Paula's gaze.

"What's going on?" Paula asked. "Isn't Adam taking it?"

Marie flashed a quick look at her boss. "He's the one who called for you. He needs you there."

A frown ruffled Paula's brow. That wasn't usual. "Did he say why?"

Marie looked at her again, very quickly lowering her eyes. "Sorry, he didn't, and I didn't ask. All I know is that it's regarding the Espinoza shooting."

She was lying, but Paula didn't want to spend time interrogating her assistant as if she were a murder suspect on the stand. She'd find out soon enough why she was so squirrely about this crime scene.

For a split moment, she hoped Vicente Espinoza had jumped off a balcony, but then she remembered he was in jail, remanded by the judge at the arraignment last week. That would've eliminated the risk to Simon Degnan's life and the need for the eleven-year-old to testify. "I wonder why Adam didn't call my cell," she muttered, checking the device again. "Send me the address, okay?"

She left without waiting for an answer. By the time she reached her car, the phone chimed with a text message with the details.

The address was only a block away from the Espinoza crime scene. She found the small street cordoned off and swarming with cops. The Cook County medical examiner's van was already on-site, the back doors wide open and the stretcher missing.

She flashed her credentials and bent under the yellow police tape, then headed to where a young officer pointed with his open palm. She walked quickly and, after a few yards, she recognized Adam's massive stature among the crowd.

He was standing a couple of yards from the focus of everyone's attention: most likely a body, a murder victim perhaps.

When she reached him, she touched his elbow to alert him. "Hey, Adam, what do we have?"

He looked past her, his eyes haunted, his stare vacant. "See for yourself," he said, leading her with a quick push against her back. She passed the medical examiner's gurney, still empty, and looked at him inquisitively. "I asked them to wait for you. I thought you should see this firsthand."

She took two more steps, and the body came into view. She gasped, instantly feeling sick to her stomach. It was Simon Degnan, lying in a pool of blood, with two bullet holes in his narrow chest. His eyes were still open and clear, the azure of the spring sky reflected in his irises.

"There," Adam said, his voice mercilessly cold. "This is what happens when you bring kids into this business, Paula."

She grabbed his lapel, about to yell at him and put him in his place, but her stomach lurched, and she heaved, covering her mouth with her hand.

"You better not contaminate the crime scene." Adam pulled her to the side, his hand gripping her elbow like iron pliers, and led her away from the crime scene crew, until he reached the side of a building. He pushed her against the wall, but she didn't care, still struggling to control her spasms.

"I was a seasoned cop with almost twenty years of Chicago streets under my belt, and you were a fresh-out-of-law-school prosecutor, nothing but guts and ambition and a brain like I'd never seen before. Remember what you told me?" He was shouting at her, his Italian accent heavier than usual.

She heaved again, unable to erase the image of Simon Degnan lying on the asphalt, covered in blood. It was on her hands, all that blood. She could've taken the case to court without his testimony, without Hobbs's knowledge, and won it on evidence only. She could've taken that chance, but she'd been too high on the promotion, on what that meant for her future, to care.

"We draw the line at kids, Paula," he shouted in her face. "*You* taught me that. No one else. All you care about is that doctor and her dead patient, when that's not even a case." He slapped his hand against his forehead, pacing in place, visibly anguished. "And I play your stupid games."

She breathed in the cold morning air, willing her stomach to settle. "It *is* a case, and I'll wrap it up and present to a grand jury as early as next week."

"Then you're crazier than I thought," he snapped. "You're risking your career for nothing. If I found out about your affair with her husband, you think her lawyer won't? Jeez, woman, you're smarter than this!"

Adam's words hit her in the pit of her stomach. He knew about Derreck. Her wheels started turning quickly, thinking what to say, how to keep him doing what she needed him to do.

"You don't understand. It's through the affair that I found out about her killing that guy."

"You serious right now?" Adam rubbed his forehead angrily, punishingly, as if his head had done something wrong. "Then you should open a formal case or quit pursuing this altogether, before it ruins your career and mine. The hospital is not going to take this lying down."

She looked past him, at the medical examiner and his assistant loading Simon's body on the stretcher, then rolling it toward the van. She squeezed her eyes shut for a moment, willing the image to vanish, but it wouldn't. It stood there, fresh in her memory.

"I'm a detective, Paula. I'm not your enforcer. I investigate legitimate cases, and when there are valid, legal reasons, I bring suspects up on charges. That's what I do. And while I was out there at that hospital, instead of working the Espinoza case, this boy died in the streets, shot down like scum. He didn't stand a damn chance, Paula, and you know it."

A tear rolled down her face. He was right. Simon's death was her fault.

"The subpoena was delivered this morning, just like you ordered," Adam went on. "Two hours later, they popped him." He looked at her and she lowered her gaze. "You used to care about kids like him. What happened? Don't tell me you're in love with that slick wannabe mayor."

His accusation infuriated her, tearing through her like a knife. "Is that what you think? Really? Is this where we are? Pointing fingers and making accusations that defy common sense? If you've lost all confidence in my judgment, and it seems you have, then maybe it's time to ask for reassignment."

A brief, stunned silence, while Adam stared at her with a gaping mouth. "You're firing me?"

"You're firing yourself." She straightened her back and pushed her chin forward. "I'm your boss, and I thought also your friend. That's why you were always welcome to share your thoughts with me freely, but today you took it too damn far. I have never crossed the line in the office I hold. Never. And yet, you speak to me like I'm a corrupt piece of shit with a secret agenda. I don't know how we can come back from this."

His shoulders dropped under the weight of her words. He stood there, speechless, while she thought about what to do. Firing him made sense, but he was involved in the Anne Wiley investigation, and that information in the hands of a disgruntled former employee was pure dynamite.

She breathed and touched Adam's elbow briefly. He didn't pull back, just looked at her hand warily. "This has been tough," she said, choosing her words carefully. "I'm willing to look past this, considering the emotional tax Simon's death has taken on us both." She paused for a moment, giving him time to process her words. "We've both said things that should've been left unsaid. And while I agree we could've done things differently to prevent Simon's testimony from being requested, I can promise you this: I've learned my lesson. In the future, I'll know to ask for forgiveness instead of permission, and I'll keep kids off the witness stand, whatever it takes."

He looked at her with a glint of doubt still lingering in his eyes. He was a seasoned cop, street-smart and wise and cunning. She couldn't tell if she'd reached him.

"How about this lady surgeon business? I met her, and she's no Ted Bundy."

"Do you trust me at all?"

He nodded, but with a telltale, one-sided shrug she chose to pretend she didn't notice.

"Then trust me on this, and I'll wrap up a grand jury case so neatly you'll think it's Christmas morning."

His eyes veered away for a moment, then landed back on her, keen, alert. "Read me in. If you trust me, tell me what you know."

Just what she was most afraid of. She couldn't tell him anything. She'd made a big mistake involving him; that much she knew. It was too late to back out of it now.

"Give me two more days, and I will," she said. "Then you'll help me decide how best to take Anne Wiley in front of a grand jury for murder."

Adam scoffed. "See, Paula? That's the issue with trust. Right now, you clearly don't trust me worth a rat's ass." He sounded disappointed, but also doubtful, suspicious even. "From where I'm standing, all I can see is that you're out to screw your lover's wife, and you're using your office to do it."

"Jeez, Adam... If that's what you think of me, we really can't continue working together."

"Well, then, convince me otherwise. Let's work this case by the book, if there is a real case in there somewhere."

"No. I want us laser focused on catching Simon Degnan's killer. The first few hours are critical when it comes to murder for hire. In case you forgot, Espinoza is locked up, so someone else pulled the trigger for him. I don't want us to waste time on the surgeon's case until this perp is behind bars."

Adam stared at her for a long moment, then turned away. "Yeah, Paula, whatever you say." Then he walked to his car, leaving her there by herself, discarded like a foregone conclusion.

Son of a bitch.

She walked briskly to her car, steeling herself, telling herself it would be all right once she had all the pieces in place. But what was she doing?

The drive back to her office was slow and tense, traffic heavy still. She chose to take the interstate, but it was just as slow as the rest of the city, with endlessly long lines to pay the tolls.

Going five miles an hour, she looked outside. The blue sky was picture perfect, not a shred of a cloud to threaten the warm spring day. In the distance, a highway billboard caught her attention. From the center of it, Dr. Anne Wiley smiled at her with her model-like face and perfectly white teeth, making the heart gesture with manicured fingers. On one of those fingers, she noticed a sliver of a gold wedding band, identical to the one she'd seen on Derreck's finger.

That perfect image was the epitome of everything she hated the most. Such a distance from people like poor Simon Degnan, lying dead on some project street, and people like her. Bile rose to her throat as anger raged through her veins.

"I swear I'll rip everything you love out of your life and set it on fire," she whispered, staring at the billboard, her hands white-knuckled, clutching the steering wheel tightly as if she was holding on to it to save her life. "I won't rest until you're left barren and alone, with nothing left to lose."

TWENTY-THREE
ALBUM

When I finally get home on Wednesday night, I feel drained after the day's busy schedule. My endless angst is taking a toll, even if I take beta blockers on a regular basis now, and I've started doing meditation. It helps, but it cannot completely shield me from sobering reality.

I'm being investigated still. A cop staked my office out. My home could be under surveillance as well, plus our phones, our internet searches... who knows what else? Maybe they've been through here, searching through my things. Or perhaps that only happens in the movies: cops entering homes without warrants and getting away with it. In real life, it can't be happening. Not to us.

Mom is at her card game, and the house, in her absence, is shrouded in silence. Derreck is still out, but said he'd be home earlier than his norm. He said something about some election meetings not happening anymore for a while, or something like that. I was too preoccupied with my own fears to pay much attention. All I remember is he's going to get home earlier, and that's all I really care about.

Then I have to take him out somewhere, maybe to the

Chinese restaurant we both love, and tell him about my fears about this endless investigation. I can't speak to him about it at home. What if they're listening? Paula Fuselier hasn't come by my office again, and neither has that hypertensive investigator, but that doesn't alleviate my fears. Quite the opposite—it's opening the door to full-blown paranoia. Although it's not really paranoia when they're out to get me for something I have actually done. It's guilt, and fear, and legitimate worry.

Since I'm planning dinner out with Derreck, I don't get undressed and don't eat. I even skip the bottle of wine that is calling me from the fridge door. I settle for a peanut butter cookie. I don't feel like eating much. It's understandable.

I climb upstairs and stop in front of Melanie's door. It's been closed for years. I'm sure Mom goes in there and cleans and dusts and what not; I'd be surprised if she didn't. But I still can't go in.

I put both hands on the lacquered wood and lean against the door, resting my cheek against it, inhaling its scent. It smells of pine and lacquer and old furniture. I close my eyes, and the sound of her laughter comes to life again, deceptively real, full of the joys of childhood. In my memories, she's singing something. "Twinkle, Twinkle, Little Star." She's singing it much slower than its original rhythm, making it sound weirdly funny, as if she's dragging through it to make it last longer. She was ten that winter, and completely crazed about Christmas. She had made lists of things she wanted and told anyone who would listen. She even wrote a letter to Santa. She didn't want much, though. Most of her list items were to spend time with her sister, to sing songs with her, to brush her hair with her new, bejeweled brush, to sleep with her sister on Christmas night.

With me.

Her love filled my heart with such joy. Yearning to remember even more, I say goodbye to the closed door and go downstairs, into my den.

The room feels colder than I expected. Its floor-to-ceiling window lets the cold inside faster than any other windows in the old house. I shiver and wrap myself in the shawl I leave there for that reason.

I sit in the Dutch armchair behind the desk and invite memories to come crashing in, welcoming their arrival like they're old friends. I reach for the left-side desk drawers and pull open the bottom one. That's where I keep the large photo album of my childhood. I take it out and lay it on the desk. Its shiny covers reflect the desk lamp's light in shades of warm white, edged with rainbows. It smells of dusty plastic and the chemicals they used for photos back in the old days.

It smells of home, of family.

I don't spend much time looking at the photos from when I was still an only child. The only one that grabs my attention is one where my father is holding me on his knee at a family dinner that I remember nothing about. There aren't too many pictures of him: he was the one usually holding the camera, his absence from the album the price we paid for his diligent documentary work.

With every turn of a rustling page, I grow older, and the colors grow brighter.

I always wanted a sister. My parents were both working long hours, and I still recall the loneliness, the silence of the house when they were away, despite the presence of whatever nanny was babysitting—usually nice, polite young women who didn't care much about me. Some were students, who used the time to study or read on the living room sofa. There were others who preferred to watch TV, the odd ones who slept, and one who liked to cook so much she actually made dinner for the entire family. None of them spent any time with me.

When I was younger, I believed that this was why my parents adopted Melanie—because I wanted a sister so badly. My adult mind tells me they must've wanted another child just as badly. But Mom had a hysterectomy a few years after giving birth to me, and adopting was the only way they could make our shared dream happen.

They didn't tell the teenage me they were looking into adopting. They didn't tell me anything while they were out there, filing paperwork and getting approved. Mom never said a word when she started spending more time in the bedroom that was going to become Melanie's, cleaning, renovating, furnishing, and decorating it to be ready for her arrival. Being fourteen at the time, I had just discovered dating and Backstreet Boys, and "Quit Playing Games" was blaring nonstop on my Discman. And I had just started high school. I was so taken with all that, Mom could've brought a unicorn into that spare bedroom, and I wouldn't've noticed.

I flip another page and smile, Melanie's joyful expression so infectious I can't help myself. It's another photo that was taken the day of her adoption, this one capturing the moment she was told. There's immense delight, and surprise, in those wide-open eyes, the gaping mouth stretched into the loveliest of smiles. She shines against the dreary background of the orphanage's backyard, which is filled with other kids roaming around, curious, some watching warily, as if we were predators lurking in the shadows, others with hopeful, pleading glances.

I love that photo. It represents the moment I first saw Melanie. Dad had caught her at the center of the image, the ugly, mean-looking attendant out of the frame. I remember her. She was a stocky woman with large breasts who wore stained, blue, hospital garb. I remember her because she never smiled; at the time, I thought how terrible it must've been for those kids to be around her, an adult who couldn't look at them with the tiniest bit of kindness. Thanks to Dad, she's not in my favorite picture of Melanie.

I'm about to turn the page, but I can't bring myself to leave that picture behind. Careful not to damage its edges, I remove it from its cellophane pocket and set it on the desk, leaning against a book. I want it in my office, framed, right next to the other one. I spend way more time in the office than in the den, and I'd like my little sister with me in more than one picture.

I flip another page and reminisce. In most of them it's the two of us, doing stuff together. Playing hide and seek in the backyard. Opening presents on Christmas morning. Me, getting fitted with my prom dress, while Mel was lifting its hem, trying to wear a piece of it herself. That day she cried because she couldn't go with me and my boyfriend to the dance. I let her brush my hair for a while. She still loved doing that; it made her happy.

Then another one, me driving the car with Dad in the passenger seat, and Melanie popping her head between the front seats, her tongue out and stained purple from blueberry ice cream. That one was taken the day I got my driver's license, a learner's permit. I was sixteen. She was eleven, a firecracker of a girl, nothing to remind us of the terrible ordeal she'd endured.

My parents put her in therapy. I didn't know at the time what it was for. In their typical overprotective manner, they told me it was to help her adapt, after having lived in foster homes. Looking at another photo of just Melanie, taken when she wasn't aware, when she was standing at her bedroom window looking outside with a hint of melancholy in her eyes, I realize I never knew how she came to be orphaned. One day I might ask Mom.

She was in therapy for about three years, most likely for post-traumatic stress. Dad found someone good, a gentle therapist who wore a kind smile on her face whenever we dropped Melanie off to see her. It was Mom and I dropping her off. Mom stopped working about a month or two after the adoption and stayed home. She probably wanted to be there for the little girl, ready to notice the first sign of trouble and intervene.

There were no signs of trouble that I can recall. Melanie

seemed to be a happy, healthy child, playing hard, laughing even harder. She was doing well in school; she was smart and didn't seem to have any issues focusing on or catching up with her education. For what she'd missed I was a readily available tutor.

She seemed fine. Not a trace of anything to remind us of what she'd endured.

Until the night terrors came.

The first one curdled my blood with a shriek so loud it froze the breath in my lungs. I rushed to her and ran into my parents, coming down the other side of the hallway. We found her, not fully awake, sobbing hard, drenched in sweat, pleading to stop hurting her.

She had been in therapy for about two years when they started happening. The therapist told my parents they were normal as she was finally dealing with what had happened to her. I had my doubts, but I was eighteen at the time. I don't remember voicing those doubts, just thinking them. *Couldn't that therapist make them stop?* Back then, I still didn't know the full extent of her ordeal. I still didn't understand.

They continued for a while, bloodcurdling shrieks in the dead of the night, followed by us rushing to comfort her. No one went back to bed afterward; we just hung out with her, keeping her company, chatting lightly, with all the lights on in her bedroom. Dad said looking at light erased the memory of a nightmare. I tried it on myself, and it was true.

She never had the terrors when she slept with me. But I was growing older, wanted to be on the phone with my boyfriend until late, or read magazines Mom didn't know about. I still didn't have the heart to tell her not to come into my room, but her therapist said it wasn't healthy for her to sleep with me every time.

Between therapy and the sport activities she was involved in at school, the night terrors slowly disappeared. She was growing fast and more beautiful than ever. Another flip of the page shows her at about thirteen years old, trying on dresses. Dad wanted to take all four of us to the annual fundraiser for the hospital and she was thrilled. She was finally going to be dressed like a big girl and go to a real party.

Three photos immortalize that day, and a fourth one, taken by me, shows Melanie dancing with Dad.

I stare at that one for a long time, unable to bring myself to move on. My eyes cling to the two faces I miss so much, but I also have another reason. I know what comes after turning that page.

Nothing.

The remaining photo slots are all empty.

No one took another family photo after Melanie died.

Slowly, I close the album, then put it away. I push the drawer gently to a close, painfully aware of the silence that engulfs the house my dad built with laughing grandchildren in mind.

From a distance, a police car makes its presence known with a fading siren. It still startles me: I'm still afraid of the day they'll come after me, but I'm content with what I've done.

They could crucify me for it, strip everything I hold dear away, all of it. My family, my job, everything I've ever worked for.

And I can still say it was worth it.

That bastard didn't deserve to live.

Had I known how to find the man we saw that day in the park, I would've looked for him and—and something... I don't know what, but I would've done something. I would've asked Dad to help me make him pay. But I didn't know who he was, his name or anything else, other than what I'd seen that day with Melanie in the park. A receding hairline on a man in his thirties. A port-wine stain on his forehead, in the shape of the letter R, with three drops apparently falling from the left side of the letter. It's not something I could easily forget.

Now I know his name.

I hope he rots in hell.

I push the chair away and stand, taking Melanie's photo from the desk with me to slip it into my purse.

Moments later, Derreck is home. I greet him with open arms and an invitation to dinner at the local Chinese place we both love.

My heart is heavy. I'm about to ruin his day.

TWENTY-FOUR
ARREST

It took Adam three days to dig up information on Simon Degnan's shooter. Paula had never seen him as determined, ferocious even. She looked the other way as he interrogated suspects with his gloves off, easily able to do so if it served the purpose they both shared. But in the end, it was good old detective work that prevailed, not raw knuckles and last year's phone book.

With Espinoza in jail, Paula and Adam pored over the visitors' log and the phone calls made to and from the county lockup. No one came to visit him except his court-appointed attorney with several years of experience. That lawyer wasn't the kind Espinoza could've talked into arranging a hit for him.

The phone log told a different story. They spent all Tuesday night and most of Wednesday running backgrounds on everyone who made or received calls after Espinoza had been remanded. They excluded attorneys, detainees' family members, and the toll-free numbers for a couple of attorney referral services, and were left with seventeen names and three burners they couldn't trace.

Then Adam started pounding the pavement, looking for

someone who fit the profile. To do a hit for a lowlife like Espinoza, the suspect had to be someone equally low or lower, hungry for some quick cash and with very little, if anything, left to lose.

Three of the seventeen fit the profile. They were ex-cons, one living in a halfway home, a second one a drug addict who'd just been released after serving seven years for aggravated assault, and the third one Espinoza's old cellmate from his prior arrest five years ago. Adam didn't waste any time with the first two. He placed his bet on the third. On Friday morning at about ten, he called Paula and requested the arrest warrant. She delivered it in person.

They found the suspect plastered out of his mind, collapsed on a dirty mattress in a roach-infested apartment three stories above Espinoza's. Almost ten grand in crisp one-hundred-dollar bills were on the kitchen counter, probably one or two bills missing. They had most likely been used to buy the large pepperoni pizza with extra cheese the roaches were feasting on when Adam broke down the door.

He cuffed the sorry sack of shit, then pulled him to his feet. He didn't regain consciousness, hanging limp until Adam, panting heavily, let him fall back on the mattress with a disgusted scowl.

Paula stared at the suspect, crinkling her nose. "You sure that's him?" The stench was unbearable.

Adam scoffed, gesturing at the brick of crisp hundreds on the counter. "Who else?" Then he proceeded to search the apartment for the murder weapon. A few minutes of opening and closing cabinets with gloves on, he found it stashed under the bathroom kitchen sink, wrapped in an old newspaper.

He held it with two fingers, stomping on a roach that fell from the paper. "Ah, crap... the things we do for a living," he muttered. Then he turned to Paula, grinning. "Found it." He ejected the magazine and racked it to spit out the bullet left in the spout, then took it to his nose. "Recently fired. We're good to go."

Paula looked at the man, collapsed into a handcuffed clump, head propped against the mattress, legs in the unnatural positions only hammered people could pull off. He wasn't the glamorous arrestee she was looking for, but he was, nevertheless, a child murderer—a high-profile collar. A good opportunity to lure Mr. Mayor back into the game. "Can you give me thirty minutes, Adam?"

"In this shithole? Are you kidding me?"

"Pretty please," she said, her voice tinged with a trace of firmness.

"Sure thing, boss," he said, gesturing with both his hands. "Have at it. I'll just stand here and smell the roses."

She pulled her phone from her pocket and hesitated, staring intently at the suspect. "It would be nice if he were sober for the party I have planned for him. Well, maybe not sober. I'll settle for awake and slightly aware. Will that do?"

Adam groaned, grabbed the suspect's arm and dragged him into the bathroom. There, he started the shower and doused the man's head with cold water, holding him above the tub by the collar.

The first message she sent went to Derreck's phone. It read simply, *I'm about to make a high-profile arrest, the killer of a child witness. Be here in thirty—can't give you more.* And the address. She then called Hobbs. Thankfully, he didn't pick up her call. She was happy to leave a message, informing him of the arrest. Then she checked on Adam discreetly; he was still dousing the suspect. The best he was getting from him was the occasional mumbled swear word.

She put her work phone back into her pocket and retrieved another, a burner flip phone with a few numbers coded into its memory as a text group: all major media outlets in the area.

Then she typed *Simon Degnan's killer to be arrested in thirty minutes. ASA on-site.*

By the time she finished typing the address, the perp was awake and calling Adam a slew of names. The suspect's first act after that was projectile vomiting. Paula left Adam to deal with it and stepped outside to gather her thoughts.

What if Derreck came after all? Did that mean their pact was to be resumed as if nothing had happened? Did that mean there was still a glimmer of hope he'd leave his wife one day? Or was she all the way over the line that separated common sense from pure delusion?

It depended on how much Derreck wanted to be mayor come November.

She looked out the window, next to the trash chute that smelled less terrible than the suspect's apartment. The first TV crew was pulling in at the curb. Another one arrived a couple of minutes later. But no Derreck. She checked her watch and took a deep breath of relatively clean air before stepping back into the apartment.

"How are we doing in here?" She looked at the suspect and frowned. He was curled up on his side on the floor, hands cuffed behind his back, groaning.

"He's got one hell of a hangover, but he's just like you wanted him. Conscious. Sorry I couldn't do more."

The man lifted his head and glared at her with squinty, bloodshot eyes. His three-day stubble had collected dirt and grime from the floor. His T-shirt, once blue with an orange, sports team logo, was covered in stains and almost entirely wet. She considered asking Adam to change his clothes, but eventually decided against it. She was the one who had to look good on TV. Not him.

"All right, we're good to go," she said, at exactly thirty minutes after she'd sent the text to the media.

When they emerged from the building, the media gathered

around them, stopping at a respectful distance, probably because of the smell exuded by their collar.

"Miss Fuselier," a reporter asked, "who is this man?"

She straightened her posture and thrust her chin forward. "The Cook County State's Attorney Office has served the arrest warrant for the man who shot Simon Degnan, an eleven-year-old boy, to prevent him from testifying against Vicente Espinoza in the murder of his wife."

The media clamored and drew closer, extending their mics to reach her.

"Which precinct assisted with the investigation?"

"This case was particularly close to our hearts. My investigator, Adam Costilla, and I handled it ourselves."

A nerdy-looking reporter took one step closer, getting almost in her face with a foam-coated mic. "Isn't that unusual, Ms. Fuselier?"

She smiled, a quick flicker that immediately waned. "Very. But there are cases that we just have to bring to closure ourselves. Simon Degnan was a material witness in a homicide, and we—"

"You couldn't ensure his safety?" the nerdy reporter asked. "How do you feel about that, Ms. Fuselier?"

She was about to answer when she saw Derreck a few yards away from her, approaching fast. She changed her intended direction quickly, happy to deflect attention off herself. "The safety of all the citizens of our city is a paramount concern for everyone at the State's Attorney Office. We cooperate closely with the office of the mayor of Chicago to reduce the crime that plagues our hometown. We hope this collaboration will continue past November, potentially with a new incumbent." She nodded toward Derreck, and the media followed her lead and turned their attention toward him.

"Jeez, Paula," Adam growled under his breath. "Seriously? You brought your lover here for this?"

"Shut up and smile for the cameras, Adam. You'll understand everything soon enough."

She walked with him to his car and waited as he loaded the suspect into it, while Derreck answered media questions like a pro. He seemed at ease surrounded by reporters, smiling calmly, making the right statements, his charisma strong and alluring.

"You go ahead, Adam, I'll be right behind you." He gave her a long stare, then climbed behind the wheel and drove off, lowering his window as he turned the corner.

She waited a few yards away, pretending to do something on her phone, while the reporters took their fill of Derreck Bourke, mayoral candidate and front runner in the recent polls. When they were done, they left one by one, forgetting all about her. It was as if a woman could never get the limelight when a man was present, as if his shadow couldn't be escaped. She'd seen it at press conferences with Hobbs, even with other ASAs more junior than she was. The moment a man showed up, her moment was over.

What would that look like when she ran for state's attorney in Cook County, most likely against Hobbs, if he didn't become governor before that? Whether she liked it or not, she needed a man's endorsement.

Smiling, she approached Derreck as he was wrapping up with the local news channel. The camera was off after the interview, and the reporter was blatantly hitting on him. He seemed to enjoy the attention, but visibly bristled when Paula approached.

"Mr. Bourke," she said, extending her hand. He took it seemingly for appearance's sake, but she shook his hand strongly, holding on to it for a split second longer than he might've wanted. "What a surprise to find you here."

The reporter walked away, visibly unhappy with her interruption. Her camera operator followed, and they climbed into the news van.

"Yes, what a surprise," Derreck replied, pulling away.

"Didn't know if you were going to make it." Her voice was nonchalant, giving him room to save face. "But I'm glad you did."

"I bet you are."

Surprised by his hostile tone, she looked straight at him, intrigued and worried. His presence meant he wanted to continue with their arrangement, right? Otherwise, what was he doing there?

"You're staking out my wife?" he asked in a low, menacing whisper. "Did you bug our house? Are you following her? What are you doing, Paula? Have you completely lost your mind?"

Ah... his precious Anne Wiley. There was nothing the man wouldn't sacrifice for her, and the thought of that made Paula grind her teeth. A wave of seething resentment heated her blood.

It was now or never. She didn't have the time to waste on someone who didn't take her seriously.

"Meet me tonight and we can discuss this." She smiled, resting her eyes for a moment on his lips. "Hotel room of your choosing. You never disappoint."

He slapped his forehead in a gesture of pure frustration. "Out of the question. Because of you, I have to talk Anne down from the ledge. It's not what you said would happen, Paula. You were supposed to take this case to make it go away, not send your investigators to stake her office out."

"She tells you everything, doesn't she?" For a moment, she envied Anne for yet another thing, for having someone to share everything with.

"You broke the rules, Paula, not me." Derreck said, taking a step toward his car. "I'm sorry."

He was going to walk away and leave her there. Again.

She'd had one chance at this, and she'd failed. Rage swelled in her chest, raw, demanding blood. Just this once, she wanted to be the one walking away.

"If I were you, I'd be careful not to get on my bad side." She brushed by him, touching his arm. "The only problem with destroying you is just how easy it would be."

She walked toward her car with a spring in her step, her heels sounding loudly against the asphalt of the small street, echoing against the concrete walls of the project high-rises. When she reached her car, she gave him a quick, inconspicuous look. He was still standing there, staring after her, seemingly stunned.

The game wasn't over yet. She could still win.

TWENTY-FIVE
CLOSE CALL

My days are somewhat back to normal, with a full surgery load on my schedule and an increasing number of patients in post-op. It feels eerily quiet, the peace before the storm, because I know it's not over. I can feel it.

Paula Fuselier will never give up. I saw it in her eyes.

The threat looms over me day and night, paralyzing. It makes for tense days at the hospital and silent evenings at home. Derreck spends more time with me lately, probably at the cost of things he's putting off at work, but not much is said between us. It's difficult to talk, when you fear your home might be bugged.

Derreck swept the house with a bug finder he bought from a spy store downtown, but he didn't find anything. I think he would've been more relieved had he found something; now, he doubts himself and the accuracy of his search.

All in all, our peace of mind is gone, and our enjoyment of life has vanished, replaced overnight by this constant sense of fear and apprehension. All because of Caleb Donaghy, as if he hadn't already done enough damage to my family. As if he needed to hurt us one more time before I put him in the ground.

I don't think he's in the ground, though. One of the things that still keeps me frozen in my anguish is his body, stored indefinitely in the downstairs morgue. If he were any other patient, I wouldn't hesitate to ask what's going on. But with him, the less I draw attention to myself, the better. You never know where another one of Paula Fuselier's detectives could be lurking in the shadows, listening, observing, collecting evidence to lock me up.

That's what I do these days—look at everyone with poorly disguised suspicion. Fail to trust even the most tenured coworkers, wondering whose side they're on: mine or Dr. Bolger's? Ask myself who made the call to the State's Attorney Office; was it Bolger? Or someone else? Avoid looking people in the eye, afraid they might see through the veil of well-articulated justifications and know I'm a killer.

The only safe place for me is the operating room. In there, I'm surrounded by friends and one of the three decent anesthesiologists left on the roster after Dr. Bolger's suspension. Big sigh of relief there. No one will barge into the OR to drag me out in cuffs. At least they'll let me finish the procedure for the sake of the patient, not mine.

I hold my breath each time I step out of the OR, expecting to find trouble at the door.

I know it's coming. I just don't know when.

Might even be today.

My worries are scattered by the words of Taylor Swift's "Anti-Hero." How appropriate... monster on the hill. Was I completely insane, letting myself leave Donaghy to die, because I thought it was the right thing to do? Because of Melanie, because of what he did to her and got away with?

Who named me the deliverer of punishment, this man's judge and jury and executioner too?

I torture myself with such thoughts, wondering if I even have a conscience, because I still can't feel regret. No. My conscience must be on vacation or fast asleep, not even twitching under all the self-blame I cast. All I remember is Melanie. Her bruised body. Her terrified eyes, sobbing in the park at the sight of her rapist. Her cold, limp body in my arms, five short years later.

I'm ready to start the triple bypass procedure on Mrs. Orlowski. It's been delayed for a few days because of fluctuating blood pressure. She seems particularly sensitive to stress, even after we kept her on a strict diet and medication regimen to stabilize her. We screened her again, for a slew of metabolic problems, looking for the culprit, and found slightly lower than normal thyroid levels. Nothing we can't fix.

I have a new rule in the OR. Before making the first incision, I take a step or two in front of the drape and look at my patient's face. It feels like the right thing to do, although there isn't another Caleb Donaghy out there. He was the only monster in our family's history.

Behind me, Dr. Dean is telling a story about his latest mountain-climbing adventure, and his plans to climb the Absaroka Range on the eastern border of Yellowstone National Park next year. Almost everyone laughs at his account of a campfire mishap involving another camper's dog stealing his steak off the grill. Almost everyone. I'm tense for some reason, and Lee Chen seems a little tired. In passing, I notice I haven't seen Lee smile in a while, except on that Monday afternoon after I was cleared by the committee. There must be something going on in his personal life.

I return to my position by my patient's chest, on the heart side of the drape, and hold my hand out. Madison places the scalpel in my palm with just the right pressure. We're ready to start.

After the first incision I make, I notice something is not right. Although we checked her labs multiple times, I stop and wait, holding the surgical saw inches above her exposed sternum and frowning at the rivulets of blood flowing fast, flooding the incision without the slightest sign of coagulation.

"Kill it," I say, and Ginny knows I mean the music. Chatter instantly drops to zero. A tense silence takes over, punctuated by the rhythm of my patient's heart on the monitors. I set down the surgical saw on the instrument tray and look at the edges of the incision.

There's no hemostasis.

I've missed something. Her blood's not clotting.

"Packed platelets, stat," I order, mere seconds before the monitors alert with a strident sound.

"BP dropping fast," the anesthesiologist calls. "Ninety-five over sixty."

She's going to bleed to death from the six-inch gash I opened in her chest.

Ginny rushes over with the packed platelets bag and Madison hooks it up. A second transfusion, whole blood, is hung onto her other arm. After a few endless moments, the monitor alarm stops its shrieking.

"One-oh-five and climbing slowly," the anesthesiologist says.

"Ginny, I want to see her clotting factors again. They were normal when I checked." She had fluctuating blood pressure, but that's not what I'm seeing there.

"Are we closing her?" the anesthesiologist asks.

"Not yet." I examine the edges of the incision, still bleeding profusely in the wake of Madison's suction. Her blood is starting to clot a little better, but still not fast enough.

Ginny holds the file open in front of my eyes, away from the table, so I can see her labs without touching the pages. I can't believe it. I read the clotting factors values with a sense of dread in the pit of my stomach, remembering how I skimmed through them on Monday, focusing only on the bold ones, the tests with the abnormal values. Because my mind was on Paula Fuselier and the peer review committee.

Computers are idiots. People like me, who rely excessively on computers to make abnormal values bold, are even bigger idiots. Her thrombocytes were only five units over the lower limit. The same story with the fibrinogen. Her prothrombin time came a mere second below the threshold that would've made the font bold, excluding her from surgery. Had I noticed these values, I would've postponed her surgery until her platelets were repleted and her coagulation times on the faster side of normal.

I can't forgive myself. In my line of work, being distracted is not acceptable, regardless of what's going on. M was right. You're either in the hospital, ready to give 100 percent, or you don't belong there. People's lives are at stake.

A few hours later, I leave the OR and rip the scrubs off my body, dumping them in the container by the sinks. I put on my lab coat, then head toward M's office with a determined gait. This is killing me. Not being able to talk to anyone about what's going on, not knowing what's going to happen to me, almost cost a woman her life.

I storm into M's office and find her on a phone call, something about next month's fundraiser. On her desk, by the phone with a twirled spiral cord, there's a framed picture of her holding the hand of a giggling five-year-old girl. Her daughter? At forty-seven, she's a little too old for that. Maybe she's not too young to be a grandmother.

The TV on the wall by her desk is broadcasting the five o'clock news with the sound so low I can't hear much. I pace nervously, staring at the TV absent-mindedly. They're saying something about an arrest in the shooting death of some witness.

M looks at me and immediately ends the call. "What the hell happened?"

My throat is dry, but the urge to unload is overwhelming. "I almost killed my patient," I blurt out. "I didn't notice the coags were borderline, and I opened her up, and—" I rub my forehead and close my eyes, at a loss for words. How can I explain in a minute or two the whirlwind of guilt and anxiety that's racing through my head?

"Who's the patient?" M asks, her eyes shifting toward the computer. She probably has the surgery schedules already open, because she strikes a few keys and asks, "Orlowski, for the triple bypass?"

I nod, feeling faint, yet a strong fight-or-flight response to her question brings a familiar tremor to my muscles.

"What's her status?" Her voice is rushed, pressuring me. M's always in a hurry. Today is no different.

"She's—she's in post-op," I stutter. "She'll be fine."

"You opened the chest of a patient with suboptimal clotting?"

I nod, feeling blood draining from my face. "I gave her packed platelets, whole blood, the works, right there on the table. It was either that, or close her and tell her we failed, and we'd have to try the bypass again in a couple of days after she gets her platelets up." I look at her eyes, dark and serious and sharp, and shudder. "I made a call to continue with the bypass. I know it was risky, and I'm sorry."

She looks at me intently as if to see what I'm made of. Her lips are pressed tightly together, her hands steepled on the desk in front of her, perfectly still. For a moment, all I can hear is the faint sound of the television.

"You made the right call," she eventually says. "The patient's not dead. You didn't open the hospital to liability by cancelling the procedure after the first incision. No one has to know about this, especially if your team can keep their mouths shut." She pauses for a moment, her eyes glinting with something undefined. "But let me be clear, you got lucky today. And luck can be a real bitch if taken for granted."

She stands and walks around the desk with steps as large as her black pencil skirt allows, then sits on the sofa and pats the seat next to her in a silent invitation. I sit, awkward, far toward the corner, noting how unusual this is for her. I've seen her sit on the sofa with other people—donors, visiting lecturers—but never me. I don't know what to think.

Across the room from us, the television is running a commentary from a local reporter. Then an ad segment comes on, for cream cheese.

"Anne, someone in the State's Attorney Office has a definite hard-on for you, for reasons I can't comprehend." I stare at her, unable to offer any insight. "But you will get your act together, if you want to still have a career, here or elsewhere. I don't need to tell you that if you lose another patient while you're under their microscope, that's it for Dr. Anne Wiley. You won't be able to practice at all, or if you do, it will be in some remote place in Alaska treating frostbite and perianal abscesses."

"I understand." Her harsh words rattle me, but they're not surprising. I welcome the scolding; it could be the kick in the butt I need to get my act together. And yet, my eyes burn with tears. If there was ever the wrong time for having a meltdown.

"Is it about him?" she said, pointing at the TV.

Derreck's electoral ad is running, right after a Tide ad about how stains love clothes.

He looks good on television; the screen loves him. For a moment, I forget where I am and watch the ad as if I've never seen it before. He's dressed in a navy-blue suit with a gray-blue shirt that matches the color of his eyes and a darker Armani tie in shades of a blue checkered pattern. He's seated comfortably on a wrought iron chair at a local coffee shop, talking casually about how the third-most populous city of the United States has become the new capital of crime. Without exaggerated gestures, and in a somber yet pleasant tone of voice, he promises action against crime, a tough stance to control the war zone his beloved city has become. The ad asks for a vote of confidence and confidence in change, a word game I had advised against using, a few months ago when he first came up with the idea of using crime as leverage for votes. I didn't think the cheesy slogan would work; the polls subsequently proved me wrong.

"Do you think the mayor could be coming after you to get to him?" M asks, as the ad comes to an end.

I look at her, not realizing I'm wringing my hands until my fingers crack and hurt. "I honestly don't know, but it's probably going to bring both of us down. Unless—"

M leans toward me, eager to hear what I have to say. "Unless what?"

My thoughts aren't clear yet, not ready to be shared. But I'm starting to shape something up. "I don't understand how they knew that Caleb Donaghy died."

The moment I say this, M's jaw drops a little. "Ah," she says. "Good point."

"I always thought Dr. Bolger called them, but what if he didn't? He was partly responsible for that surgery. In retrospect, even if he hates me a whole lot, I don't believe he's dumb enough to call attention to a patient who died while he was in the room."

"What if he did, though? He seems blinded by his chauvinistic hate of successful women. Don't think I haven't tasted his poison myself." She scoffs with contempt.

I shake my head slowly. "I doubt it, because of the timing. The State's Attorney Office was called *before* we had the autopsy findings, before Bolger knew for certain it wasn't something he might've done wrong. The call was made before the peer review committee." I stop wringing my hands, but it takes willpower to do it. "My gut is telling me he didn't make that call."

"Then who did?"

"I don't know," I say simply, on a long, quiet sigh. My answer hasn't changed much since the peer review, when she asked me the first time. "At least I understand Bolger's motives. As twisted and hateful as they are, I understand them. But if he didn't call, I can't see anyone with a motive."

M tilts her head and smiles. "I can think of a way to find out, if we're lucky enough and the call was made from a hospital extension. I'll get a report from IT. Then, if we find whoever did it, you can ask them why."

I nod and fidget, wondering why she hasn't kicked me out yet.

"Do you want to stop operating until this shitstorm blows over?" she asks, in her typical blunt style.

"No," I reply, the urgency and hurt in my voice unmistakable. "Please don't suspend my privileges. It would kill me. This life, my job, is everything I live for. You can't take that away from me."

What I don't say is that losing my surgery privileges would be seen as suspicious by the ASA, fueling her conviction that there's something fishy about Caleb Donaghy's death.

She holds her hands up in the air. "All right, I won't. But we can't have any more screwups. Is that clear?"

I stand. "Crystal," I reply, before she waves me off with the same impatient gesture she probably uses to send her grandkid to brush her teeth.

On the way back to my office, I find myself wondering what M will do if she finds out who made the call to the State's Attorney Office.

TWENTY-SIX
SUBPOENA

Another weekend of relative silence passes by quickly. Pretending that everything is all right is one of the hardest things I have to do. I want to speak with Derreck about it, about what could happen, and what I should do. But the thought of having a bug in the house kills all appetite for virtually everything. We are automatons, going through the motions in half-phrases or mumbled words, avoiding conversations like paranoid characters from *1984*-like flicks.

Mom stays mostly in her room, reading or watching TV. We still eat together, and Derreck stayed home the entire weekend. Sunday night, he takes me out for dinner at a small pizza place where he knows the owners and can request a certain booth.

There, our heads together in frantic whispering, I ask how I will know when it's all over. Will the State's Attorney Office call me and tell me the investigation is closed? He said that never happens. Worse, such investigations can sometimes take years to conclude. Then he again asks my permission to speak with Mitch Hobbs, the Cook County state's attorney.

I decline, thinking M will take it very badly if something

goes wrong and the prosecutor can add the attempt to influence the investigation to the list of offences. He reluctantly agrees, saying it's probably safer that way, but he doesn't seem convinced. I eat very little pizza, even though it's mouthwatering and loaded with artery-popping cheese deliciousness.

All I can think of is how much longer until I breathe normally again.

I listen to Derreck explain the mechanisms of mayoral races, only half paying attention. Some pizza patrons recognize him and point fingers or greet us; some grin and just walk past us, staring. One scowls; he's probably a fan of the incumbent.

Noticing these people's reactions are brief interruptions in my chain of thought, stuck in the same hellish loop over the one question no one can answer: why didn't Caleb's heart start again? Why was it so inert, so deathly still after I flushed it with warm saline?

I might never find out. Somehow, that isn't acceptable.

By Monday morning, I have a plan.

It's not the greatest, and Derreck will probably rake me over the coals for it, but I just *have* to know what stopped that heart from awakening. The two weeks and three days that have passed since I sent Caleb Donaghy to the morgue, spent in heightened anxiety and pure anguish, have generated an identity crisis of sorts.

Am I a killer or not? Did I take his life, or was I just willing to?

Some might say it doesn't really matter, since I acted as if his heart was viable, removing its chances to start beating again. After seeing his face, the open-heart massage I gave him would never have helped, as less than two minutes later, I rushed and declared him dead, terrified he might still live.

That's why I have to know if that heart was viable. I have to. Otherwise, not knowing will slowly drive me insane.

I sit at my computer, as soon as I finish my rounds, and start typing an email to the Cook County medical examiner who performed the autopsy on Caleb Donaghy. After introducing myself and explaining my reasons, in a short paragraph I list the procedures I'd like to perform on Donaghy's body, to further investigate his heart's failure to restart.

Yes, it's ridiculously stupid, like kicking a potential hornets' nest. His autopsy report exonerated me, and I'm extremely grateful that happened. Anyone with an ounce of common sense would just let it be.

That's why I ultimately save the message in my drafts and decide to sleep on it for a day or two. Maybe I can figure out a different way to find out if that heart was viable, without poking this ugly bear. Or perhaps I could finally accept that my actions, viable heart or not, were what made me a killer, and stop seeking exoneration. Although the law disagrees. If a man is killed in a car crash for example, then is stabbed by someone who thinks he's still alive, the knife wielder can only be charged with desecrating a corpse. He wouldn't, technically, be deemed a killer.

Maybe neither would I. But who am I kidding? Definitely not myself.

When I raise my eyes from the computer screen, I see Paula Fuselier grinning crookedly at me through the glass wall of my office. My blood turns to ice.

I can't believe she's back. Derreck was right. It could take forever to know we're in the clear. Probably well past November, if this witch hunt is election-related after all.

Then a thought rushes through my brain as the prosecutor enters my office. Maybe someone made another call about the close miss with Mrs. Orlowski last week. I dismiss the concern; no one knew about that other than my surgical team, my new anesthesiologist, and M. I'm willing to bet my life none of these people would call the State's Attorney Office on me.

I stand and meet her close to the door. I don't want her

anywhere near my desk again. "Ms. Fuselier, isn't it?" I look straight at her without smiling.

"You know it is."

"I'm afraid I can't speak with you in the absence of counsel. You wasted a trip."

"You can listen though," she says, coldly, moving past me and letting herself drop into one of the chairs in front of my desk. She crosses her legs and bounces her foot rhythmically, almost hitting my desk.

I want her gone.

She's not going anywhere. Instinctively, I cross my arms at my chest and lean against the wall, staring at her.

She takes her sweet time checking herself in a small mirror before speaking. "I'm here as a courtesy, to let you know we have a subpoena pending for all your surgery videos."

I resist the urge to ask what for or how far back. Per Derreck, even questions can be used against you in a court of law. Not just statements.

She pulls a small notepad out of her pocket and smiles sheepishly. "You must forgive me; some of these things are difficult to remember." She clears her voice and continues. "As far as I know, your average CPR time in the operating room with the heart on pump was forty-three minutes before declaring death."

I shrug. "I've never called time of death on any patient before Caleb Donaghy. You have no idea what you're talking about."

Yet the numbers she's quoting are exactly what M quoted in the peer review session. So it *was* Dr. Bolger after all, ratting me out, not once, but twice. No one else but him was present both for the Donaghy surgery and the peer review committee.

My heart sinks. The last thing this woman needs is a reload of ammo like Bolger must've provided.

"Oh, yes, my mistake. Says here average of forty-three

minutes before NSR. I thought that was, you know, doctor speak for deciding when someone is dead."

"NSR means normal sinus rhythm. As in alive, not dead." I can't help the sarcastic tone of my voice. I should shut up already.

"Oh, okay, that makes sense. So, we're getting a subpoena to find out how this surgery... no, how this *resuscitation* was different. We'll compare all the other recordings to this one and map them out, show every move you made differently. For instance, here, it says that you usually deliver an epinephrine shot straight into the patient's heart, but this time, you didn't."

That sense of foreboding I barely got rid of renews and seeps through my body, weakening it. Who would've known such details, other than Dr. Bolger? M would've never jeopardized the reputation of her hospital if she needed to harm me. When M wants to hurt someone, she fires them, and it's usually well-deserved, more like reprimanding than hurting. She's not a sociopath, and she doesn't need anything else other than the power of the function she already holds.

The prosecutor is about to ask me something else when Madison storms through the door. "Mrs. Molinari needs you in post-op, stat," she announces, standing in the door, keeping it open. I frown for a moment, taken aback by the fact she used a male patient's name with a Mrs. in front of it.

Then I realize she came to my rescue with a fictitious reason.

I walk out, knowing she'll evict Paula from my office or call security if she fails to do so in less than three seconds, per M's abundantly clear instructions.

I stride quickly to the treatment rooms next to the OR. I find an empty one and slip inside, locking the door behind me and pulling the curtains shut. Then I collapse on the chair, breathing heavily, choking with tears of fear and desperation.

This isn't going away.

I have to run, to get out of here and go someplace safe, even if for just an hour.

TWENTY-SEVEN
DEN

When I left the hospital, without saying a word to anyone, I thought I was leaving early. But it was already dark outside. Still, I kept my head low as I headed for my parking spot, afraid that the prosecutor might see me. In fact, it was I who wanted to avoid seeing her, nothing more: the human version of an ostrich and his head proverbially burrowed in the sand, while his big, feathery butt is left hanging out for the entire world to see. That's why, despite my lowered head, several colleagues wished me a good night on the way to my car.

But I didn't see her, didn't run into her, and, as far as I can tell, she doesn't know I ran from her.

The moment I close my car door and start the engine, tears flood my eyes, and I let a sob climb out of my chest. I knew this was coming, but that doesn't make it any easier.

I'm not ready. I've come to terms with what I've done, with what that makes me, but I can't bring myself to accept a future behind bars, locked away from everything I hold dear: my family and my job. I would die. But as I slide into the heavy traffic of the early evening, a disturbing thought snakes its way into my mind. People die hard. They think they're going to die if this or that happens, but, in reality, they don't. Nature finds a way to keep them alive against all reason and all personal willpower even, because it's written in our DNA to survive at all costs. No, it's safe to say I would live through many years of pain and suffering and desperation before I'd actually die in prison.

That's a horrifying thought. For a deeply unsettling moment, I contemplate taking my own life while I still can.

Then I breathe. *It's not over yet,* I tell myself enough times to start believing it.

I stop at a small street stoplight and wait for it to turn green. It's windy out there and drizzly, but not heavy enough to start the windshield wipers. Fallen leaves and sprigs hit the windshield occasionally, carried by brutal wind gusts. The sound is unsettling, as if extracted from a horror movie soundtrack. But then I catch a glimpse of a twig, slammed against the windshield for a split second before it blows away. There's a bud at the end of it, still tiny but already green, the promise of spring to come.

I haven't looked at trees in more than two weeks. I haven't run in the mornings either. My life stopped being normal the moment I saw Donaghy's port-wine stain. I stopped living the moment he did, in surreal, poetic symmetry.

Derreck's car is not in the driveway when I arrive home. I didn't expect it to be: he's rarely home before six, though lately, he usually makes it before six thirty.

When I step into the living room, I find Mom at the stove, stirring a pot of boiling pasta. The air smells of cilantro and sauteed onions and freshly grated Parmesan. No meat for dinner still; that's Mom's way of showing she cares. Unnecessary, but heartwarming and precious.

I linger in her hug, but there's no more time for crying. *I need to know.* Lack of certainty is driving me insane, especially with this prosecutor nipping at my heels, hoping I'll stumble and fall, turn into easy prey she can butcher at will.

"What's wrong, sweetie?" she asks, pulling away enough to give me a long gaze. Her brow ruffles slightly with worry. I smile and kiss her cheek.

"Nothing much," I say, dropping my purse on a chair. "I have something I need to do before dinner."

"I'll keep it warm," she says, returning to stirring the pasta. A moment later, her phone's timer goes off, and I hear her turn the stove off as I enter the den.

I find the peace I need so badly in the quiet, cozy room filled with memories and my father's strength. *What would he say? What advice would he give me?*

I sink into the Dutch armchair and close my eyes for a moment, imagining a conversation with him. He speaks to me in a stern voice with undertones of pride, and calls Donaghy's death *justice well served, albeit too late.* I'm not delusional; our dialogue is all in my mind, and I write the entire script. Still, I write it in his voice, trying to sprinkle in as much of his wisdom as possible. So, I keep listening, my eyes closed, my mind wandering freely, ready to take his ideas and put them into practice.

Try to figure out what's what, he says, *before jumping to conclusions. You still don't know what happened. And if you don't know, how could this prosecutor woman know?*

I open my eyes wide. He's right. No one knows who Caleb Donaghy really was except Derreck, and he would never betray me. If Paula Fuselier wants to prove a crime has been committed, she has to prove motive. I will run this by Derreck, but I'm reasonably sure I'm right.

I fire up my laptop and wait impatiently as the screen comes to life. I open a browser window and type Donaghy's name, then start typing Melanie's, but my fingers freeze above the keyboard.

What if I'm being watched, and that includes the internet searches I run? What if this ASA doesn't know of any correlation between Caleb Donaghy and my family, but by running this search, I tell her there's something worth looking for?

As long as Paula Fuselier believes that Caleb Donaghy died on the table the way some heart patients sometimes do, all she can do is try to have my license suspended. And I have a decent chance to stay out of jail. Unless I do something stupid and give her more evidence.

But am I really being watched? Is the house bugged? Would someone do that to people like us without a warrant? Derreck is the front runner in the mayoral race; such an attack would have consequences.

But not if his wife is found guilty of murder, the devil's advocate in my head is quick to answer.

Worry flushes over me like an icy-cold shower. If the house has been bugged, we don't know when. It's possible it happened before I told Derreck and that means she knows.

I try to remember the conversation I had with Derreck that night, when I was sobbing hard in his arms, not making much sense. What did I say, really? Did I actually say—

Yes. I did. I said I knew him. Not at first, but I knew him, and I also said I rushed calling time of death. But I couldn't explain who he was... I remember I just broke down, sobbing in Derreck's arms, and he didn't need words to figure out who my patient was.

Not knowing is driving me insane. It takes over my entire mind, making it spin in place like the spinning pinwheel on my Mac's computer screen when it freezes.

This woman seems motivated by something personal. No way it's just a phone call she received from the hospital, like M assumes. What I've seen in her eyes is deep hatred, fueled by something I don't understand. Maybe she knew Caleb Donaghy, although his body still lies unclaimed in the hospital's basement morgue. If that heartless monster was someone she loved, she would've probably given him a proper burial by now.

"Dinner's ready," I hear Mom's voice from the kitchen. "And Derreck's home too."

I close the browser window, biting my lip in frustration. I can't even do this much in the so-called privacy of my own home: to find out if there's anything out there, floating on the internet, that could prove a connection between Donaghy and Melanie and me.

As I turn off the light and walk out of the den, a pang of anxiety stabs me as I remember the email I drafted for the medical examiner on my office computer, asking him to further investigate Donaghy's heart.

I have to delete it first thing tomorrow, before it gets sent out by mistake or gets read by the wrong people.

I should've never written it.

TWENTY-EIGHT
RUN

I lie awake, staring at the ceiling, watching shadows chasing one another as moonlight shines through the crown of the pine outside the window. The wind is still gusting, pushing and pulling at the tree's long branches, sometimes brushing them against the window.

But it's not the noise that keeps me awake.

Derreck sleeps soundly by my side, his minty breath landing on my face softly, a reminder I'm not alone and that I am loved. His arm rests on my stomach, but I don't mind. I can't close my eyes; the best I can do is lie still so as to not wake him. He's been tired lately, drawn, black circles under his eyes compromising his usual appearance of strength and nonchalance.

I'd be a complete fool to imagine what I'm going through doesn't affect him.

Figure it out, my father would've said, *for the both of you.*

I remember him teaching me about figuring things out, or, in his own words, the "differential diagnosis, life edition."

"It's about placing smart bets," he'd said, his eyes shining with excitement as they always were when he was teaching. "If you're healthy, you're not going to bet you'll need surgery next year. You might still need it, if something unforeseen happens, but your safest bet is to maintain your health. Go where the probabilities tell you, make smart bets with your assumptions, and always," he punctuated, his index finger waving in the air, "*always* be honest with yourself."

It's time I figure things out before the state's attorney's rabid dog figures them out for me.

Eyes wide open, I relive Caleb Donaghy's surgery, every detail, every moment. After watching the recording so many times, it's not difficult. Once I recognized him, I recall returning behind the drape, my hand hovering above his chest, slightly trembling.

I had wanted to rip his heart out of his chest for what he'd done to Melanie. I didn't. I kept my cool and pretended to continue resuscitation for two more minutes, then called it quits.

No one noticed my pretense at resuscitation, not even Dr. Bolger, or I'd already be in jail.

The safest bet is that Paula Fuselier doesn't have a thing on me she can use. That's what logic and common sense indicate. Occam's Razor too, with its medical version: *When you hear hoofbeats, think horses, not zebras.*

I'll start living my life again, acting as if nothing happened, as if all those hoofbeats were just another routine horse. The ASA can't figure out it's a zebra unless I draw the damn stripes on it myself. No more getting flustered in the OR or rushing out of the hospital with my head hung low. No more emails to the medical examiner or tearful admissions of guilt in M's office. None of that crap.

Okay, that's one answer to a really big question.

The second question remains unanswered for now.

Yes, I wanted that monster dead after I saw his face, but, before that, I need to understand why his heart didn't restart. If it's something that could save me, I can use it. Or, if it's something detrimental, at least I'll know to steer clear of it.

The alarm clock on Derreck's night table reads 3:37 a.m., displayed in big, green digits.

The perfect time for a morning run.

I slide from underneath Derreck's arm, and he groans quietly, then turns on his other side. I wait for a few moments, until his breathing is steady and shallow, then I sneak out of bed.

The usual morning shower I skip for now, afraid the noise could wake him. I just grab my tracksuit and my favorite pair of sneakers. As an afterthought, I add a warm scarf to the pile of clothing. The night air might still be too cold.

I run my usual path through Lincoln Park, the three-mile loop entirely deserted with the exception of a person sleeping on a bench. My breath puts vapor in the air with every step as I pant, struggling to complete my run after having skipped it for almost three weeks. It's amazing how quickly bad behaviors take ownership of people.

As soon as I'm done, still wearing the tracksuit and sneakers, I drive to the hospital, where I can take a shower and put on the spare set of clothing I keep there, just in case. I find the hospital's corridors empty. The occasional nurse hustles by in gum sole shoes, barely acknowledging me as I make my way to my office.

My first order of business is to start my computer and delete the email I had drafted for the medical examiner. It's still there... then it's not: deleted, then deleted again from the deleted items folder.

Showering and changing takes me a little under fifteen minutes, then I'm ready to dive into my next order of business. I have under three hours until I have to start my rounds, then at ten, I have a valve replacement on a nineteen-year-old boy.

It might not be enough time for what I have to do.

I take my red Donaghy file and open it, timelining the man's stay in the hospital, a sketch in pencil on sheets of paper pulled from the printer by Madison's desk. I jot down all the events in a person's hospital stay, based on the routine I know well. Meals. Blood draws. Rounds. The whole shebang.

Once I have the events mapped out, I start looking at hospital records for the entire duration of his stay. Which rooms he occupied. Who changed his sheets. Which nurse's aides helped him shower. Everything he ate and who served his meals. All the medications he was administered. By whom. Where. How often, how much, and what side effects were observed, if any. Finally, who prepped him for surgery the morning of, shaving his chest and his beard.

Whatever crippled that son of a bitch's heart, I'll find it sooner or later.

TWENTY-NINE
HOBBS

Paula's desk was cluttered with law books, some of which she'd extracted from the boxes she'd packed so neatly preparing for her move to the fifth floor. Some of them were still open, others closed over bookmarks improvised from sticky notes bearing scribbled comments.

Adam had stopped by a couple of times, probably checking in to see what her priorities were, but she'd waved him off on each occasion without speaking with him. He couldn't help with her issue; he wasn't a lawyer. Just a cop.

No one could help her. She needed to help herself this time, and she couldn't find the way. She was a sore loser at best. Better said, she didn't know *how* to lose. Having fate slam the door in her face was not an acceptable outcome for the Anne Wiley investigation.

Teeth grinding, she went over her notes, looking for any legal loophole to make the subpoena for Dr. Wiley's surgery records stick. No judge would sign it in its current form. What probable cause could she invoke? A gut feeling? Any sane judge would laugh her out of their chambers.

But she'd seen the glimmer of fear in Anne's eyes when she

mentioned the subpoena. She'd seen her turn pale when she read out the notes about the time spent resuscitating prior patients. Paula knew she was on to something but couldn't prove anything yet.

Since she'd returned from the hospital the day before, she'd been desperately digging for legal precedents that would allow the subpoena to slip through, if she found a friendlier judge or someone who owed her a favor. In yesterday's clothes and having caught only a few minutes of shut-eye on the couch in her office, she had to admit bitter defeat.

She had nothing she could use.

Anne Wiley would get away with killing her patient, and Derreck would never leave his wife.

Why would he, when his mother-in-law's deep pockets funded his mayoral aspirations? How could Paula ever compete with that?

She grabbed the *Criminal Law and Procedure Handbook of Illinois*, a softbound edition with a blue cover, and threw it across the room with a groan of frustration. It slammed against the wall and landed on the floor, its pages rustling as they settled, guilty for not providing a way out of Paula's legal impasse.

Moments later, Marie's head popped in at the doorway. "Everything okay?"

She managed not to shout at her assistant. "Yes, Marie, I'm fine. Just dropped something."

Marie looked at the book with doubtful eyes, then at Paula, but didn't say anything. She picked up the book and took it to Paula's desk.

"Hobbs needs you in his office," she announced, collecting two empty mugs with dried remnants of yesterday's coffee.

"When? Now?"

"He just called." She looked warily toward the corridor. "He didn't sound happy."

Fuck. "All right," Paula replied, smoothing her hair with her hands and tucking in her blouse before putting on her jacket. She applied lipstick quickly, then grabbed an embossed folder that contained a clipboard with a notepad and a pen, and walked out past Marie.

"Adam wants to speak with you too, when you have a moment," Marie shouted behind her. Paula just raised her hand with her thumb up without turning her head. She'd deal with Adam later.

The elevator ride to the fifth floor was a short one, not giving Paula too much time to think why her boss wanted to see her. Most probably it was about an arraignment she had scheduled for later in the afternoon. She hoped that's what it was, but her stomach churned with every floor chime.

Hobbs was pacing his office when she entered, his charcoal suit jacket abandoned on the back of his chair, his shirt sleeves rolled up, his gray tie loosened. A deep frown ridged his brow and didn't vanish when he looked at her. He gestured toward one of the chairs in front of his desk and she sat quietly, expecting nothing good.

He stopped a few feet away and stared at her for a moment. The silence in his office was loaded. "Before I tell you just how disappointed I am, let me start by informing you that you're being officially investigated for abuse in your role as assistant state's attorney. You're suspended effective immediately."

She froze, speechless for a moment. What the hell had happened? "May I know what this is about?" she managed to ask, sounding calm and not too fazed.

"For employing this office's resources for what appears to be a personal agenda."

She stared at him, completely dismayed. "Sir, I can assure you—"

"We're talking about your so-called investigation into the death of a patient at Joseph Lister University Hospital, while being operated on by a Dr. Anne Wiley." His eyes glinted steel. "Ring a bell now?"

She fell silent, thinking hard about what she could do to manage this train wreck.

But Hobbs wasn't done talking. "Her name must sound familiar to you, since you're sleeping with her husband, Derreck Bourke. On government time, as it happens."

Oh, it was *way* worse than she'd expected.

Adam, damn you to bloody hell. How could you do this to me?

He'd turned on her. The sting of betrayal hurt badly, ripping through her chest like a disease. No one else had known what she was up to. Adam Costilla, her most trusted colleague and friend, had ratted on her, spilling his guts to Mitch Hobbs, a man who had the power to squash her existence like a bug.

Slowly coming to terms with what had happened, she shook her head, wondering if any of her future plans were salvageable. The text of a meme she'd recently seen kept spinning in her mind. *If you're going through hell, keep going.* She'd laughed when she'd seen it, but then had to agree it had value. Wisdom, even. No matter how difficult her current bind, she had to keep going forward. As if she'd been one hundred percent honest and lawful in her actions and intentions.

Hobbs groaned as he leaned against the desk, crossing his arms. "To make it worse, you invited your lover, the husband of someone you're investigating, for a joint press conference at the site of a high-profile arrest." He looked away from her for a moment, visibly appalled. She could see he was clenching his jaw tightly. "He's running against the current mayor, Paula. Our office absolutely *cannot* get involved. What were you thinking?"

She tried to stand, but he stopped her with a hand gesture.

"Sir, I can explain."

"Really?" He scratched the roots of his receding hair.

"Then you're one hell of an attorney, because I don't see how that's possible. You questioned hospital employees without a case number and without attorneys present, even after you were warned by hospital officials not to. Let's start there... how do you explain that?"

He wasn't going to let her speak. It was in the inflection in his voice, a thirst to see her bleed for embarrassing him, for making his office look bad. Still, she had to try.

"They didn't need their attorney present. They were not subjected to custodial interrogation. And I can explain why—"

"That's a very fine line you're toeing, Paula. I'm not a clueless idiot." He paused for a moment, while she lowered her eyes. "You mean to tell me what they said during those interviews cannot be used against them in a court of law?"

"Yes, but legally—"

"Don't you *dare* begin to explain the law to me!" he bellowed. She promptly clammed up. "If this bogus case of yours ever gets argued in court, whatever you discovered could be thrown out, because you were told to speak with their employees only with their attorneys present, and you deliberately decided not to."

She nodded, unwilling to risk opening her mouth again. She had the urge to stand, feeling vulnerable sitting with Hobbs's tall frame towering over her. It was psychological: she wasn't afraid he would pounce on her physically, but the effect was unpleasant, making her seem small and exposed.

As if he read her mind, Hobbs resumed pacing the office, running his hand through his hair once or twice, seemingly preoccupied by something he wasn't sharing. Then he took a seat behind his desk with a long, pained sigh. "It seems your motivations for questioning Dr. Wiley were purely personal in nature, fueled by jealousy. I also have it on good account that the hospital cleared Dr. Wiley of any wrongdoing through its peer review process. The Cook County medical examiner did the patient's autopsy himself and found nothing. Care to explain any of this?"

She waited, giving him time to change his mind and continue with his questions, but he was just staring at her, his eyes squinting with anger.

"Yes, I'm having an affair with Derreck Bourke, the surgeon's husband," she said, keeping her voice calm and level, as if she had nothing to hide and nothing to be ashamed of. "During the course of this affair, I was made aware that the patient's death was not random, but intentional."

Hobbs ran his hand over his chin, cupping it with his fingers. "And how, exactly, were you made aware of this issue?"

She hesitated for a moment. "Um, pillow talk, sir. I was—"

"Also known as hearsay." His voice was dismissive. "The surgeon's husband is a lawyer, not a doctor. I don't believe he's qualified to know why a patient dies during cardiovascular surgery."

"My intention was to probe and see if there was a valid reason for concern. All I've done was to try to—"

"Get rid of the competition?" he scoffed, his voice filled with searing contempt. "Wouldn't that be nice, to have the future mayor of Chicago caught in your little web of lies and deceit?" He tilted his head for a moment, thinking. "Got to give it to you, this is brilliant. On one hand, you're helping his career by getting him face time on television. On the other hand, you're cleaning house, making sure the missus is history. What were you thinking? That she'd see one of these interviews on TV and learn her better half is in cahoots with the prosecutor who's trying to put her in jail?" He whistled in mock appreciation. "If I were this woman, I'd divorce his sorry ass the moment I saw that happening."

Yeah, that had been part of her plan, but it didn't matter now. She wasn't going to be able to achieve her goals, and that filled her with searing rage.

"All right, I've heard enough," Hobbs said, looking tired suddenly, drained and disappointed. "You'll have to account for all the times you visited Joseph Lister on government time and provide a reason for each interview and the summary of what was discussed. In writing, in a formal report you'll submit by the end of the week. You'll also have to account for each hour you spent out of the office when you weren't in court, going back a year."

"A year?" She reacted before she could control herself. "How am I supposed to remember—"

"Don't you have a planner?" Hobbs asked, his voice dipped in sarcasm. "Or maybe you didn't write down all those pillow-talk debriefing sessions at fancy hotels, so you wouldn't leave a paper trail?"

She lowered her head, deeply humiliated. Her cheeks burned.

"Your promotion is on hold for a year," Hobbs added coldly, "pending the result of the formal investigation into your conduct. If you're found guilty of abuse, your employment will be terminated with cause."

It was all coming apart. Everything she'd worked for, everything she'd planned so carefully, all of it falling to pieces faster than a house of cards.

But there was one sliver of hope that she could still make it all work. If she could get Anne Wiley on the hook for murder.

"Then I have nothing left to lose if I ask you this," she blurted, looking at Hobbs with a silent plea in her eyes. "Please allow me two more days to prove to you this wasn't jealousy or payback or a scheme to get my lover divorced. If you ever had a gut feeling that didn't let you sleep at night, then you'll know what I mean. I know this surgeon did something she shouldn't have. I'm betting my career she killed a man. Not by accident, or because some people die during surgery, but intentionally. She murdered her patient behind the smoke screen of a risky procedure. All I need is to find a little bit more evidence, and I can bring her in front of a grand jury." She stopped for a moment to draw breath. "Please, sir. That's all I'm asking for, two lousy days. And if I fail, I'll save you the trouble of firing me. I'll resign."

Hobbs studied her with keen eyes that glinted with anger and discontent and something else, perhaps curiosity.

"It's not nearly enough," he whispered, between clenched teeth. "If you fail, I'll have you disbarred." Paula held her breath. "You have twenty-four hours."

THIRTY
ADVICE

I lie naked in Derreck's arms, spent, yet restless, my knee thrown over his legs, my head nestled on his chest. His fingers run through my hair, slowly hypnotizing me, attempting to extend the blissful state he must think I'm in. But I'm not... I'm tormented inside, his gentleness jarring when I crave the slap of the belt against my skin and the searing pain it brings. That pain soothes me, feeds my need to feel what Melanie had felt, although I know I can't even come close to the dimensions of her ordeal. But I didn't dare ask Derreck for it, not today, not when our lives are in complete upheaval because of me.

I will myself to lie still, and, for a moment, I doze off, the transition from glow to slumber not easy to resist.

I start back awake immediately, my racing thoughts unwilling to cede the battle to the dark hours of the night. I shift gently and open my eyes, as if it were morning already, not almost midnight.

"What's up, baby?" Derreck asks, in a low whisper. "Bad dream?"

I chuckle with sadness. "Bad reality." I'm tempted to tell him how I feel about this madness that has engulfed my life and is threatening to consume it whole, but I remember speaking is not safe in our house anymore.

Derreck senses my concern. "I had a security team do a complete sweep of the house, the garage, everything. The house isn't bugged. As far as they could tell, it was never bugged. They even swept your car in the parking garage at the hospital."

I lift myself a little, leaning on my elbow. "Did anyone see them?"

"They're pros, Anne, the best aspiring politicians can hire." His smile is relaxed, reassuring.

I lie back down, my fingers trailing his chest, taking it in, the joy of knowing our words have not been recorded, our lives have not been invaded, at least not here, in our home.

"What's on your mind?" he asks, his voice conquered by sleep. He's about to doze off, but still wants to talk to me, to listen. A tiny smile of gratitude stretches my lips; I'm so fortunate to have fallen in love with the young law student back then, instead of some boring, self-centered doctor with a god complex. I laugh a little, thinking that marrying a lawyer instead of a doctor came with huge benefits in my workplace too, as I don't have to look at all the young and pretty nurses with jealous suspicion.

"Care to share?"

"Uh-uh," I say, refusing to fuel his ego. He's already self-assured enough. "I love you. That's all you need to know." I reach to kiss his lips. He wraps me in his arms and closes his eyes. Mine pop wide open again. There's not going to be much sleep tonight.

Every chance I had today, I analyzed the events, procedures, and people who interacted with Caleb Donaghy, looking for patterns, trying to determine if anything, no matter how small and insignificant, had been done wrong since his admission. But I have nothing that can explain why his heart refused to restart.

"Okay, out with it," Derreck says, pushing himself higher up against the pillows. He looks at me with the gaze you give a hurt child.

I veer my eyes away for a moment, not sure what to say when he knows everything that's on my mind already. But maybe this isn't about informing him, about keeping him up to date with events and developments. He doesn't need to know every bit of information about Donaghy's heart and every single worry-fueled thought that crosses my mind. "It's this woman's unrelenting hunt for me that throws me. I can't understand what fuels her desire to ruin my life."

Derreck's body tenses as I speak. I'm ruining the moment.

"Has she spoken with you again?" His eyes are keen, analytical.

"Not since yesterday."

He props himself up in a sitting position, leaning against the headboard and muttering an oath. "What the hell? She was supposed to talk to hospital counsel, right? Not to you?"

"Yeah, she was. But she came into my office yesterday, and she had numbers, Derreck. Statistics about my surgeries, things no one would know, except—"

I stop midsentence, seeing how intense his gaze has turned. I know my words must be upsetting, but I didn't expect him to be so mad about it. I see a vein on his forehead, throbbing with his pulse, indicative of systemic elevated venous pressure. His jaw is clenched shut, and his pupils are dilated more than the dim bedroom light would justify.

"This woman, I can't fucking believe it," he mutters.

"I've never met her before, so it can't be personal," I say, reciting the thoughts that have been swirling inside my mind for days. "She seems to be some random prosecutor who was assigned to my case and is using it to build up her career. At least that's what I'm thinking. You know, me being the heart girl and all." I laugh quietly, but there's no humor when I do.

"Listen," Derreck says, looking into my eyes with scary intensity. "I don't want you to say another word to this woman. Not one word, you understand? Not without the hospital's attorney present. And I believe it's time I make some calls."

It takes me several minutes to talk him off the ledge and make him promise he won't call anyone. I'm confident it would only make things worse. Much worse.

He finally falls asleep, and I doze off too, tempted to set my phone to buzz me awake early but deciding against it, for Derreck's sake.

When I open my eyes again, it's still dark outside. Shadows are dancing on the ceiling, slower than the night before; the wind gusts have subsided. The clock on Derreck's night table reads 3:07 a.m.

Time to get up.

In a repeat of yesterday's routine, today I plan better. I take the tracksuit and sneakers with me, but also a clean suit with a couple of fresh shirts and a pair of comfortable shoes.

The three-mile run in the cold morning air refreshes my mind and invigorates my body. It's less painful than yesterday, my awakened muscles grateful for the renewed exercise routine. Then I head straight for the hospital.

I have one more thing I need to look at, and it's better that not very many people know about it.

My first stop is the basement, where hospital security has its offices right next to the morgue. The corridor is perfectly empty, humming with the sound of old, crappy fluorescent lights. It smells damp and moldy down there. As I walk quickly toward the security office, I notice water dripping from the thick, hot-water pipe fixed on the wall. Condensation.

I knock twice on the security office door, then I walk in. It's a suite, almost completely dark. It's not even five in the morning.

Far toward the left, I see the bluish flicker of monitors, and I hear the rustling of a food wrapper being torn. That's where I need to go.

The security officer is a young man in his early twenties. He's leaning back in an ergonomic chair, eating a KitKat with one hand and playing a card game online with another, completely oblivious someone's there.

I clear my throat softly and smile.

He jumps to his feet, disfigured by sheer panic for a split second. "What the...?" I'm still smiling, and panic washes off his face, replaced by a widening grin. "Oh, it's you." He grins some more, looking hastily for a place to drop his snack and deciding to discard it in the wastebasket under his desk. Then he wipes his hands against his pants. "The heart girl," he adds. He's fidgeting, probably anticipating a handshake. I don't disappoint him, although very few doctors still do handshakes these days. A fine tradition, only it stopped being smart a few virus mutations ago.

"I'm Mike." His hand is a bit clammy, probably from the surprise of my visit, but his grip is firm and enthusiastic. "What can I do for you, Doctor?" He's eager to please, just like his colleague from the morgue did last week. I'm guessing they might be friends.

"You might've heard I lost a patient a couple of weeks ago." He nods, not taking his eyes off mine. "I want to make sure nothing unusual happened with him the night prior to the surgery. Is there any way we can do that here?"

"Oh, sure," he says energetically, as proud of the security system he's monitoring as if he'd invented it himself. "Let me show you. We record everything, and we don't purge files for two whole months. When did your patient die?"

I give him the date, and he starts looking for the files in the system's archive.

He seems so thrilled with my apparent interest that he

explains everything he's doing. "We have the data archived by date, then by floor and room number. Corridors are labeled C01 and so on, elevators are E01, parking has codes for levels instead of units, because it's only one parking lot, but it has multiple levels. Basement levels are B, and the higher the number, the deeper the basement level."

"Yeah, got it." I only half listen to what he's saying. I'm holding my breath, waiting to find out if anyone came near Donaghy the night before he died. He was fine in pre-op the next morning, but... I just want to know.

I give him the four-digit room number where Caleb Donaghy stayed the night before his surgery and watch the screen, my hands together in a white-knuckled clasp.

The recording displayed on the screen is unexpectedly clear and in color. The system must be new. Once the recording starts, several buttons appear on the screen. Some are control symbols I recognize from years of playing videos, like fast forward and play, others I don't understand. I watch him work the interface.

"The recordings are saved in segments, usually eight hours long. The system does that, so we don't have to worry; there are thousands of cameras in this hospital, we'd never be able to keep up. See here?" He points his cursor at one of the buttons I don't understand. "This button shifts forward to the next segment, very useful if you want to investigate something going missing. First you figure out in which batch it appears, right?" I nod and smile, apparently all I'm required to do for a while. "So, what time would you like to start?"

"Say, eight in the evening prior."

He clicks on the screen, switching to the prior segment, then does a search for the time code and positions the video right where I need it.

I look at my patient, sleeping on his back, probably sedated.

He's still unshaven and wearing that baseball cap. The room is dimly lit, and the TV is off.

Mike hits the fast forward button several times, accelerating the speed of the playback with every click. "Because nothing really moves in this view, we can do this really fast."

I check my watch, a bit worried. Mike's "really fast" still takes some time. I'd like to leave the basement before anyone sees me and starts asking questions.

When his phone rings, I jump out of my skin and take my eyes off the screen for a moment. He silences it really quickly and looks at me apologetically. "It's nothing. I'm on break now, but I can—"

"I don't want to keep you," I say. "Go ahead, I'll be here, watching him sleep."

He nods and touches his pocket, where the cellophane of a pack of smokes rustles. "If you find something, write down the time code and I'll be back in a few minutes to help you." He walks away, then immediately turns around and says, pointing at the screen, "Don't touch these two buttons. The scissors deletes a segment, and the little square imports a segment in its place. Big trouble if you touch those."

"I won't touch them, I promise," I reply. Why would anyone build these functions in a security system?

My face must be an open book, because he laughs awkwardly and adds, "It's for training purposes and certain cases, like if we have VIPs in here, or Tom Cruise." His grin fills with pride and he straightens his back ever so slightly. "My credentials are really strong. I made shift manager last week."

"Congratulations," I say, then turn my attention back to the screen.

He walks away, and a moment later, I hear the suite door close.

The rest of the recording shows absolutely nothing, except my patient tossing and turning, and the scheduled nurse coming in at two to check on his vitals. But when she leaves the room, through the open door, I see a nurse whose silhouette I recognize. I freeze the playback and stare at the screen, while a shiver runs down my spine.

I close that playback screen and pull up the corridor view for the same time code. The nurse is wearing blue hospital scrubs and seems to be heading straight for the emergency room. She's wearing gloves, a mask, and a bouffant hair cap, but a strand of blonde hair had escaped, landing on her shoulder. She's walking slowly, with a gait I recognize, straight past Donaghy's room.

From one camera feed to the next, I follow where she's going. She doesn't stop until she reaches the operating rooms, then I lose her when she enters the one where Donaghy died.

"Oh, no, please, no," I mutter in a broken, choked whisper. Gasping, I switch the feed to the operating room view and watch with my hand pressed against my mouth, breathing heavily.

On the screen, the nurse approaches the pump machine and opens the refrigerated compartment where the cardioplegia solution is stored, awaiting the next procedure. She takes out a large syringe from her pocket and takes the needle cap off. Her back is turned to the camera, but I have no doubt in my mind she's injecting whatever she brought with her into the cardioplegia solution port. Then she slips the syringe back into her pocket and leaves everything just the way it was.

I don't have much time, but this decision is an easy one to make. I hit the scissors button, and the screen prompts me to confirm I'm sure I want the segment deleted. I hit yes, and the screen turns to static, but the little square button is still there. I hit that next and import a segment from a few days earlier. The operation completes smoothly, and I breathe.

Then I remember she walked down some corridors, and probably had her car in the parking lot. One by one, I replace as many segments as I can, stopping short of deleting yet another one when Mike returns.

My hands are shaking, and I can't steady my breath.

"Were you looking for something?" he asks, finding me in the segment selection screen.

"Yes," I say, sounding calmer than I feel. "I wanted to see the video from the night before that. I remembered he was in the hospital for two days."

He takes over the mouse and easily finds the file, then starts playing it at ten times the actual speed. "What do you suspect?"

I sigh, a hint of relief starting to unknot my tense muscles. "People lie to us all the time, you know. You tell them they can't eat salt before a procedure, and they hide two bags of chips in their backpacks."

"Ah, I see." Then he smiles and says, "I thought you were looking for a cold-blooded killer." His laughter fills the room and I laugh with him, hiding the jolt of anxiety that rips through me on hearing his words. "You know, I want to be a cop some-day," he adds, and for a while, we talk about his career, while the playback takes forever to complete.

The prior night video doesn't show anything. No one came inside my patient's room, and he didn't eat any chips either.

Not that it matters. I could've found him poisoning himself with donuts sprinkled with digoxin on that video, and no way in hell I'd mention it to anyone.

There's too much at stake.

THIRTY-ONE
NAME

When I get to my office, a quarter after eight, I greet Madison and then sit at my desk, resting my forehead against my fanned fingers and my elbow on the red Donaghy file. I look at Melanie's pics, the old one on my desk since forever and the new one I brought from home last week, now in a matching silver frame. My little sister smiles at me from the photo with the eyes of a child whose dreams have come true. It's my brief escape from reality, before it hits me again.

I still can't come to terms with what I've just seen. With what I've done. I've deliberately removed evidence from a security system. A crime punishable by time in prison, right there with evidence tampering and obstruction of justice. If I get caught, I'll never see the light of day again.

Madison brings me a steaming cup of coffee and I grab it from her hands as if it were a lifesaver and I were drowning in high seas. It warms up my fingers and soothes my fraught nerves. Eager to have the caffeine flowing through my body, I blow on it briefly, then burn myself taking a sip.

I'm only half listening to Madison's review of the day's schedule, my thoughts racing, dissecting what I've just seen.

And deleted. I keep repeating to myself, over and over, that no one will ever know what I've done. It's funny how I keep digging myself deeper and deeper, but I didn't have a choice.

M storms through my door in her typical fashion, interrupting Madison's review. She waves her out unceremoniously, then leans over the desk until she's inches away from my face. "You've got one hell of a problem," she says, keeping her voice lowered. She never does that.

My stomach takes a dive. "What happened?"

"The security office rang. They know who called the State's Attorney Office." Breath gets caught in my lungs. She doesn't wait for me to ask. "Lee Chen. Can you believe it?" She slaps her hands together in a gesture of pure astonishment.

I breathe, relieved it's not about my early morning visit to the security office, then it hits me. "*Lee?*"

I didn't see that coming. I'm absolutely devastated that someone on my own team could do such a thing.

But I'm grateful to know how the storm named Paula Fuselier had started. There's nothing worse than not knowing.

M is nothing if not quick to action. "Call Lee Chen in here, stat," she shouts toward Madison. My assistant picks up the phone, while M takes a seat in front of my desk and crosses her legs. Then she shoots me a warning gaze. "Let me do the talking, all right?"

When Lee Chen comes in with Madison by his side, he's pale and looks as if he's going to get sick and throw up all over my carpet. M waves Madison off again, but she doesn't go farther than her desk, with only glass doors between here and there.

"All I need to hear from you right now is why," M says, leaning forward as if she's about to pounce. "I know you made the calls to the State's Attorney Office. I just don't know why."

Calls? There were more than one? My heart sinks. I look at Lee, deeply disheartened.

His chin is trembling and he's barely standing. "I'm so sorry," he eventually says, his words a mere whisper. "I had no choice. They caught me, you know, and my mother doesn't have a green card."

"They caught you doing what?" I ask, and M promptly glares at me for breaking her silence order.

"Just a damn DUI." He sobs with his mouth open. "But they knew about my mother. They offered a deal, and I took it. My mother can't go back to China. She'll die." He looks at me pleadingly. "I was so happy when they cleared you. Please forgive me."

"Who's 'they'?" I ask, and this time M doesn't scold me with a glare. "Who offered you the deal?"

"That prosecutor who's been coming here. Paula Fuselier."

No. I didn't hear that. It means she was out to get me long before the Donaghy surgery. But why? Goose bumps raise my flesh in sheer terror. "When was that?"

"Last year, in October."

That doesn't make any sense. "What did she have you do?"

He lowers his eyes and clasps his hands in front of him. "Call her whenever something went wrong with your cases. I only called her once, I swear. I didn't call her about the Orlowski coag mishap."

My jaw drops and I can't think of anything to say.

"You're lying," M snaps. "One thing I will never take from my employees is dishonesty."

"She called *me* the second time around. Told me to dig up something she could use from Dr. Wiley's case history. I knew what you said during the peer review, and how well you defended that decision, so I gave her your resuscitation stats. That was the second call, I swear."

M's hand lands on her forehead. I can relate... my head is spinning too. "How the hell did you hear what went on in the peer review session?"

He shrugs but doesn't raise his glance. "Everybody's talking. It's because Dr. Bolger was such a pain, and our Dr. Wiley—"

"Enough!" M shouts, raising her hand. "You'll report to the downstairs lab and take permanent third shifts until I decide what to do with you. You're free to go."

Lee grabs the door handle like a sleepwalker, then turns to me and whispers, "Please forgive me, Dr. Wiley. Just know I won't be able to forgive myself." He bows his head deeply and disappears. In the adjacent office, Madison's mouth is gaping.

M stands and I follow suit, although the room is spinning with me, faster and faster. But then M winks at me. "I'll make sure he doesn't quit on us. We need him on our side if this ever gets to trial. His testimony could prove this was a setup. Oh, and I have to speak with counsel about his mother's immigration status. If we fix that, they can't toy with him anymore." Then her smile wanes. "I suggest you figure the hell out what's going and why the State's Attorney Office is handing out deals to nail you. I don't think I want this kind of complication messing up things for my hospital. Are we clear?"

She doesn't wait for my answer, just leaves, leaving in her wake a maelstrom I can barely survive. She put me on notice, plain and simple.

Figure this mess out, or lose my tenure.

I don't even know where to begin.

THIRTY-TWO
TRUTH

I wrap up the rest of my day as quickly and effectively as I can, putting off several administrative tasks or delegating them to Madison. She's glad to help and keeps a stiff upper lip after what she learned about Chen. I can tell she's deeply upset about it. I will probably never be able to trust anyone again, but that's not at the center of my mind right now.

When I head out of the hospital, the sun's still above the horizon, a rare sight lately. It's a cloudy, gloomy day with light drizzle and a November feel, but I welcome the light of day. It does nothing to brighten my mood, though.

When I get home, I find Mom curled up on the sofa with a fashion magazine in her lap. She stands and gives me a hug and a smooch on my cheek. This time, I pull away quickly and look at her, searching in her eyes for answers so I don't have to ask the questions.

She smiles with her usual kindness and a hint of sadness, then tucks a strand of my hair behind my ear, the way she used to when I was a child. I close my eyes for a moment, wishing I was still five. When I open them, I'm still an adult, a forty-one-year-old who's struggling more than I'd ever thought possible.

I don't know how to tell her what I saw. She waits, sensing something is wrong, patiently giving me the time I need to collect my thoughts. In her eyes and the firmness of her jaw, I see the same strength I've relied on all my life.

Tears burn my eyes. "You knew," I whisper. "You knew who my patient was."

She shoots a quick glance toward the den as her smile withers. Through its open door I can see my laptop on the desk.

She holds my hand with trembling, knotty fingers and sits on the sofa with me by her side. "Yes. But do you know why it mattered?"

I swallow hard, remembering Melanie's bruised legs. Words from her autopsy report start swirling in my head. "Yes, I do."

Mom takes my frozen fingers to her face and rests her cheek against them. "Oh, sweetie, I had no idea you knew about Melanie."

"Since the first day she came to us," I whisper, unwilling to say such things out loud in the eerily silent house.

"And you didn't say anything?"

I smile through tears. "I was a dumb teenager, Mom. I heard you cry that night, and I thought you wanted to send Melanie back."

She gasps and covers her mouth with her hand. "How could you think that?"

"Just for a few days, don't worry. I guess I was afraid to lose her, that's all. She was all mine, you know. My new little sister." Mom squeezes my hand and leans back, closing her eyes. Sitting like that, she seems so vulnerable and frail. I haven't notice that frailty about her before... it had crept up on me when I wasn't paying attention. "I understand why you cried that night. But why were you arguing with Dad?"

"We weren't arguing," she says, softly. "We were debating what to do. It was obvious the poor child had been sexually assaulted. We wanted to have her examined but didn't want her traumatized again. When I gave her that bath and I saw those bruises, I thought I was going to die. She saw me crying, poor thing, and she was so ashamed. She begged me not to be mad with her." She wipes a tear with the tip of her finger. "Can you imagine that?"

"So, what did you do?" I've been asking myself those questions for almost thirty years, but never dared to ask her.

"Bill sedated her. He took a big risk, but he didn't want her traumatized again. We did the examination ourselves, while you were sleeping. You can't imagine..." Her breath shatters and she takes a moment before she speaks again. "The next day, we went to the police. They spoke with Melanie, but she refused to say anything. She was so ashamed and afraid, as if it was her fault somehow."

I never knew they took Melanie to the police. No matter how hard I rack my brain, I don't remember her ever being gone from my side, but it was possible; I'm not doubting that. I just wish they'd told me.

"They investigated her foster parents, but without her testimony and an official medical examination, there was nothing they could do."

"You could've sedated her again for the medical exam—"

"It didn't matter," she replies, bitterly. "Too much time had passed to be able to retrieve any usable DNA, and anyway, DNA wasn't on everyone's lips back then, like it is today. They had nothing." Her lips quiver for a moment. "But we learned her foster father's name. Caleb Donaghy. Not a name I'd ever forget." Her voice turns harsh when she says it. "The police looked at several foster parents, because she had a few. We knew her bruises were too fresh to have been anyone else but the last foster family she had, mere days before we adopted her. It was that and the fact that she'd run away from her foster family. Twice, actually. And no one bothered to ask her why, or to just look at that poor baby's bruises."

"What if that monster raped other girls too? Pedophiles don't change. They don't just stop. Did anyone bother to ask the other girls he fostered?"

She shakes her head under the burden of her powerlessness and guilt. "There was nothing we could do. Bill even hired a lawyer, who in turn hired a private investigator, hoping to catch him doing something illegal, so we could get him kept away from children." She squeezes my hand. "We tried, sweetie. It kept me up for years and haunted my nightmares." She sniffles and looks away for a brief moment, then back at me. "It took your father four years of begging people to listen, of making phone calls and asking for favors, to get that man removed from the foster parent directory. That's all we could do."

A beat of silence, haunted by yesterday's monsters and today's heartbreaking reckonings. Somewhere between us, in the transparent space of my memories, my little sister smiles at me, encouraging me, telling me everything will be all right.

"Then, one night, as I was bringing you some tea, you were working on your patients' case notes," she continues, telling the story in softly spoken words, the voice of someone who's at the end of a long, exhausting road. "His name was right there on your screen. The name that has haunted me every day of my life since Melanie. Through some screwed-up twist of fate, he had to be your patient." She lets a long sigh escape her chest and looks at me with visible anguish. "I'm so sorry he had to die on your table, sweetie." She stifles a sob that makes her chest heave. "But he had to die."

She wraps her arm around my shoulders, and I let myself be drawn closer, burying my face in her hair and taking in her perfume.

"Yes, he had to die," I whisper, then hold her as she sobs, our tears mingled together. "I made sure of it."

THIRTY-THREE
GUILT

Five short words, and they free my soul more than I thought possible. Keeping this secret from Mom has been weighing me down immensely.

I bring her a glass of wine after struggling a little to uncork the sweaty bottle of Pinot Noir. Then I pour myself one, filling it generously, and join Mom on the sofa.

I need some time alone to realize how I feel about all this. The events of the past three weeks have made me wonder who I am and what cloth I'm cut from.

I consider Mom and me, sitting on our sofa, drinking wine, and ask myself, *Who are we, really? How does what we've done change who we are and how we'll live, going forward?*

It's not an easy question.

Mom takes a sip of wine and sets the glass down on the coffee table. "Tell me, how did you know who your patient was?"

My eyes stare into nothing for a while. "I knew something was wrong the day we adopted her. She had those bruises... but I was a kid myself. I didn't know what to make of it. I thought she'd been beaten or had hurt herself somehow. You cried all that night, and I was terrified for a while that something was awfully wrong." I bring my wineglass close to my lips but don't touch it yet. "It was, only I didn't know exactly what." I smile at Mom with gratitude. "Then Melanie started going to therapy, and I drew my first half-baked conclusion that she'd been beaten or abused."

"I had no idea you were so aware of things," Mom whispers, staring at her arthritic hands. She's wringing them slowly, rubbing the pain out of them as much as she can. "You should've said something."

Yes, I should have. Children, especially teenagers, can be stupid like that. They carry the weight of the world on their shoulders unnecessarily, or at least prematurely. "Then we went to the park one day, and she started crying when she saw him sitting on a bench. I remembered his birthmark, nothing else. It's unique."

"That's why she didn't want to go to the park anymore? She cried her eyes out one Sunday when I wanted to take you girls." I nod. She puts a hand on her chest as if to steady her heart. "I wish I'd known."

"I didn't know his name then. I didn't know who he was until I saw that birthmark again, when he was lying on my table with his chest wide open." I shake my head, the memory of that day still raw in my mind. "A TV show I saw when I was about sixteen opened my eyes to the possibility of Melanie having been raped by him. She fit the symptoms, her behavior the day we brought her home, everything pointed to the fact her bruises were more than just a beating." I play with the wine in my glass, making it swirl around, reflecting the light with glimmers of ruby. The restlessness of the liquid matches the upheaval in my heart. "Do you remember how scared she was of Dad? She didn't want him to touch her or hold her hand."

"It took Melanie about a year to understand your father was

nothing like that man. The day she reached out for his hand, he was crying tears of joy."

Bittersweet to know that about Melanie and Dad, a tiny, precious piece of her brief life with us I'd somehow missed. I feel happy for both of them, decades too late. The devastation of the time and lives we lost gets to me, making me tremble like a leaf in November wind.

"I promised her, Mom," I whisper in a tearful voice that doesn't seem mine. "That day in the park, I promised her I'd keep her safe forever." I shake my head in disbelief, reliving memories too painful to put in words. "She slept in my bed that night and so many after that, and I swore that man would never come close to her again."

"I'm so happy she had you by her side." Mom squeezes my hand with shaky, gnarled fingers. "Doing what you did for her. You were her guardian angel."

I take her hand in mine after I put the wineglass onto the coffee table. "But I *wasn't* there, Mom," I confess. "I promised her that man would never hurt her again... and he did."

"No, sweetheart, it wasn't your fault." Tears spring from her creased eyelids, squeezed shut as I speak.

"It was." I raise my voice. "I should've known. The day she died, I was old enough to know. I was in premed, for crying out loud. I was an adult, dating, having sex, understanding things way better than she could." I lower my head to hide my tears. Loose strands of my hair fall on my face, and she tucks them away as if I were a child.

"No, baby, it wasn't your fault."

"I should've known," I repeat stubbornly, not allowing her to forgive me when I haven't yet forgiven myself. I pull my hand from hers and stand, then start pacing the floor like a caged animal. My fists are clenched and held in front of my chest as if I'm getting ready to fight for my life, but I'm fighting *with* myself, not for myself. "When she told me she was going out on her first date, I was thrilled for her. I was so happy, thinking she'd have a chance at a real life, with a boyfriend, and later a husband, a family, some kids of her own." I scoff, stomping my foot down and glaring at Mom as if she's the one who screwed up. "You know what I did before she left that night? I did her hair and makeup. Her *hair*, Mom!"

She listens to me and looks at me with kindness and understanding and immense sadness. She doesn't ask anything, doesn't rush me. She's just there for me, like she's always been.

"I let her have my circle skirt, the blue one, and my white blouse with ruffles. She liked that skirt so much, do you remember?" She nods and wipes a tear from the corner of her eye. "She was twirling and twirling, laughing so hard you could hear her from downstairs. And then I did her hair." The smile that had lit my eyes remembering her swirl in an undulating wave of blue chiffon dies, snuffed by anger. "It didn't cross my mind for a single moment to warn her about boys."

The weight of what I failed to do is so overwhelming I still struggle to talk about it. I pace around some more, trying to find the right words.

"Her boyfriend was a year older than her and nice enough, but still a boy. He was going to make a move sooner or later, right? Kiss her, maybe touch her legs, her breasts... I knew that! And I didn't think to tell her that not all men are the same, not all of them are Caleb Donaghy." I gesture angrily with my hands. "I still don't know how to live with it."

Mom stares at me with eyes rounded in agony, flooded with tears. Her trembling hand covers her mouth again, silencing a soundless wail.

"What's worse is we never told you where she was going. She wanted to keep it a secret, and I was..." My voice breaks and I have to steady myself before speaking again. "I was so deliriously happy to see her dance like that, getting ready for her first date, a little in love with a boy. I wanted so desperately to believe she was fine, healed, that maybe she didn't remember what that man did to her when she was little." I breathe deeply as the darker memories invade my mind, mercilessly ripping me to shreds of guilt and grief and anger.

"Come, sit here with me," Mom says, but I'm not ready yet. There's a tremor in my legs that drives me to run, but there's nowhere to go. For as long as I'll live, I'll have to carry the weight.

"I should've talked to her..." I suppress a sob that swells my chest. "I still can't go upstairs to her room, you know. We were so happy there. I can still see her laughing. I close my eyes and I see her dance like a dervish, twirling in my blue skirt, flapping her arms as if she wanted to fly. Spinning and spinning and spinning until she'd run out of breath and let herself fall on the floor in a sea of ruffles and colors and happiness." I swallow hard, unable to stop but hurting with every word I say. "Then I remember her body, the weight of it, how it felt in my arms, cold, lifeless, so heavy. I lifted her up, but it was too late. I was only gone ten minutes, just to take a shower."

I stop my pacing, looking at her bedroom door, a sliver of glistening oak at the top of the stairs. There are shreds of dark memories I don't put into words. My shrieks for help when I found her, hanging from the bedpost. Dad's rushed footfalls, then his stunned look as he took her inert body from my arms, prying my hands open to let her go. Mom's heart-wrenching wails, guttural and coarse. Somewhere in that whirlwind, my own voice, calling out her name, refusing to let go.

"I didn't even notice how upset she was when she came back. I would've never left her alone. I never thought she'd end her life. I keep reliving those hours, that day, and wonder how I missed it."

Another tear rolls down my mother's cheek. "Oh, baby... you didn't. I remember it perfectly, and she didn't seem upset. We talked with her boyfriend a few days after the funeral, and he told us she suddenly started crying while they were watching a movie and wanted to go home. Probably he touched her, like you said, triggering all sorts of negative emotions and memories she'd repressed, or perhaps it was something in the movie. But none of this is your fault. Caleb Donaghy killed our Melanie the day he first assaulted her."

"You know, I tell myself that all the time. It's easier than looking at myself in the mirror, knowing what a terrible thing I did. I could've spoken to her, maybe taken her on a double date at first or asked her therapist how best to handle this. Yes, Caleb Donaghy killed my sister, I have no doubt in my mind, but I was one hell of a clueless, selfish bystander, letting it happen right in front of my eyes."

Mom's chin thrusts forward just a little. She reaches out for her glass of wine. "I'm glad he's dead," she whispers.

I sit by her side and take my glass from the coffee table. The wine is warm now, but I don't care. "So am I."

"There might be video," she whispers, looking at her wineglass. "Of me, you know, in the hospital."

"It's gone," I reply casually, as if I'm telling her I took the trash out. "Almost all of it. The worst parts, anyway."

I look at her and see no worry in her eyes, just peace. I haven't seen her at peace in a long time. "Now all we have to do is be perfectly quiet until the storm passes."

She nods, her blonde hair waving on her shoulders. She always had such beautiful hair.

I have to ask, otherwise I'll be spending countless nights tossing and turning. "What was in the syringe?"

She's not offended by my question, just surprised, as if I should have figured it out by myself. "Potassium, what else?"

I raise my eyes in silent gratitude as Derreck's car pulls into the driveway, shooting slivers of headlights between the drapes. The cardioplegia solution was also potassium, but a lower concentration. No one could ever detect the initial concentration based on the autopsy of the body, after I'd flushed that heart with saline for two minutes. An exceedingly high concentration of potassium kept it from starting again, effectively poisoning it during the procedure.

I raise my glass and whisper, "To justice."

Mom raises hers. "And to Melanie."

When Derreck walks in, he finds us tearful and holding hands on the sofa. His brows ruffle with worry. "What's going on?"

Mom answers calmly. "Nothing to worry about. Just girl talk, and we got a little mushy reminiscing."

He looks at me as if asking the question again without using words. I smile at the man I'm so in love with. "Nothing, babe, we're okay."

I'm not sure how much of what happened today I should tell him. Some secrets are not mine to share.

I don't know what will happen, while this Paula Fuselier seems so adamant on bringing me down. She could find the original cardioplegia solution bag, the one Mom injected with potassium. Do they retain such used consumables after patients' deaths? I realize how little I know about this. Maybe the cardioplegia bag is now at the Cook County medical examiner's office, on some forensic lab table. Basic analysis would show the solution concentration was wrong. From there, they could look at the videos and if they looked hard enough, they could find the recordings I didn't delete. Then Mike, the newly appointed shift manager, would casually mention I was there in the dead of the night, looking at videos, and that he left me alone just for a few minutes.

One thing I do know, and it terrifies me.

Tonight might be the last night we spend together.

THIRTY-FOUR
VIDEO

The TV is on and we're back on the sofa, after having a light dinner Derreck fixed for us—a delicious Greek salad with kalamata olives and lots of thyme, served with saltine crackers and a cheese omelet.

I didn't eat much, my thoughts filling me with anxiety so unbearable I can barely stand being around my family. I recite the FEAR acronym in my mind, molding it into a secret mantra, hoping it will make it all go away. *False evidence appearing real. That's what anxiety is.*

Then maybe that's not what drives the shivers down my spine. My evidence is as real as can be, and cops could be banging on my door any moment now.

As long as Paula Fuselier is continuing her investigation, we're all at risk.

On the surface, we're so calm and seemingly relaxed, watching TV together with glasses of wine in our hands. Derreck tops the wine from a second bottle of Pinot Noir he uncorks with ease. He starts with mine and I hold the glass out until he fills it almost to the brim. Alcohol is a no-no for anxiety, but it takes my edge off. And I don't have anxiety... I have a legitimate concern for my safety, my mother's safety, our future; our lives, even.

We're watching a crime show. I rarely have time for that kind of thing and it'd already started when I turned on the TV. It's more Mom's taste than mine. The show makes the viewer root for the cops, depicting the killer as a contemptible, despicable bad guy. *Is that what I am? What Mom is?* If other people watched the show of my life, would they root for Paula Fuselier? Or would they agree a monster had been kept from harming other girls? It seems wine does nothing to alleviate my crisis of identity.

There's a commercial break, and Derreck uses it to get a bowl of pretzels. He's probably still hungry. Unlike us, his stomach isn't churning with fear at the thought of cops barging through the door any minute.

Another ad begins, and I recognize the soundtrack. It's one of Derreck's, the one they keep showing, about his commitment to cut crime rates in half and make Chicago a safe place again. I know every detail, so I close my eyes and escape it, tending to my inner monsters for a moment, pleading with them to let me breathe.

"How's it going?" Mom asks, as Derreck returns. "Are you winning?" I look at her, surprised at her interest. She's smiling, seemingly completely at ease, as if nothing has happened. "What are the polls saying?"

He's beaming, despite visible tiredness around his eyes. "I'm the leading candidate as of right now, ahead of the incumbent by seven percent. Seven is not much but... it's a good place to be at the beginning of April." He takes her hand to his lips like a perfect gentleman. "I couldn't've done it without you. Your financial and moral support have been amazing."

"Ah, rubbish," she replies, smiling widely. I can tell she's flattered by his words. "You're the best son I could've hoped for, Derreck. I have every confidence you're going to win this thing."

He raises his glass. "Hear, hear." We all take a sip, while I try to silence my inner voices. He might win this, unless his wife gets arrested, his mother-in-law too.

"I'd be more than happy to host a fundraiser for you," Mom offers. "I can get this place cleaned up nicely, hang some bunting from the staircase and the second-floor handrail. Maybe up there too." She points at the tall living room windows. "Memorial Day would be a good time to do that, wouldn't you agree?" He nods and fidgets a little, shifting in his seat. He seems a bit uncomfortable, but Mom doesn't seem to notice. "I know a few doctors with deep pockets who'd really support a strong, anti-crime stance."

"That's wonderful," he replies, just as the ad ends. He seems uncomfortable talking about this with Mom, and that's a little strange. But I don't worry much about it: we all have off days, and I have other, more acute things bothering me.

"I didn't get a chance to tell you, I found out who called the State's Attorney Office about my patient," I say, trying to keep my voice casual but sounding tense, almost grating. They both look at me intently. Derreck's brow creases. "It was Lee Chen, out of all people. He's my surgical nurse," I clarify for Derreck, who might not remember.

"So, someone did call the SA's Office, huh?" he mutters, more to himself. For some weird reason, he seems almost relieved. He downs the rest of his wine and grabs the bottle to top off his glass.

"Yes, someone did, but seems Lee didn't have a choice. He was blackmailed into doing it."

"What?" A dark cloud washes over Derreck's face. Mom seems to be holding her breath.

"They caught Lee with a DUI and he was offered a deal," I say, noticing how every word I say is making Derreck angry. "That's the part I don't understand yet, but M is looking into it with our legal counsel. Lee said he was offered the deal in exchange for any incriminating information about me, *months* before my patient died. It happened last October."

Derreck springs to his feet and rushes into the kitchen. There, he opens the fridge and stares inside as if looking for something. After a long moment, he comes back with a bottle of Grey Goose and a couple of shot glasses. He puts them on the table and offers me one, but I decline, again noticing how enraged he is. He fills a glass with vodka and downs it in one swig. Then he fills it again.

"What's wrong, baby?" I ask, but I already know. Finding out your wife has been targeted by the State's Attorney Office like a mobster can't be easy. In moments like this one I wish he'd just call it quits with politics and choose something peaceful as well as meaningful to do with his life. But I'm being selfish.

"Everything is wrong," he mumbles, rubbing his forehead. "I'll start making some calls." I raise my hand as if to stop him, but he counteracts with another hand gesture. "I have to. This is getting out of control and can't continue. It's my career, okay, but it's your life, *our* life. I can't just lie down and take it."

Before I can answer, my phone chimes with a message alert, but I choose to ignore it. A moment later, it chimes again. It could be an emergency.

I reach for my phone and find a message from M. She has never texted me before, in all the years we've worked together. Her first message says, *Watch this right now* and there's a link. Her second message simply repeats the word, *Now* followed by three exclamation marks.

"What is it?" Mom asks.

"M sent me a video. I don't know what it's about." I realize I'm afraid to open the link.

Derreck brings his head next to mine. "I want to see it too," he says, "unless it's something medical."

Between the two of them, I can't delay. I tap the link and it loads a news article with an embedded video. Dated four days ago, the article speaks of an arrest made in the case of a young boy's murder. I've heard about it before, I realize: the boy was going to testify in another murder trial. I look briefly at Derreck, wondering how this has anything to do with me. Why is M sending me this?

He's pale and his forehead is covered in tiny beads of sweat. He's staring at the small screen with poorly disguised horror written all over his face: the kind people exhibit when watching a deadly car crash. He's trying his best to not show it, I can tell, but it's there, in his dilated pupils, the tension in his jaw, the hands clasped so tightly together his knuckles are turning white.

"Hit play, sweetie," Mom says.

I do it, wondering what Derreck could be anticipating with such angst. The video is a press conference held by none other than Paula Fuselier, in front of a decrepit high-rise somewhere downtown, on a street I'd never drive on. It's not a large gathering of newspeople. She's answering questions about the victim being a material witness her office failed to protect. Better said, she's *not* answering those questions, deflecting poorly and contradicting herself.

Then the video cuts to Derreck answering questions about crime and his mayoral campaign, from the same group of people.

He was there, with that woman.

My breath gets caught in my chest and my heart starts pumping hard under the flush of adrenaline. I watch the video, afraid of what each new second will bring. On the tiny screen, Derreck answers the media's questions, but then it cuts to a distant view of Derreck and Paula talking: just a couple of seconds, not more. Seeing the woman who's been trying to bring me down standing so close to Derreck hits me like a fist in my stomach. He seems distant in the video, angry even, and a little stiff. Usually, when he wants to make people comfortable, he leans forward a little bit, so he doesn't tower over them. With her, he's as upright as he can be.

When I look up from the phone screen, I see Mom staring at me with a pained expression in her eyes. "Who's that, sweetheart?"

I look at Derreck, but his head is lowered still. "It's the assistant state's attorney I keep telling you about. Paula Fuselier."

"Oh, you know her?" Mom asks Derreck innocently. "I must've missed that somehow."

When he looks up at me, he's perfectly calm, composed, reassuring. "I told you I know *of* her. We run into each other at the occasional event. I can't help who I find at crime scenes and press conferences from the State's Attorney Office. But I offered to speak with her, and you said no. The offer is still on the table."

Any suspicions I might've had wane and die. He did tell me all that. "No, I still think M would fire me if I meddled in this in any way."

Derreck seems relieved. Maybe one day he'll tell me what about.

Today is not the day to grill him. But there's one question I can ask: not of him, but of M.

I switch my phone to the messenger screen and respond to her message. *How did you get this?* I ask.

Moments later, I get her bone-chilling reply.

Anonymous sender.

THIRTY-FIVE
A KISS

No one stopped Paula from entering Anne's office that Wednesday morning. She'd done her homework well. Anne and her busybody minion, Madison, were in surgery until about eleven. Paula had about half an hour to kill, but didn't want to miss the opportunity to catch the surgeon right after the procedure.

She didn't have a good plan. She didn't have any plan, really, just an idea, a last hope to turn things around, based on the emotional distress Anne must've suffered seeing her beloved husband chatting and doing press conferences with the woman who'd been trying to destroy her. Then, when she was at her most vulnerable, she could interrogate the surgeon one more time, and hopefully, this time she'd cave.

It was thin. So thin it didn't really exist, less than gossamer in the wind, but she had nothing else to go on. If this plan failed to deliver, Hobbs would see to it that she'd be disbarred, and her career would be over. As for Derreck... he was history. If he'd ever loved her, that was over and had been for a while. She'd been incredibly wrong about him. Derreck Bourke liked to be straddled in bed, but nowhere else. He'd thrown her off his back like a wild, untamable bronc.

Her entire strategy had imploded, leaving nothing behind it but the ashes of her life. Slipping her hand inside her pinstripe jacket pocket, she felt the cold grip of her gun. At least she had that... One way or another, Anne Wiley was not going to get away with what she'd done.

She sat at Anne's desk and propped her feet up. She hated everything about the room: the floor-to-ceiling window behind her flooding it with natural light, the bookcase double-stacked with well-thumbed medical volumes, the faint smell of lavender air freshener and coffee, the fine leather of her chair. Derreck looked at her from an eleven-by-fourteen framed portrait on an upper bookcase shelf. He was smiling lovingly in the picture, his beautiful face relaxed and a few years younger.

He'd never smiled at her that way.

Some people just have it all. Even if they don't deserve any of it.

A red file with the hospital's logo was the only item on the desk that was work related, apart from a laptop. She lifted the lid and tried to log in but failed; it was password protected. No surprise there. But she left it fired up and open: one more thing to throw Anne off emotionally. If she had anything to hide on that computer, Paula would know about it from Anne's reaction.

Other than those two items, everything else was personal. A large, lacquered pine cone, who knew from where or what significance it had. Nevertheless, if Anne kept it there, it must've been important to her. She felt the urge to stomp it under the soles of her high-heeled shoes.

Two, small, framed pictures were set on the desk toward the left. Paula looked at them for a long moment, taking in every bitter detail. She hated Anne's face even as a teenager. Who the hell gave her the right to laugh in the sun like that, with her long, blonde curls and her pearly white teeth straightened to perfection? She picked up the photo and stared at Anne's face, wishing she could scratch her eyes out, even if only in the picture. A thin layer of glass protected it, and she wasn't ready to start breaking things just yet. She put it back on the desk, gently, unnervingly so, unable to take her eyes off it. Then she looked at the other and froze. Transported, she picked it up and brought it closer, breathless, slack-jawed.

Approaching footsteps outside the door interrupted Paula's thoughts. She put the picture down and leaned back comfortably in the seat, expecting Anne. Instead, Derreck stormed in.

Instinctively, she put her hand in her pocket, feeling the grip of her gun, clutching it tightly. If it was the last thing she could do, she would pull that trigger.

"Son of a bitch," Derreck muttered, staring at her from the middle of the room. "I can't believe what you're doing, Paula. You're throwing your life away. And for what? A fucking affair?"

"That's all I was to you? An affair?" Paula whispered the words softly, hiding her emotions the best she could.

Derreck stared at her for a moment. "What are you doing here?"

"My job," she replied coldly, walking around the desk and stopping a couple of feet from Derreck. She could smell his aftershave, the scent of it bringing back memories of passionate nights and broken promises. "Your wife broke the law, Derreck, and I have no reason to keep cutting her any slack, since you and I are over." He didn't flinch, just stared at her as if she were crazy. She hated that, almost as badly as she hated being left behind, discarded like yesterday's trash. She inhaled slowly, filling her lungs with air to keep the searing, aching frustration at bay. "What are *you* doing here?" She smiled the way she used to when they were both naked under the covers. "I didn't expect the pleasure of your company."

He scoffed and made a dismissive hand gesture to show her that wasn't the case. "I went to your office to find you, and your investigator, Adam Costilla, told me you were here, against direct and specific orders from Hobbs. He begged me to stop you from doing whatever it is you're doing." He ran his hand through his hair quickly, nervously. "What the hell *are* you doing, Paula?"

She stared into his cold, blue eyes looking for the tiniest trace of warmth, of lust even. She would gladly take lust over the hateful, arctic stare. Maybe it had been just an affair and she'd been wrong all along, but it had been good while it lasted; for a little while at least, she'd felt lucky and beautiful and wanted and spoiled, just like his damned wife must've felt every day. Then it all went away, because of Anne. And she didn't even know about the affair.

Well, maybe it was about time she found out. A tiny smile bloomed on Paula's lips.

"I heard you blackmailed her coworker to rat on her," Derreck hissed, shooting careful glances left and right. "What the hell was that about?"

She laughed bitterly, keeping her eyes on the corridor through the glass walls. Stepping a little to the left and turning, she drew closer to Derreck. He kept his distance, but in doing so, his back was turned to the glass wall. He wouldn't be able to see Anne approaching.

"Don't tell me it's the first deal you've heard about in your entire legal career. State's attorneys always waive smaller charges in return for information on more dangerous criminals."

"And that's my wife to you? A dangerous criminal?"

"How little you know," Paula replied calmly, shooting a quick glance at the clock on the wall. Anne was due back any minute. If Madison arrived first, then there would be trouble and her plan would go to hell once more. "You don't know anything about the woman you married, Mr. Mayor."

"Don't call me that."

"Changed your mind? Are you not running anymore?" She tilted her head and played with a strand of her hair, batting her eyelashes, shamelessly flirting.

He ignored her advances, but the situation seemed to be getting to him. He tugged at his tie knot and rested his hands on his hips. "Paula, let me tell you what will happen. You will leave with me now and stop coming here. Hell, if you have a damn *heart* attack you don't come here for medical assistance! This, whatever this is, ends now."

"Ooh, I love a man in charge," she whispered, just as she caught a glimpse of Anne approaching her office. She stood on the tip of her toes and wrapped her arms around his neck, then kissed his lips passionately.

He tried to pull away, but she'd interlocked her fingers behind his head and held his mouth close to hers while she arched her back, grinding against him, her body touching his from head to toe in what would've appeared to be a heated embrace.

He broke free of her, shoving her away, but not before Anne had seen what Paula wanted her to see.

The door opened, and Anne entered. She seemed pale. Paula smiled, licking her lips lasciviously. At least she'd scored this much of a win. For a long, delicious moment, she took in the intense pain she saw in her eyes, absorbing it like much-needed sustenance after decades of famine.

"What's going on here?" the surgeon asked, looking at Derreck, who was wiping his mouth with his sleeve. "What does this mean, Derreck?" Her voice slipped toward higher tones and trembled a little.

Paula took the gun out of her pocket and pointed it at Anne's chest, turning carefully so she wouldn't be seen from the hallway. "Sit down, Dr. Wiley."

THIRTY-SIX
GUNPOINT

I feel... *gutted.*

I never thought it was possible so much pain could strike so suddenly and intensely, and still leave me standing, drawing breath.

There was something in the way this woman touched my husband—the way her body met his as if they were old acquaintances—a something I know will now be forever etched in my mind. He pushed her away, yes, but only after a split second's hesitation. If Paula Fuselier had never touched my husband before, she'd be shoved away forcefully, her back slamming against the bookcase, knocking the breath out of her lungs. She wouldn't be smirking at me with the air of a victorious conqueror, a pillager laying waste to my life.

Not my Derreck. No. This can't be happening.

The gun in Paula Fuselier's hand doesn't scare me that much. Other things do, like losing Derreck's love and devotion, our life together. The way we were until this morning is gone forever and will never return, even if I try to forget, forgive, or do whatever I can to salvage what's left of our love.

My knees feel weak, and I struggle to remain standing.

Where's Madison? What's taking her so long? One look through that glass wall and she'll know there's trouble. She'll call security, and this will be over in seconds.

I remember wondering some time ago how people know when it's the last time for anything. A peaceful dinner. Making love. Saying hello to a loved one. They simply don't. There's no such thing as a premonition. I would've sensed this nightmare coming. I would've sensed Melanie's decision to end her life. I would've sensed *something,* not just let myself be pinballed through life, out of control and unable to change my direction, drifting and drowning on endlessly stormy waters.

A chilling thought brings a shiver to my spine. I *did* feel something last night, watching that video. Maybe I felt something before, but decided to not pay attention to it, discarding the input of my sixth sense, refusing to recognize its value. It's atavistic, a remnant of that gut feeling that kept our ancestors from stepping on snakes or crossing into the path of a mountain lion. There are no mountain lions in Chicago, but the gut doesn't know that. It will still speak to us about other snakes. If we listen to it.

"Sit down," Paula says, gesturing with the gun toward my office chair. I walk around the desk slowly, my knees still uncertain.

Once I sit, I feel a bit more confident, the chair supporting my weight. My knees can be weak all they want now; it doesn't matter. All I know is *I* can't afford to be weak, not anymore.

"What do you want, Paula?" I stare directly at her and see the eyes of an emotionally disturbed person, frantic and jumpy; as if I needed to confirm the diagnosis, and the gun aimed at my chest isn't enough.

I can't look at Derreck though. I can't bring myself to make eye contact, but I can sense he's looking at me.

He takes a step closer to Paula and touches her shoulder, probably trying to deflect her attention from me. "You should probably know I filed a sexual harassment complaint against you this morning. I met with your boss, Mitch Hobbs. He was very interested to hear what I had to say. Whatever you pretend you're investigating here is over."

She squints with rage and points the gun at him, then closes the distance between them, pushing the gun against his chest.

Oh, no. I hold my breath. If she pulls the trigger now, the bullet will pierce his heart and he'll be dead before his body reaches the floor.

"You son of a bitch," she whispers slowly, one word at a time. "I'll end you."

Holding on to the edge of the desk for support, I stand and ask, "What do you want?" An immense sadness chokes me right then, at the worst possible moment, bringing a slight tremble to my voice.

She turns her attention and the aim of her gun to me, away from Derreck's chest. I breathe.

"It's right in front of you, and you still don't see it, do you?" Her voice is loaded with such immense hatred it makes my skin crawl. What have I ever done to this woman?

Instinctively, I look at Derreck. He's in front of me, the only thing in front of me I still care about.

"Not him." She laughs. "Her." She points at one of Melanie's pictures, the one I've only recently brought from home. I stare at it in disbelief, but she reaches over the desk and picks it up.

"Take your hands off my sister's photo," I say in a low, menacing voice.

"*Your* sister?" She laughs hysterically, the barrel of her gun moving up and down with her cackles. "I tried to take something from you the way you took from me. I waited for a year for someone to die on your table, for you to make the smallest mistake, so I could come after what's yours the way you took what was mine." A beat of tense silence. "Melanie!"

My mouth gapes in disbelief. "Melanie?" I whisper, a million questions in that name.

"For twenty-five years I looked for my sister after you came and took her away from me. Twenty-five years, and all I had was the memory of your face with your blonde curls and white teeth and carefree smile. Not your name, not anything that could've helped me find her, just your face. I studied law, thinking I'd become a prosecutor and get her adoption records unsealed. But no, even as an ASA, I couldn't talk the judge into letting me see who took her from me."

"Who was Melanie to you?" I ask, although the icicles in my blood tell me I already know the answer.

"She was *my* sister! *Mine,* not yours. Not yours to take!" She raises her voice, but I hear distinctive undertones of pain. "She was the only family I still had. Damn you, Anne Wiley!"

A flurry of thoughts swirl in my head. I feel dizzy and nauseated. The woman pointing her gun at me is Melanie's sister. Her own flesh and blood. For a split second, I want to hug her and hold her in my arms, as if a part of Melanie could somehow come back to me after all these years.

Then a cherished memory creeps up on me, its altered meaning chilling my blood once more.

I recall Melanie's letter to Santa in the first year she spent Christmas with us. She wished to spend time with her sister; to sing songs with her; to brush her hair with her new, bejeweled brush; to sleep with her sister on Christmas night. And I was thrilled, enchanted beyond belief, thinking her letter was about me.

It wasn't.

She was asking Santa to let her see her real sister once more.

My heart breaks at the memory of little Melanie, giving me her letter to mail with such high hopes in her eyes. I wanted to believe she loved *me* that much. Now I just wish she would've said something.

"I never knew Melanie had a sister," I whisper, fighting back tears. "Nobody told us. They just said she kept running away from her foster home, and some other girl helped her."

With a lopsided, sad smile that looks more like a grimace, Paula puts the framed photo in front of me and taps with her fingernail against the glass, next to Melanie's face. "That was me. See the resemblance now? It was right in front of you, and you never saw it."

My knees are shaking again, and I have to sit, slowly, unwilling to let go of the desk until I feel the chair beneath me. I take the photo and bring it close to my eyes, studying every little detail I already know by heart. In the forefront is Melanie, the day we adopted her, laughing and looking straight at us. In the background, several other children are playing, running; some are crouched on the ground, playing in the dirt. But one girl, about twelve, is looking at Melanie and us from near the trunk of a tree. She has a few loose strands of long, brown hair on her face, and her full lips are pouting. There's immense sadness in her facial expression, sadness I've noticed before and discarded, thinking it must've been because this girl didn't get adopted, but Melanie did.

I was right, but, oh, so wrong.

The woman in front of me has that girl's lips, only a little thinner now and covered with glossy, pink lip stain. Her hair is the exact same shade of brown and still long, but done neatly in an elegant, professional style. And her eyes, the same shade of brown as Melanie's, are tinged with sadness and flooded with rage.

"Twenty-five years of searching, of asking, of pounding the pavement looking for you, so I could see my sister again." Her voice is cold now, factual, the emotion gone, the rage still there. "Then, one day, as I'm stuck in traffic on the interstate by the West Loop, I see you. Smiling with those perfect teeth of yours, telling me about life from a full-size highway billboard." She chuckles bitterly. "I nearly drove into a truck that day, trying to make out your name from that distance, Dr. Anne Wiley."

My heart breaks for her, although she's made my life hell. "I had no idea—"

"Shut the hell up," she snaps, making a threatening gesture with the gun. "Do you think I care about anything you have to say?" I pull back, dismayed. "First you took my Melanie, then you killed her!"

I stare at her with eyes wide in shock. Derreck is pacing in place, rubbing his forehead forcefully as if to smooth out his brow. I signal him to keep his distance.

"We didn't—"

"You had *no* idea what she was going through," she shouts, leaning over the desk until she's inches away from my face. I can feel her heated breath on my skin. I instinctively pull back, but that only makes her angrier. "Twenty-five years of searching, then I finally found you," she says, "your address, your hospital, everything there was to know about your perfect little life. Then I ran a document search for your address and last name, only to find Melanie's death certificate." Rage washes over her face in waves: unresolved grief, bitterness, heartbreak. "Can you imagine?" she asks, looking straight at me, her eyes filling with tears. "I'd even bought a plush teddy for her, just like the one you didn't let her take when you stole her from me." Her lips are trembling with stifled sobs. "Five years, that's how long she lasted with you." She stands and straightens, regaining a measure of self-control, of calm, but she's anything but. "That day I swore I'd rip everything you have from your life, and crush you with my own hands after you've lost it all."

Each word she says is a dagger that stabs through my heart. Everything I thought I knew about Melanie was wrong. My parents would never have separated sisters at adoption; they would've taken them both, and I would have loved having a second sister. If we only knew.

Remembering Melanie's desperate cries when just she was loaded into our family car, before leaving the orphanage, is heart-wrenching now that I understand why. Her sudden bouts of sadness, especially in her first two or three years with us, the way she looked out the window sometimes... it all paints a different picture now that I know about Paula.

Paula should be satisfied: she has ripped almost everything from my life, the things I loved the most. Derreck... and now Melanie. My memories of her are recast under the discoloring shadow of *what if* and *who knew*.

"You really had no idea," Paula scoffs. Probably she reads my pain on my face. "How ignorant can you be?" She looks at me as if I am worthless, a piece of trash in her way. "But I don't care about that. You still killed her, whether you knew she had a sister or not."

I look at her with sadness. "We tried our best to make her happy. She had therapy, everything she needed, a good school—"

"You didn't understand what she was going through!" she shouts, slamming her fist against the desk. "How could you know? If it doesn't happen to you, you can never understand. But I did. I could've been there for her, helped her cope."

Her words ripple through my mind, seeding doubt and guilt beyond what I already carried. Could she be right? Had we not adopted Melanie, would Paula have understood her struggles better than I did?

Either way, she has the right to know.

"We knew," I say, quietly. "We found out about the abuse on her first night at home."

Paula's right hand, still holding the gun, drops a few inches. "You knew?" A sob shudders through her body. She breathes it off, then her rage returns. "I don't care, like I don't really care about your stupid patient. But for Melanie's death, you're going to pay." The hand holding the gun takes aims at my chest again, firm and steady.

"Please, put the gun down and let's end this," I whisper. "We both loved her very much. I'd love to—"

"Don't begin to think you and I have anything in common. I hate everything about you, even the air you breathe. I hate it for keeping you alive."

"—show you pictures of her growing up," I continue undeterred. Somewhere, beneath the surface hardened by years of grief and anger, is sweet Melanie's flesh and blood. I could never hate her or resent her or wish her harm. "There's video too."

"You think it matters now? Do you think you and I can walk out of here and become best friends?" Her raised, derisive tone gets the attention of a passerby in the corridor. He looks at us but doesn't slow his pace. "I promised I'd rip everything you care about out of your life, and I meant it. This sorry schmuck"—she jerks her head scornfully toward Derreck—"was just the beginning."

"Wait a minute," Derreck says, paying zero attention to the gun.

I look at him intently, urging him to not interfere. Maybe I can still reach her.

"He was an easy target, your Derreck," Paula adds, and I wish she'd stop talking. "He's been sleeping with me for seven months, right after the hospital fundraiser you hosted." She stares at my gaping mouth and laughs. "Yeah, I was there. Watching, seeing who you cared about, making a list. A hit list."

"You fucking bitch," Derreck says and moves toward her, but she points the gun at him and he freezes in his tracks.

Seven months! The room is spinning with me, faster and faster.

"How do you feel now, Dr. Wiley?" She laughs maniacally. "Should I call a doctor? Are you about to have a heart attack? It would be so easy, huh? My job would be done here, and Derreck and I could go back to our favorite suite at the London-House for a fuck and a nightcap with hors d'oeuvres."

"Please, no more," I ask, tugging at the collar of my blouse as if it's strangling me.

"And the funniest thing is, you paid for all those hotel rooms, didn't you? He was broke when he met you, just a spine-less, gutless wannabe with a law degree and student loans up his wazoo. But you, you're loaded, you can foot the bill for his career aspirations. Of *course* he loves you." She laughs again while I die inside, inch by inch. "I wish you both all the happi-ness in the world."

I bend over, feeling the need to curl up.

"Oh, but wait, that won't happen," she says, winking at Derreck. "This is your last day on this earth, Dr. Wiley."

Derreck's body tenses as if he's ready to pounce. I stare at him pleadingly and he lets his shoulders drop a little.

With the last bit of strength I can muster, I look at Paula with understanding. "We loved the same girl, with all our hearts. You shouldn't hate me for loving your sister."

"Why?" she asks, tilting her head to one side.

"Because she loved me very much. I can show you." My comment stirs Derreck up. He slaps his forehead and stomps his foot against the carpet.

"Shut the hell up," Paula shouts, but her voice is tinged with tears. Seemingly angered by her own weakness, she swipes everything off my desk with one move. Melanie's photos land on the floor with the sound of shattered glass. The pine cone she gave me for my fourteenth birthday rolls over until it stops by Derreck's feet.

And Caleb Donaghy's red file flies open, scattering its content all over the floor.

I'm so close to reaching her, despite Derreck's disapproving glare. But he lost the right to approve or disapprove anything during the seven months he's been cheating on me.

I'm about to plead with her again, when I notice her demeanor. Her face has turned pale, her hands are trembling, the gun seems too heavy for her to hold. I follow the direction of her horrified gaze and find Caleb Donaghy's photo, the one I took in the morgue.

I don't understand, or maybe I do, but it doesn't fit.

"Who's this?" she asks, her voice a barely audible whisper.

"How can you ask who this is? He's the patient you've been accusing me of murdering."

"*This* is Caleb Donaghy?" She crouches down and picks up the file and the scattered papers awkwardly, still holding the gun. "I only saw his DMV photo," she whispers, more to herself than to me, "with a bad toupee and a beard and glasses. I had no idea..."

I stand and come near her, holding my hand out for the file. "This is the man who died on my table," I say, gently. "I thought you knew."

When she looks at me, I don't recognize her anymore; but I see a bit of Melanie in her: the haunting look she had in her eyes when she saw Donaghy on that park bench.

I finally understand.

Melanie wasn't the only victim of the man lying in the hospital morgue. Just one of the many.

"I'm so sorry you had to endure such an ordeal," I whisper, gently. "You and Melanie were too young, too vulnerable in the hands of that—"

"Shut the hell up," she snaps, but her voice is not nearly as cold and slicing as before. She takes Caleb's photo to the paper shredder by the wall. The whirring lasts a mere second and the photo is gone. "I'm glad he's dead."

I take a giant leap of faith. "So am I. For Melanie." A beat of tense silence. "And for you."

She takes a step back and looks away, then at Derreck, the rage in her eyes waning and waxing as she fights her inner battle. "My sister is dead, and someone must pay for it. I thought that someone should be you, the rich, spoiled brat who took Melanie away from me." Her head jerks toward Derreck, but her eyes are fixed on me. "He opened the door and made it easy for me to start trashing your life."

"You mean to say I was just a pawn in your revenge scheme?" Derreck shouts, and goes for the gun. She pulls away, but there's nowhere to go: her back's against the desk.

"Derreck," I shout, staring at the struggle with eyes open in horror. I've seen the results of fights over loaded weapons in the emergency room too many times. "No! Get away from her."

He's not listening. "You used me," he growls, pulling at the gun with both hands. She doesn't pull the trigger, just fights with him. He's much stronger than she is and livid with rage. He finally grabs her wrist and twists, but the gun goes off and Derreck screams.

"Derreck!" I call again, wanting to rush to his side, but he's still on his feet, still fighting for that gun. Clutching Paula's wrist with one hand, he turns it against her and presses it against her chest.

When the gun goes off again, I scream, just as the cops barge in, all aiming their drawn weapons at Derreck.

Paula lies at his feet, a strange expression in her eyes, her chest wound bleeding profusely.

"Drop your weapon, sir," one of the cops orders. He's dressed in heavy SWAT gear that rattles when he moves. "Now, or I'll shoot."

Derreck crouches to the ground and puts the gun on the floor, then raises his hands. He's bleeding from his lower left abdomen. His forehead is pale and covered in sweat.

Madison barges in and says, "I have ER teams on the way. Sorry it took so long."

I kneel by Paula's side and feel for a pulse. It's there, but weak and thready. She's losing lots of blood and she's about to go into shock. She doesn't have five seconds to waste.

One of the cops grabs Derreck's arm a little roughly, forcing him to stand. He tries to pull away, but the cop's grip is tight.

"Hey, you can't do this to me! Do you know who I am?"

I don't think the cop knows who Derreck is.

I've been married to him for fourteen years, and I don't.

THIRTY-SEVEN
CELEBRATION

A few hours ago, Paula was recovering in ICU, sleeping, handcuffed to the bed rail, and I was by her side. The room was peaceful, vertical blinds keeping the sunshine at bay. Only the faint beeping of her monitors interrupted my thoughts.

I sat by her side, still wearing surgical garb. I stayed with her for a couple of hours after she was rolled out of the OR. I didn't operate on her; Dr. Seldon did—the rule of never operating on people we know personally came into play.

She'll make a full recovery. The bullet nicked her pericardium and ended up lodged in her rib, but didn't damage the spine. Dr. Seldon managed to retrieve it and stitched her up nicely. Out of all the places to get shot, a hospital with a level one trauma center is probably the best. I attended the operation, fully scrubbed, but didn't touch anything, per Dr. Seldon's firm request.

I didn't want to... I just wanted to be there for her, and Dr. Seldon's kindness allowed me to attend. I know it's what Melanie would've wanted. I was with Paula every step of the way from when she fell to the ground in my office, through the cardiac tamponade they managed in the ER while the OR was being prepped, through the surgery, and through a couple of hours of her recovery in the intensive care unit.

When she shifted in her sleep, I stood and took her hand, squeezing it gently. "I'm so sorry we took your sister from you," I whispered, although Paula was still out. "But I'm not sorry she came into our lives."

I checked her vitals one more time, then I left.

I didn't want to be there when she woke, afraid my presence would be a stressor she could do without. But there's no telling what the future might bring. Against all logic and common sense, I hope there could be a way she and I can stay in touch. I'd like to think of myself as a good person, someone who doesn't hold grudges and who tries to understand what trauma and loss can do to a person. Someone who can forgive.

Walking out of her room, I searched my soul and came up empty. I don't know if I can be that better person when all is said and done. Thinking of her in Derreck's arms is excruciating. I'm not sure if I'll ever be able to move past that.

She's facing charges for her actions, steep ones.

The cop who was still in my office when I returned mentioned attempted murder and seemed confused at how distraught I was about those charges. A long stare and a slight cocking of his head told me he thought I must've been a bit crazy. But then he was kind to me and helped me to a chair when my legs finally gave up. Madison took over from him and ushered him out of there like a schoolboy.

Paula could get life in prison. I asked the hospital counsel, and he explained things I only partly understood, about how premeditation and the discharge of a firearm during the commission of a Class X felony could mean decades more spent in jail.

As I sat by her side, searching for Melanie's features on her pale face, I swore to myself I'd fight any charges she might be given with the best of my abilities.

She's suffered enough.

Unfortunately, now it's my turn. My life has been upended in a devastating way. Derreck's wound is superficial, but what we had together is over, burned to the ground.

I drive home in a state of continued stupor. *It's Wednesday, and Mom's not home on Wednesday evenings.* I'm strangely grateful for that, realizing just how much I need time for myself, to think, to grieve, to process everything that happened today.

But first, there's something else I need to do.

As soon as I enter the house, I climb upstairs and stop in front of Melanie's door. I close my eyes and lean my forehead against it, letting my mind wander. After a few moments, the faintest sound of her laughter invades my thoughts, a welcome and cherished memento of our life together. With that sound fresh in my mind, I grab the doorknob and turn.

The door opens and I find myself in Melanie's old bedroom. The furniture is covered with sheets, but everything has been kept just the way it was. The floor is clean, the rug vacuumed recently. Mom must've kept it like that, not mentioning it to me, not saying one word about it. Just waiting until I was ready.

There's nothing for me to do here. Melanie lives forever in my heart. She left this room behind twenty-two years ago.

Before I head out, there's one thing I need to do. I go to the large window and pull the curtains wide open to let the sunshine in. Particles of dust swirl and dance in the rays, reminding me of a blue circle skirt and a white blouse with ruffles.

Downstairs, in the guest bedroom, the scent of Derreck's aftershave hits me hard, and I stop, staring at the open closet.

I know what I have to do. I just don't know if I can.

He's not home yet. After the hospital stitched up his super-ficial wound, he was taken downtown to the precinct to give a statement. He's not looking at charges; his self-defense claim will stick. He was still waiting for his attorney to show up when he last texted me.

I didn't reply. I don't want to reply to him ever again.

I just want him gone, out of my life forever.

Maybe you could maintain for about a second that he was a victim of Paula's revenge scheme. Maybe he was, but he wasn't forced to cheat. He could've said no. He didn't. That, to me, is a life-altering offense.

There's no coming back from seven months of cheating.

As I pull out a suitcase and unzip it on the bed, I realize my gut told me about the affair a long time ago, when I noticed he was coming home smelling fresh after a twelve-hour day. In fact, he was coming home after sleeping with her, the fresh smell being the showers he was taking in the hotel afterward.

That mystery is solved.

Now I have to figure out how to best untangle our lives. A chill descends on my spine when I recall Paula's disparaging words about my husband. What if they are true? What if he won't let himself be kicked out of the house, mere months from being elected mayor? He has so much to lose.

I let out a pained sigh and sit on the bed by the empty suitcase.

Money. That's usually the answer. I'll offer him money to go away, and keep everything quiet until after the elections. Then I'll divorce him and make sure he doesn't get too much out of it. Thanks to Paula, I can prove his infidelity. I know to look for snazzy riverside hotels on his credit card statements.

The sound of the laundry door opening draws me into the living room. I expect Mom to be home early, but it's Derreck.

I'm petrified, staring at him as if I see a ghost.

He's smiling, his usual charming smile at full intensity as he hands me a dozen, long-stemmed, red roses and places a kiss on my frozen lips. I take the roses, the rustling of cellophane sounding gratingly loud in the tense silence of our house, but I can't move. I should take them to the kitchen island and put them in a vase. I should scream for help. I should tell him to leave.

There's something in his eyes I've never seen before: a cold determination, the steel core I've always admired, now shining through, sending waves of fear through my entire body. I stare at him, noticing how loudly my gut is speaking to me right now.

Only this time, I'm listening.

"Hey," he says, pulling at the knot of his tie until it's loose enough to pull over his head. "I know how upset you must be." He drops the tie on the back of a chair, then takes off his jacket with a wince of pain. His shirt has a bloodied hole in it, but I can see a clean dressing underneath. He takes the shirt off, rolls it in a ball and throws it in the trash. "People make mistakes, Anne."

He takes the roses from me and leaves them on the counter, then puts his hands on my shoulders. I shiver. "People do things they can't really explain. Other times, they do things they'd rather not be held accountable for." He speaks to me gently, but I'm not fooled. My gut is screaming. "Take your patient, for example. What was his name? Caleb Donaghy?"

There it is, that name the sword of Damocles hanging over my head, holding me hostage. He's not going to take a career-ending blow from me lying down. I was a fool to imagine.

Ice shards travel up and down my spine as I recall everything I told him about Caleb Donaghy. It doesn't matter now that it wasn't my decision to call time of death early that killed him. I could never tell anyone who did. And today, he's learned even more, from Paula and the things I told her about Melanie, from her reaction to seeing Donaghy's photo. I just proved to my attorney husband I had motive for killing Caleb Donaghy.

"I don't know if I can forgive you, Derreck," I say, knowing I'm probably wasting my time. He kicks off his shoes and sits on the sofa with a satisfied groan. He's not going anywhere. "I want a divorce."

He doesn't flinch.

"The thing about forgiveness," he says, "is that it can be learned. Time heals all wounds, including the devastating pain that you must be feeling right now. Time erases people's memories, you know, especially if those people really want to forget. And I do." He looks straight into my eyes until I lower my gaze to escape him. The offer comes across loud and clear.

"What would you like to do, then?" I ask, looking at him again with as much determination as I can. I'm not going to take this lying down either.

He springs to his feet, wincing a little and touching his side where the bullet grazed him. "What do you say we celebrate a little?" He heads over to the fridge and extracts a bottle of wine, one of the more expensive ones. He uncorks it and fills two glasses as I stand there, staring in disbelief. Then he hands me a glass and raises his in the air. "To us, my dear wife, to you and me, together forever."

I raise my glass and clink it against his, feeling nauseated and faint.

He grins and winks at me. "And to Caleb Donaghy."

As I watch him drink, a smile blooms on my lips. My beloved husband assumes, in his cold-hearted arrogance, that he has me defeated and forever silenced by the threat of what he knows about Caleb Donaghy. He believes I'll bow my head to his will and cunning, and continue to be a faithful and devoted wife to the future mayor of Chicago, walking by his side as he ascends to power using my family's money.

Over my dead body, my dear cheating, lying husband.

I can see it on his composed face, in his relaxed demeanor, he thinks he's got away with it. But then again, so did Caleb

Donaghy. Until he landed on shelf #6 in the hospital basement morgue.

You see, only one of us here, in this room, knows at least a dozen ways to make a heart stop without leaving any forensic evidence.

And that isn't him.

A LETTER FROM LESLIE

A big, heartfelt **thank you** for choosing to read *The Surgeon*. If you enjoyed it and want to keep up to date with all my latest releases, just sign up at the following link. Your email address will never be shared, and you can unsubscribe at any time.

www.bookouture.com/leslie-wolfe

When I write a new book I think of you, the reader: what you'd like to read next, how you'd like to spend your leisure time, and what you most appreciate from the time spent in the company of the characters I create, vicariously experiencing the challenges I lay in front of them. That's why I'd love to hear from you! Did you enjoy *The Surgeon*? Would you like to see other similar stories? Your feedback is incredibly valuable to me, and I appreciate hearing your thoughts. Please contact me directly through one of the channels listed below. Email works best: LW@WolfeNovels.com. I will never share your email with anyone, and I promise you'll receive an answer from me!

If you enjoyed my book and if it's not too much to ask, please take a moment and leave me a review, and maybe recommend *The Surgeon* to other readers. Reviews and personal recommendations help readers discover new titles or new authors for the first time; it makes a huge difference, and it means the world to me. Thank you for your support, and I hope to keep you entertained with my next story. See you soon!

Thank you,

Leslie

www.LeslieWolfe.com

 facebook.com/wolfenovels

amazon.com/stores/author/B00KR1QZ0G

bookbub.com/authors/leslie-wolfe

ACKNOWLEDGMENTS

A special, heartfelt thank you goes to the fantastic publishing team at Bookouture. They are a pleasure to work with, their enthusiasm contagious and their dedication inspiring.

Very special thanks to Ruth Tross and Christina Demosthenous, who make the editing process a pleasant experience and who are the best brainstorming partners an author could hope for.

A special thanks goes to Kim Nash and Noelle Holten for tirelessly promoting my books across all channels. Alba Proko is the wonderful audio manager who turns my written stories into audible recordings, nurturing the productions throughout the process and making me proud of each and every one of them. Your work with my stories is nothing short of inspiring.

A huge shoutout for the digital marketing team, who work seamlessly and tirelessly in ensuring that every book launch is better than the one before. You are simply amazing.

My warmest thanks go to Richard King and his enthusiastic efforts to bring my work to other markets in translated versions and perhaps, one day, to the screen. A heartfelt thank you for everything you do and for your keen interest in my work. It's much appreciated.